Opening Strains

Passionate Beats trilogy, book 1

Arell Rivers

OPENING STRAINS

Book 1 in the **Passionate Beats** trilogy in the Untamed Coaster series

ARELL RIVERS

Copyright ©2025 Tarnished Halo Publishing LLC

Published by Tarnished Halo Publishing LLC

2025 Edition

ISBN (digital): 979-8-9869346-3-1

ISBN (print): 979-8-9869346-4-8

Arell's Team

Editing:

Plot Coach Theresa Leigh, The FairyPlot-Mother, http://www.fairyplotmother.me

Developmental Editor Trenda Lundin, It's Your Story Content Editing, http://www.facebook.com/ItsYourStoryContentEditing

Editor Nancy Smay, Evident Ink, http://www.evidentink.com

Proofreading: Roxanne Bluin

Cover design: Dar Albert, Wicked Smart Designs, http://www.
wickedsmartdesigns.com

✿ Formatted with Vellum

Rehab and Restraints: A Bad Boy's Reckoning

One stupid jump onstage at Untamed Coaster's rockumentary premiere, and I'm out of commission. Pulled groin? More like a damn disaster. And the only person who can fix me is Jenna Westfield. *Jenna*. The ex of our late keyboardist, who added her to the Do Not F*^% list that survives even though he's no longer here. And the only woman who made me question my no-strings rule from the moment I met her.

Two weeks in the Hamptons at her clinic, and I'm a goner. Falling not only for her, but also her warm, welcoming mom, a whole damn life I never knew I wanted. But she's holding back, those haunted eyes telling a story I can't quite read. Professional ethics, ghosts of the past, and my own mother's constant nagging keep us apart. Then, one stolen kiss changes everything.

Suddenly, I believe we could have an actual relationship. Almost buy into her ideal that UC is my "found family." However, the paparazzi are vultures, branding her a "Black Widow"—and she splits.

Now, I'm alone on tour, wondering if I blew my only chance at something real.

Contents

Chapter One

The mask I often wear—front man for the multi-award-winning Untamed Coaster—slips over me as I tug on the door. Inside the conference room, Jeremy Davis, reporter for the *Record News*, awaits. Usually Luke Allen, our manager, either does these by himself or I join him, but he's busy today, so I get to do this interview alone. Whatever. After more than a decade, I can handle any question thrown at me.

"Hey, Jeremy, nice to see you again."

"If it isn't Bennett Hardy, in the flesh." The journalist, a few years older than me, stands. He extends his hand, and we shake. "Looking good."

"You too." Adjusting my rings and leather bracelets, I take in his appearance. His hair, which used to be shoulder length, is now short. While I remember when he was scrawny many years ago, he's filled out. Yet his piercing hazel eyes remain, reminding me of his profession.

While I settle into a comfy chair and open a bottle of water, Jeremy sets up a recorder and takes out a notepad. "Ready?"

I incline my head. The sooner we start, the sooner we end. I can already picture my reward, complete with unlimited Manhattans and a random brunette with a nice rack. My stomach reminds me I didn't have lunch, so I add tacos to my prize.

"As usual, I'm going to ask you questions and feel free to answer them as you see fit. I'll make sure to clean up any grammar issues. We at the *Record News* are interested in getting behind public-facing information but we don't traffic in gotcha situations. We aren't a tabloid."

Appreciating his honesty, I take another sip of water. Truth is, I wouldn't be here if he were working for a lesser magazine. "Fire away."

He plays with his shorter hair. Probably still getting used to it. "The buzz around your upcoming movie *Untamed Coaster Unleashed* is staggering. I think the public is excited to see the rise, fall, and rebirth of UC. It's okay if I refer to the band as UC, right?"

Why I need to give him permission to use our initials every time we sit down is beyond me. "Everyone on the inside does."

Jeremy makes a note. "All of the rumors swirling around the movie have been positive, although the subject matter is quite deep. I was lucky to get an early screening of the film and can attest to how powerful it is."

It *is* a great fucking movie. Quinn Walker, the director, went above and beyond.

Jeremy continues, "At the beginning, UC was riding high, selling out stadiums with no obstacles in your path. Until Darren Hilliard, the band's original keyboardist, overdosed. At that point, everything collapsed. Can you give me some insight into what it was like back then?"

Our keyboardist died. How does he think it was? "Darren's death truly was awful for the band. After all, he was the one who invited me into UC, when we were all working at Amazing Amusements." *Really, Bennett. Why did you open this door?*

"The amusement park." Jeremy's eyebrows raise. "Tell me about it."

And he walks right through. "You want to hear about how I joined UC?" *Please say no so I can get to the fun part of my day. And tacos.*

Jeremy motions for me to continue. I sigh as my hopes for a quick exit fall off the music stand.

Here we go. "Well, the summer before senior year in high school, I worked at the amusement park with the guys. We were all assigned to the Untamed Coaster ride. I was the operator while Darren, Río, Coop, and 007 ensured all the riders were safe and the coaster was ready.

"I've already brought up Darren, your original keyboardist. Could you give me a quick rundown on the others?"

Is this necessary? "Sure. Río is River Sullivan, who plays drums, and Coop is short for Cooper O'Shea, UC's guitarist. I think you can figure out how we came up with their nicknames. As for 007, that's Pierce DeLuca on bass. I actually dubbed him that since both he and the actor Pierce Brosnan, who was playing James Bond when we were born, have dark hair and blue eyes." *Proud of that one.*

"Clever."

I soak in the accolade. When he doesn't say anything else, I add, "Yeah, well, at the beginning of summer, they heard me singing along to 'Gives You Hell' by The All-American Rejects. The song was being piped into the amusement park before it opened and it spoke to me. You see, I had been thrown over by my girlfriend so she could attend the senior prom with my then best friend." *Why did I share that detail? I never ever share that detail. At least I managed not to blurt out Lissa's name. Or Curtiss's.*

Jeremy sits straighter. "Ouch."

Annoyed at myself, I stare at the ceiling for a couple of beats. I wave. "Old news. So, the guys were impressed with my voice. After work, they invited me to join them at a local sports bar." I lean toward him, as if sharing a deep, dark secret. "One they knew didn't card." We both laugh.

Latching onto the safer topic, I continue, "Anyway, I showed up and a band was playing, and they were good. That's when Darren

told me all the guys played instruments and had formed a band themselves, but their lead singer had left for the military, so they were
looking for a new front man. I didn't know it at the time, but my audi-
tion happened when I sang The All-American Rejects song earlier in
the day."

"And the rest is history?"

"Basically. It took some deft finagling"—in terms of introducing
me to a bunch of young ladies at the bar who convinced me I was hot
enough to assume the role. Back then, I needed reassurance. I soon
left Lissa's betrayal in the dust when those chicks were all over me.
Got rid of my virginity, too. "Finally, I did agree to drop out of high
school and join the band."

We share a smile. After consulting his notes, Jeremy asks, "Let's
step back for a second. How did your parents like the idea of your
quitting high school to be in a rock band? I mean, you were only
seventeen, correct?"

*Not going down this rabbit hole. One trip down memory lane was
enough for this interview.* "I was, yes. My father had passed away
from a heart attack a few weeks before all this went down, so he never
knew. As for my mother, I made sure she was taken care of. Because
the other guys already had graduated, Darren rode me hard to get my
GED."

I can still picture Dad lying on our hallway floor, pleading with
me. *"Promise me you'll always look after Mom." With tear-filled eyes,
I'd responded in the affirmative. No way would I deny a dying man,
one whom I loved with my whole heart, his final wish. At that moment,
it didn't matter that the woman in question had chastised me all my
life, blamed me for something it was impossible for me to have done,
and was mentally unstable. He added, "You've always been such a
good—"*

He never finished his sentence.

To this day, I want to know what he was going to say.

Have I lived up to my promise to him about Mom? Well, I made
sure she was safe and secure. Even if our parting back then—

No. More. I squeeze my thigh.

"I'm sorry for your loss."

I allow silence to chase itself around the four walls of the conference room.

"So, uhm, when did you name the band?"

A relieved chuckle escapes. Thank God we're moving on. "I didn't. You see, Untamed Coaster was the original name. The guys didn't tell me until I agreed to join, though."

"Nice." He grins. Water slides down my throat as I wait for his next question. Which comes quickly. "In the movie, you talk about the famous huddle you do before all your shows. Care to shed some light on it?"

Uncomplicated territory. "Of course." *See. I can be easy-going.* "It's a throwback to our Amazing Amusements days. Before I could start the ride, I had to check in with the guys to confirm that it, and the guests, were all set. When they were satisfied, they raised their fists into the air, which prompted me to shout, 'Strapped, locked, and loaded, are you ready to roll with Untamed Coaster?' It sort of stuck. Now we use it to remember where we came from and to get hyped to rock the crowd."

Smiling, Jeremy flips the page on his notebook. "I'd like to change the subject a bit. I understand one motivation behind the movie is to introduce Tristan Lambert, your new keyboardist, to the general population. How has his transition been?"

UC's PR team prepared me for this question. I puff up. "Once we decided to offer Tris the position, which was a grueling process, it took some time for him to gel with us, as Quinn shows so well in the movie. But he's one of the band now, for sure." All the details about our hunt for a new keyboardist were depicted in minute detail in the film, so no need to go into them now. Although, discussing video applications and live auditions would be preferable to running my mouth off about my mother, my former best friend, and ex-girlfriend.

Jeremy interrupts my thoughts. "What dynamics within UC have changed with Tristan's introduction?"

I ponder his question—one I haven't thought about much. "First of all, he's great on the keys. However, Tris is his own man, without a doubt, and has different traits than Darren had. For example, he's quieter than Darren was, but still manages to get his point across." Like when he got UC to agree to some embellishments to Darren's song, "Crushing Blow." None of us wanted to change a note in the song, but his ideas were freaking good. *What else can I say?* "Plus, the ladies sure have welcomed him into the band." I don a smirk.

Without missing a beat, Jeremy asks, "Speaking of, any woman catch your eye?"

This, again? My palm raises. "Me? No one woman in particular—there's way too much going on in my life. In case you missed it, we're preparing for our upcoming tour." I rest for a second. "When we're introducing Tris to the world."

"What a tour it promises to be. You'll start in America then fly over to Europe, right?"

Score! Diversion succeeded. "Yes. Our first shows are in New York City, and we play venues throughout the United States before we hop across the pond to Europe, then Australia and South America. There's even talk about hitting the Far East, so stay tuned."

"We sure will." Jeremy reviews his notes. "Before I let you go, I need to circle back to Darren's death. We know he passed away in a Florida hotel room. What more can you share with us?"

Luke warned me to expect a proctologist exam, but why? I hate reliving this shit. The whole world knows Darren was prescribed Oxy following his wrist injury. Overdosed. As much as we are able to determine, that night he took a pill prior to going out. Between the drinks and joking around with everyone, he must've forgotten and took probably two, three or more before falling asleep. As a result, a panicked 007 called me to Darren's room. *Get your mind in the game and finish this interview.*

I take a deep breath. "It was in the early morning. I was in my own room when I got a frantic call from 007 that Darren was in trouble." This is accurate. No need to share I had left a redhead's room only a couple of hours before, thank you very much. I do send off another thanks to the universe she didn't try to cash in on the timing of our tryst.

To stall, I tip up the water bottle. Jeremy stares at me expectantly. "I ran down the hall and met 007 in Darren's room. We tried everything we could to revive him, but he was gone." My fingers close around the UC pendant I always wear. "I called the rest of the band, who rushed to his room. As a goodbye, Coop led us in singing 'Amazing Grace,' then I reached out to the hotel to take care of the details. I also had the unenviable tasks of calling Mother Hilliard as well as his girlfriend, Jenna Westfield."

Jenna. She had given all of us UC pendants the Christmas before. I loosen my fingers and drop the necklace. The woman who, Darren informed us in no uncertain terms, was on our *Do Not Fuck* list. A list never to be crossed, no matter the fact he's no longer on this plane.

Despite sitting with a journalist, memories stir. The first time I met Jenna, everything about her entranced me. We were at a club, and she was all alone. I ordered her a glass of wine and gave her the cherry from my Manhattan. When she took it and winked at me, I fell in lust. She quoted *The Godfather*, and it was upgraded to love. Although she somehow believed the second movie was better than the original. I shake my head. I will never get over that.

Then, Darren appeared, kissed her, and broke up my stupid white-picket fantasy. Turns out, Jenna had been the physical therapist he'd been raving about for months, who helped rehab his wrist injury. Once the professional relationship ended, their personal one took off.

Jeremy clears his throat. *Focus, Bennett.* "As you can imagine, they were not easy calls to make. But we got through it, together, and now with Tris in the band, we're carving out a new identity for UC."

In a lower voice, Jeremy says, "Thank you for sharing these intimate details. I didn't realize you were the one who took care of all the items on the terrible to-do list, including calling his mother and girlfriend."

"Our manager, Luke Allen, wasn't at our hotel that night, so the responsibility fell on my shoulders." We're all members of the same band, yes, but I don't do friends. Not since Curtiss . . . makes my life easier. Besides, following Dad's death, one thing I've learned well is to detach and run on autopilot. Getting shit done is the main reason why I'm the *de facto* lead of UC—it would take the band forever to pick a restaurant, let alone handle any heavy stuff. I lift the bottle of water to my lips.

"Have you kept in touch with either of them?"

Do not go near the hornet's nest that is Jenna Westfield. "We still talk with Mother Hilliard. She's an amazing woman who raised Darren and his sister as a single mother. In fact, we're planning on seeing them when UC's tour is close to her home."

He looks happy with my answer. "How wonderful. I'm sure his mother's thrilled to see the band succeeding."

I consider his comment. "She is. She knows Darren's right there with us, rooting for our continued good fortune."

Jeremy flips another page in his notebook. "Great. And how about his girlfriend, Jenna?"

A more detached tone emerges from my throat. "We haven't spoken with her since the funeral, as her connection to us was through Darren."

My mind jumps to the awful call I had to make to her when Darren died. I remember dialing her number—the one Darren himself proudly had shared with the band when they officially came out as a couple.

"I'm calling because I wanted you to hear this from one of us before it comes out in the media."

"Oh boy. What did Darren do now? Dance on some table? Trash a hotel room? Hijack a cop car?"

Her laughter rips something inside of me. "I wish." *I pause.* "I'm so sorry to tell you this, but Darren passed away in his hotel suite this* morning." I rush to ease any of her possible outrageous fears. "He was alone."

"No!" she screams. "When? How?"

If only I had any answers. "I'm not sure exactly when. He left the club pretty early last night."

She jumps in. "He called me. We—he was alive when we hung up."

I refuse to mention the pill bottles on his nightstand. "All I know is 007 phoned me around nine this morning from his room, and Darren was already gone. He was in his bed, wearing boxers."

"Because he promised me he would."

Alright, not going there. "He also had your UC necklace on. I'm so sorry, Jenna. Know that Darren loved you very much. He never flirted with any other girls. In fact, just last night, I saw a bunch of women surround him and guess what he did? He whipped out his cell and showed them photos of you."

Sobs come through the phone.

I lift up the UC necklace to show Jeremy. Hopefully this will be a needed distraction. "However, Coop, 007, Río, and I still wear these pendants that Jenna gave to us the Christmas before Darren passed. It has UC's logo on it." I pause. "We even had one made for Tris when he joined the band."

The reporter sits forward and examines my necklace. "What a nice gift." After a minute, he reviews his notes while I take the opportunity to tuck it away, together with Jenna, where she belongs. "I have one final question. How about telling me about *Untamed Coaster Unleashed.*"

Thank you for this softball. "The movie debuts worldwide next Thursday. Quinn, who I mentioned before, was our director and she captured our return to the stage with perfection, in my humble opinion. You'll see our trials and all we went through in replacing Darren. It's a pretty wild ride."

Jeremy turns off the recorder. *Made it!* Even though I let this one get deeper under my skin than most, at least now I can move on with my life. And tacos.

"I think that about covers everything." He collects his notebook. "Thank you, Bennett, for sharing some time with me. As I said before, I loved the film and am looking forward to attending its premiere. I wish you all the best."

I finish my water and stand. *Play nice and get out of here.* "Thanks so much for having me, Jeremy. Here's a tip . . . UC is planning to perform after the movie." I tap his shoulder. "See you on the flip side."

Chapter Two

I stand beneath the massive screen, send heartfelt words to Quinn, the genius director behind *Untamed Coaster Unleashed*, and blow her a kiss. To my surprise, she sends it back at me, so I do the right thing and toss it to her boyfriend Callum MacMurray—who is the owner of the fine whisky establishment where our career restarted. Tonight, though, is the band's grand nationwide reintroduction, like our manager Luke promised us it would be. It's time to show the nice crowd here what we've got.

I adjust the microphone and nod to each of my band members. A shirtless Río—when does he ever wear a shirt?—bangs the beat to "Upside Down" and our set begins. Even though we've been putting on shows for sellout crowds since our return at Callum's whisky distillery, it's different performing tonight in a movie theater. The lighting, the sound, the energy are unique. Quinn's movie amped us up to oversized proportions.

We finish our first number one and launch into our next song. I walk from one side of the stage to the other, waving to people I recognize in the crowd. Most fans abandoned their seats and have moved into the aisles. I bet this cinema hasn't ever rocked like this before.

Coop's guitar is on point. When it comes time for his solo, I stroll over to him. With a chin bob, he steps around me and takes center stage, his sunglasses and hoop earrings glinting under the lights. I take this opportunity to turn around and lean behind Río's bass drum to down a bottle of water. We're tight. Our music's speaking for itself. This is where we belong. I catch Luke's gaze from backstage and he gives me a thumbs up.

With my throat soothed, I return to Coop and stand back-to-back with him. He's in the zone, and the crowd is eating us up. Finished with his solo, I sling my arm around him. I shout, "Let's hear it for Coop!"

The wall of noise that comes back warms my heart. Next to me, Coop whispers, "We got this."

He's right. We've made it back. Perhaps not better than ever, but newer, with a slightly different edge. Coop, Río, and our bassist 007 have come a long way since that awful morning two years ago. Tris stepped into our former keyboardist Darren's shoes with his own spin. I refuse to dwell on the loss of our original band member. Time marches on.

I listen to UC's instruments as the song finishes on a high note and thank everything holy that we made it back. I have no other career path and can't imagine my life without performing, without being *the* Bennett Hardy. This persona saved me from unimaginable torment.

"Did you enjoy the movie as much as we did?" My voice reverberates throughout the theater. Cheers return back to me. "Who wants to keep on rocking?"

Tris starts playing "Crushing Blow," and I almost freeze. This song is all Darren. Amend—*was* all him until Tris put his own spin on it. Now it's both new and old at the same time. An ode to Darren and a nod to our new sound. UC has risen from the ashes.

Next to Tris, I attack the lyrics more intensely than I ever have. The band picks up on my exuberance and the beat hits a little harder. *Nice.* I strut across the stage, wishing we were able to put in an extension here so I could venture out into the audience. Even crowd surfing wouldn't work given the layout.

So, I make do. With the lights as hot as they are, even without a light show, it's time for me to follow Río's lead and strip out of this wet shirt. Not like I do ab exercises for my health. Well, I guess I do . . . I place the microphone into its stand and unbutton my shirt. Ladies in the crowd scream, but I can't tell if they're singing the lyrics with me or shouting as my bare torso comes into view. Whatever. I'll take either.

I toss the material off to the side, causing my UC necklace to bounce, and a roadie runs over to retrieve the shirt. We launch into another song. Holding the mic, I strut around the stage, taking time to share space with 007. Even though he's not returned to the same demeanor as before Darren left us, 007's found a new footing. Maybe it's the fact he now wears Darren's studded belt? In any case, he's the talisman for all of us. We'll never be the same but we're still kicking ass.

I make my way over to the drums, enjoying Río's pounding beat. If it weren't for his oversized personality, we wouldn't be here today. He cuts through the crap with a style all his own, whether it be in music or life. The drummer hits various cymbals at least a dozen times, then spins his drumstick, ending with it pointing at me.

My head shakes. What a ham. *Thinks the guy wearing leather pants, ten rings, and as many bracelets.* I pull the mic away and snort, earning a rimshot from Río. Grinning, I look out onto the crowd, feeding on their energy.

Because I can, I say, "You're the reason we're here. We kept on moving forward—even when we didn't want to—'cause we could feel you all rooting for us. We love playing music, and we're thrilled you came to watch a movie about our reintroduction into polite society." I grin. "Or not so polite!"

The crowd, our fans, cheer.

I seize this moment to introduce the UC band members. With a bow toward Río, I say, "River Sullivan's on drums. Who here wants to swim in his river?"

Ladies scream, earning a smirk from our drummer.

When they quiet a bit, I shift my attention to 007. Not wanting to disrupt the balance of the band, I offer, "Pierce DeLuca plays the bass better than anyone else in the business. Give it up for our own 007!" To squeals, 007 spikes his chin toward me then takes his solo.

"Next up is our newest member, Tristan Lambert. As you know, Tris beat out a whole host of other keyboardists to get this spot. We're lucky to have him with us, as he brings his own twist on things. Show some love for Tris!"

The resounding approval from the audience rivals that received from the other band members, which further reinforces how right we were to pick him to join UC. For his part, Tris's lips tick upward in a smile showing how happy he is to be here with us. He deserves it.

I walk over to the guitarist. Coop plays a riff from Led Zepplin as I approach, showing off his mad skills. Stopping next to him, I say, "This guy on guitar here is Cooper O'Shea. He keeps us on our toes, always with wise advice . . . even when we don't ask for it."

People laugh as Coop ends his spotlight with "Have a Nice Day" by Bon Jovi. I clap. Gotta give him props, he can be funny when he wants to be.

"Coop's a real comedian when he has a guitar strapped around him." Chuckling into the mic, I start to introduce myself, but have to pull away as I'm laughing too hard. This return—the movie and our getting back on stage—is exactly what I needed. What the band needed.

"What I was gonna say is I'm Bennett Hardy."

I open my naked arms wide, and our fans lose their shit.

Even though I'm enjoying their response, I have one final thing I need to share. The audience needs to hear it, and so does the rest of the band. My lungs fill. "Not going to lie. What you saw in the movie was a pretty accurate description. Losing Darren was awful. Truly one of the darkest days of our collective lives." I glance upward. "We like to think of our return as us being guided by him from above."

I step back.

From the crowd, clapping rings out.

The guys and I exchange glances, confirming we're all still all right. 007 is the last to join in, but his smile says it all. We're back and we're here to stay.

I raise the microphone again. "We have one final song to play for you all. It's the song that played over the credits of the kickass film done by Quinn Walker you just watched. Let's make sure all the folks in surrounding buildings know Untamed Coaster is in the house. Are you ready for 'Refocused Destiny'?"

Before me, people jump up and down, screaming our band's name. Individual member's names. The song's name. I'm high on their enthusiasm.

Río's beat is hard, the exact right tone for this song. Our destiny has been refocused by adding Tris, as well as with Darren's guidance from the other side. The view from here is spectacular.

I race around the stage, checking in with each of the band members and the audience in front of me. The night—the red carpet, the movie, this performance—is one for the history books. We've never sounded better.

Turning to backstage, I shoot Luke a grin. This time, he gives me a double thumbs up in return. Even our manager knows we've made giant steps forward.

I spin to face the crowd and give the ending of the song all I have. After my last drawn-out note, the band takes over with instrumentals rising into a crescendo. Despite never having practiced any of this before on a stage like this, we (metaphorically) blow the roof off. When the song's about to end, I leap into the air, tossing my fist overhead, my legs outstretched in a split rivaling an Olympian. When I land, the music ends as if my jump were the final exclamation point.

The lights go out.

Panting, I put the microphone back into its stand and take a stride toward the center stage to join the band in our bows. "Fuck!"

My scream is drowned out by all the noise in the building. I don't even think Coop, standing closest to me, heard.

I take another tentative step and a searing pain races through my leg.

Our fans call out to me.

When we hit our mark, I force my lips to smile and wrap my arms around the guys. Wave at the crowd. Blow kisses. Bow for the ovation.

All the while, my insides scream in pain.

We turn and march into the greenroom. With all my concentration, I keep my gait steady.

Coop exclaims, "Let's give them another wave!"

I long to yell no fucking way, but the other guys already have turned. Unmoving, I remain frozen until Tris calls out, "Come on, Bennett. They want to see us one more time!"

It's not his words but rather his excitement that forces me to capitulate. Well, that and the fact nobody knows about the freaking agony I'm in.

On my good leg, I spin. "Coming!" With every other step, blinding pain runs up my leg. I put as much weight onto my good leg as possible, schooling my features into excitement.

"This is amazing," 007 says under his breath.

As one, we raise our hands high and wave to the audience. We take three more quick bows before I say, "Let's leave them wanting more."

Without waiting to see if they follow me, I force myself to walk as if I'm not in excruciating pain. After what happened with Darren, UC's fans can't witness my vulnerability.

Darkness descends as we enter backstage. Hugs are exchanged but I don't bother. Instead, I allow myself to limp to the nearest chair, toss the *Record News*—featuring Jeremy Davis's article—onto the floor, and flop into it.

Leaning against the backrest, I utter to no one, "Thank fuck I made it."

Our manager approaches, yelling, "That was a phenomenal performance. The band's never sounded so good."

My hands move toward the inside of my thigh. Freaking hurts like a mother.

At my side, Luke drops my cell onto the table—following an unfortunate incident with a call in the middle of one of our gigs, we now have to turn them in before taking the stage. His head tilts. "Hey, what's up, B?" Every time he uses this nickname for me, I find it disconcerting . . . still I don't correct him. No way will I return the overly friendly favor, though.

Because the truth's going to come out anyway, I admit, "I think I landed wrong when I did that jump."

Luke chuckles. "That was some crazy-ass shit out there. It worked like a charm, though." He pauses. "Wait. What did you say?"

Through gritted teeth, I repeat, "I landed wrong. My leg fucking hurts."

"Oh crap." He comes around in front of me while others mill about the room, congratulating each other and slapping backs. "Where? What hurts?"

I point to my inner thigh. "I'm not sure what I did. I can't put any weight on my leg."

He runs his fingers through his shoulder-length light brown hair, a couple of shades darker than mine. Which is now plastered to my face following our performance under the lights. "Let me get you a footstool."

A minute later, one materializes under my foot. No idea where it came from, but I don't give a shit. I just want the pain to stop.

"Could you get me some Advil or something?"

"Already on it, B." Someone passes him pills and some water, which he hands over to me.

"Regular Advil, right?"

Luke's eyebrow goes up. "After Darren, you have to ask?"

Stupid question. He's well aware how Darren died. I shut my eyes to block out the rest of the awful period. I take the meds and wait for them to work.

The others in the band are on a post-show thrill. They're high-fiving all around me. I want to jump in, but know I need to give the pills time. Then I'll be ready to party.

"I loved the part of the movie about the rock-climbing wall." Coop nudges 007 in the stomach, then lifts his sunglasses to the top of his head. "Did you see how you helped Tris? Hearts were flying out of your eyes."

007 shakes his head. I keep my own counsel, but agree with Coop. The outing was a turning point for the band. From the chair, I offer, "Perhaps not hearts, but definitely smiley faces."

007 takes our ribbing for what it is. Genuine giddiness that UC is back in business. "Well, I didn't see you assholes coming over to help the poor guy out. Tris was in dire need of someone to give him pointers."

Tris chimes in, because he's now a part of the band. "Yeah. 007 at least helped me get my feet under me. You three didn't do anything but make fun of the inexperienced rock climber."

"Hey," I stick up for myself. "Keyboardists are hard to come by. We would've helped you out. Eventually."

They laugh and I'm back in the zone. I stand and take one step on my bad leg and realize my huge mistake. With a grimace, I fall back into the chair.

"What's up?" Coop attaches himself to my side.

Cat's out of the bag, so no use hiding any longer. "I landed wrong during the last jump. Luke got me an Advil, so I'll be better soon. Guess the meds need more time to work."

"Where does it hurt?"

I gesture towards my inner thigh.

Coop makes a big issue out of wiping his brow. "Whew. For a minute there, I thought you were pointing to your junk. Where would you be without the snake in your pants?"

Luke interrupts our laughter. "Since I have you all here, I wanted to give you some news. Rather, Kenneth Dumont from Platinum Records is here, and *he* wants to give it to you." He turns toward a tall, tanned man with a good amount of salt-and-pepper hair—heavy on the salt.

He raises his hand. "Hey, I'm Kenneth Dumont, your new artist relations rep at Platinum. I've been behind the scenes for a while observing you guys, and have to say, the label loves what we've been seeing. The movie itself is fantastic, and you're the real deal."

We look at each other, wondering what he has up his sleeve. We don't have to wait too long.

"The label's been working with Luke and have almost all the details finalized." Kenneth looks at each one of us. "We've added stadiums to your upcoming tour that starts in two weeks. Any new dates will be arenas only."

I hold my breath. Holy. Shit. A summit I never thought we'd see again. We had embarked on our third stadium tour when Darren died. Now we're going to do it all over again. We've been prepping to play places that hold up to seven, eight thousand—maybe ten—but nothing compares to stadium seating of over fifty-thousand. Wembley holds ninety. What a fucking trip this will be.

The guys all look as shell-shocked as I feel—slack-jawed and wide-eyed. All except Tris, who's never done it before. Freaking amazing way to start a career.

Kenneth continues about our opening bands, cities, and modifications to the set design. I try to absorb it all, but am gobsmacked that this is happening again so soon.

Luke adds, "You all better rest up, because we're getting underway in two weeks. We have a lot to do before then, so take this long weekend to party because you deserve it. Monday we'll work out the kinks to alter our plans for huge arenas!"

I jump out of the chair and share hugs with the band. The pain is still excruciating, but I don't care. This is too big.

"We have a movie and a stadium tour. Thank you, Darren." 007 kisses his fist and raises it to the sky. We mimic his action.

After hugs are shared all around, including with the new rep from Platinum, I collapse into the chair once more. My hand rubs my thigh. Fuck, this hurts.

Luke approaches me. "Any better?"

"I wish." The guys debate where to go to celebrate and whom to do it with. But for my bum leg, I'd be right in the thick of things.

"Let me get you an ice pack," Luke offers.

I sigh. "Sounds good."

Our manager adds, "I think someone should take a look at it. To be safe, all right?"

I roll my eyes but agree. After all, we're leaving on a stadium tour, and I need to be one hundred percent. "Fine. I want this fixed so I can go out and party."

Luke clamps his hand around my shoulder. "Soon."

Chapter Three

Kenneth hands Luke a bottle of Dom. The cork springs free and glasses are passed around to the band, our techs, and roadies. While not my first choice of drink, this news calls for a special celebration.

Chico, our guitar tech, approaches me holding an ice pack. "Luke said you needed this?"

I toss back the bubbly. "Yeah. Twisted something out on stage. The ice should help." He passes me the pack, and I return to my chair to put it in place.

"You all rocked it out there. It's great for you to be back on the big stage. Where you belong."

The pack keeps falling off my thigh, so I put the glass down on a side table and position it better, keeping my fingers on an edge. "Thanks. It was a great time."

"You had the audience in the palm of your hand," Chico notes. "Like old times, right?"

I pause for a moment. "It was heady, for sure. Hearing them echo our lyrics never gets old."

"I can only imagine." He points to the pack. "Is this helping?"

Shrugging, I resist the urge to remove the ice pack. "I don't know. It doesn't really bother me when I'm sitting. It's only when I'm up and moving."

He looks like he wants to say something else, but the band joins us at my chair. Twirling his gold hoop earrings, Coop asks. "Leg still effed up?"

"Not when I'm sitting," I reply. "If only it would stop hurting like a scorned groupie when I get up."

"I bet it was that crazy-ass jump you did," a shirtless Río pipes up. "Have to say, from my vantage point behind the drums, it was fire."

I fidget with the ice pack. "Thanks. It certainly felt right in the moment."

Tris fiddles with what appears to be a friendship bracelet. Never noticed it before. "Hope you didn't do anything to your groin muscle, dude. That shit takes forever to heal. My uncle pulled his and wasn't right for like a year."

A groan from all of us goes up in response. 007 smacks him behind the head. He adjusts his studded belt—the one that used to be Darren's—and in the worst Austrian accent known to mankind, says, "It's not a tumor."

The groans turn into chuckles. "I'm sure it's nothing," I placate the band. "A little ice and some Advil and I'll be on the dancefloor in no time."

"Sure hope so," Río chips in, then takes one step to the side. "On second thought, with you on the sidelines, that means more girls for the rest of us. Hope your leg is out of commission for a long while."

I purse my lips. "Then I won't be performing at the concerts." I shrug. "Guess you don't want to go on tour."

Río scratches his nose. "Hope your leg is back after the weekend. I have no problem picking up the slack and entertaining the fairer sex for the next few days."

He bumps against Coop, who agrees, "Yeah. We certainly can take a few additional ladies each to make up for your being missing this weekend. It's not a hardship."

"Call dibs on a blonde!" 007 adds unhelpfully.

I turn toward Tris, who has yet to capitalize on his apparent good fortune. "Redheads are my favorite," he murmurs.

I force a laugh over all their antics. "Sorry to disappoint you all, but my money's on partying with you tonight. However, I might take my celebration to a private location and not share any of the women."

Coop holds up his phone. "I know you think this is nothing, but do you want me to call anyone?"

"No." Everyone who needs to know is right here in the room. I don't have any other people in my life. It's better this way. My small circle of acquaintances suits me.

Río frowns. "Are you sure? You never talk about other friends because, hey, when you have UC twenty-four seven, why do you need anyone else?" The group laughs. "But what about your mom? Shouldn't she be notified?"

"There's nothing to tell her. I'm fine." I play with the end of the ice pack. In truth, she's the last person on earth I'd call if I needed help.

Río replies, "Message received, buddy." He hits me on top of the ice pack and shooting pain screams throughout my body.

"That fucking hurt," I hiss.

"Sorry man," Río says. "I thought it wasn't so bad."

Through gritted teeth, I answer, "When it's left alone."

Brows together, Coop leans toward me. "Are you sure you're all right? Want me to get a doctor?"

"Luke is," I pant, "getting someone." I take several deep breaths.

Noise around me stops. One by one, each of the guy's mouths shut. I follow their gazes to the threshold, and my own mouth seals.

All the air in the room disappears.

My brain seizes.

Why on earth is *she* here?

Luke ushers Jenna Westfield toward me. Our manager and Darren's ex whisper between themselves. Tris's head tilts. Río's brows pull together. Coop's eyes reach his hairline. 007's face glows red.

I bite my inner cheeks.

Luke draws our attention. "Guys, we were lucky to have a physical therapist in the audience."

"Administrator," Jenna corrects him.

He continues without acknowledging she spoke. "We need to get Bennett checked out."

Hands on hips, chest pumping in and out, a red-faced 007 stares her down. In a bellow sure to be heard several states over, he howls, "Get someone else."

I don't want Jenna to touch me.

I don't want to revisit our initial conversation.

I don't want to be gut punched by Darren, even from the grave.

Still, if Luke brought her to check on me, I'm pretty sure there were no other options. I need to take control of this situation. And fast. "Guys. I'm sure it's nothing. Remember, Darren praised her work with his wrist injury. I'm going to let her take a quick look at my leg, and then we'll all be on our way."

Luke shoos the rest of the band away from us, muttering something about giving us privacy. He literally has to push 007.

Above the jackhammers pounding through my body, I manage, "Hey, Jenna."

"Bennett." She removes the ice pack from my thigh. Of course, I'm still wearing my black leather pants from performing, but they're going nowhere. On the other hand, my torso is bare. Wonderful.

Over the leather, her hands skim my legs. She kneads my upper thigh. She manipulates my leg, causing a bit of discomfort. A bit? It fucking hurts! I remind myself she's doing an exam, nothing more. To keep my thoughts away from the no-go zone, I imagine the most boring task I can—a meeting with my CPA.

This distraction works for a minute, until she tells me to stand. Unsteady, I rise out of the chair. Relying on my good leg, I stand before her and she continues running tests.

She pulls my leg away from my body and tells me to push against her hand. I try, and maybe succeed a little, but the pain is blinding. My ass lands in the chair again.

"What I thought," she whispers to herself.

"What is it?" I ask.

Her pink tongue licks her lips. "I'm no doctor, but if I had to guess, you have a grade two groin pull."

I repeat her diagnosis. "How long til I'm normal again?"

"Normal?" Her eyebrow quirks. She replaces the ice pack on my thigh, which is throbbing from all the work she put it through. Which honestly, wasn't much.

Being in Jenna's presence again after two years is playing havoc with my mind. She's Darren's. *Was* Darren's. Seeing her in the movie was one thing, but now in person? It's messed up.

"Assuming I'm right, you'll be healed in no time."

I melt into the chair and take a long look at her. She's thinner than I remember. Than even in the movie. Her sandy blonde hair is longer too, which she's wearing in a ponytail. Not the stylish cut she used to sport.

I can't allow myself to chronicle her other changes. "What does 'no time' mean?"

"I think you should see a doctor."

My clenched fist bangs on the chair's armrest. "All because of a stupid jump?" From the corner of my eye, I notice Luke starting in our direction.

In a voice quieter than I remember, she says, "Injuries can happen anywhere, Bennett. People get hurt in their own homes all the time."

"Whatever." I wave my hand as Luke joins us. "I repeat my earlier question. How long until I'm better?"

Jenna glances from Luke to me. "A grade two pull usually takes three to six weeks recovery time."

I suck in my breath. "No way! I have two weeks until our first sold-out concert!"

Chapter Four

I don't have three weeks to get over this stupid groin pull, never mind six. I don't even have *two*. UC's going on tour in fourteen days, and I damn well have to be there.

My reaction draws all my band members and most of the crew and roadies over to us. In all the hubbub, I lose sight of Jenna. Probably for the best.

"What's up?" Río pipes up.

I turn my head away, which spurs Luke to tell the group. "Jenna thinks our boy Bennett has a stage two groin pull, with a three- to six-week recovery time frame."

My eyes rise to the ceiling. This cannot be happening, so close to our re-emergence. I won't let it.

Coop shakes his head. "Dude. We need you before then."

"I know." I force my gaze to my bandmates. "I know. I'm sure Jenna was wrong. Luke here will take me to a doctor tomorrow and I'll get checked out properly. There's nothing to worry about."

As the frontman for UC, I can't sit and let the music go on around me. I need to be running around the stage hyping the crowd. Jenna has to be wrong.

One of the new roadies who handles lighting leans over and whispers in my ear. "I know how you could get over your injury quickly."

Hope sparks. "Really? How?"

He makes the peace sign, brings it to his mouth and sticks his tongue out. "You could do the physical therapist. Bet you'd be perfect in no time."

"Fuck no!" I push him away from me. With an even louder volume, I tell him and anyone listening, "I'm not doing Jenna, and neither is anyone related to the band. *Do Not Fuck* list, remember?"

007, who's been sporting a sourpuss since Jenna was brought into this mess, adds his own two cents. "That woman is off-limits. She's not a part of this tour or our band, and has nothing to do with us." As Darren's best friend, 007 took his death the hardest. Irrationally and without another outlet, it seems like he's transferred his anger from Darren's overdose onto Jenna.

I point at our bassist. "What he said."

Luke hops into our group, which is wound so tight you could bounce a quarter off it. "All right, now. I've got limos ready to take us to the afterparty where we're going to mingle with some Hollywood elites, influencers, and reporters. Remember, we could be photographed at any time, so be on your best behavior." He directs his last sentence to Río who raises his hands like he's innocent.

No matter what shit's going on, these guys are a good bunch to have at your back. At a distance, of course.

While the rest of the entourage streams through the green room, a woman's arms steal around my neck. "Bennett."

I get a whiff of raspberry and gardenia perfume, and know immediately who has me wrapped in her arms. Turning, I kiss her cheek. "We're all beyond thrilled with how your movie turned out, Quinn."

I let her go and she steps away. Next to her, Callum, dressed in his homeland's tuxedo—meaning a kilt—reaches out to shake my hand.

I raise my chin toward Quinn. "You got a keeper."

He wraps his arm around her. "Don't I know it. We're actually going to Scotland to do a film about my family soon."

"You're in amazing hands." I mean all this praise, and more. I direct my next comment to Quinn. "The way you captured our struggles didn't feel intrusive. You showed our progress like it really was. The absolute reason why you're going to win an Oscar."

Quinn giggles. This lightness in her is new—and a welcome facet of her personality. I'd bet my left nut Callum had something to do with bringing it out. "I don't know about an award, but I'm thrilled you liked the finished product." She cranes her neck. "Have you seen Jenna anywhere? Someone from your team pulled her away and I haven't seen her since."

I swallow. "Yeah. Well, that was for me." I point to my leg. "I managed to pull a muscle and a roadie brought her to check me out."

Her boyfriend asks, "Is everything okay?"

I sigh. I can be real with these two. "I'm hoping Jenna's diagnosis is wrong, Callum. She said I'll need six weeks to heal and we're going on tour in two. Luke's taking me to a doctor tomorrow."

Quinn hugs me again. "I hope everything gets fixed up for you. Rumor has it your upcoming tour is going to include stadiums. I have no doubt but that you'll be in tip-top shape for it."

"Thanks. This is so surreal." I tap my thigh. "I'm sure I'll be fine soon. To answer your earlier question, though, Jenna disappeared after checking me out and I think she snuck out the side door of the green room."

"At least I got her to sit through the movie. If you see her again, please let her know I'm in her corner. She seems very fragile."

Fragile.

Quinn's analysis lingers long after she and Callum are pulled away. She's spot-on. Not that it matters to me how Darren's girlfriend is faring. Not. At. All.

At nine the next morning, I'm poked and prodded and pushed in all directions by the doctor before being whisked away for x-rays and an MRI. Approaching the monstrosity of a machine, I ask if this is necessary and am assured it is. Sighing, I get into it and pretend to be in a recording studio. At least it's over relatively quickly, and soon enough I'm sitting in the doctor's office again.

Luke checks his watch, and I resist the urge to know how long we've spent in this building. All I want to hear is take two more Advil and everything will be fine. However, the throbbing in my thigh warns me of a different result.

"How's it feeling, B?"

"A little worse since the last time you asked me, considering I've now been through a shitload more tests. Felt like Jenna did at least five. Do you really think all this fuss is necessary?" My left foot, attached to my good leg, taps the floor. I try to switch to the other side, but the throbbing stops me. A deep sigh comes out of my soul.

Our manager cracks his knuckles. "Listen, I've been doing some calculations. We've already sold out the early part of the tour, and the thought of rescheduling it gives me hives. If you're not up to performing, though, we don't have much of a choice. I can get my assistant on it—probably add three more to help her.

"No," I shake my head. "I'm not letting UC down. I'll be fine to tour, just you wait." Without the band, I would be nothing. I send up a prayer I'm right. *When have my prayers ever been answered?* I add, "Maybe we can put a chair off to the side if I need to take a break."

The doctor returns, carrying a huge stack of papers. He sits behind his desk and I want to throttle my diagnosis out of him. *Stop stalling, man, and tell me the verdict!*

"I've reviewed all your tests. The good news is you're in fantastic shape, which is a definite plus."

"He hits the gym at least six times a week," Luke supplies.

I don't let my gaze wander from the doctor, who seems somewhat impressed with my workout regimen. I have my reasons for doing this, none of which are his business. With deliberate redirection, I ask, "So what do you think, doc? When will it stop hurting me?"

The doctor rubs his nose. "The tests show you have a groin pull, Mr. Hardy."

"Bennett," I correct him. Again. "That's what Jenna said. She diagnosed it as a grade two pull, with a three-to-six-week recovery time. Thing is, I'm scheduled to go out on tour in two weeks."

The doctor's brows pull together. "Well, this Jenna was half-right. Is she a doctor?"

"No," Luke supplies. "Physical therapist."

"Ah," the doctor says. "Good instincts. She was almost spot on, except for the grade."

I perk up. I knew it—this will all be over in a much shorter time-frame than Jenna predicted. I rub my hands on my thighs, careful to avoid my injury. "Great. I'll be fine in no time, right?"

The doctor shakes his head. "Unfortunately, that's not the direction this is going. You actually have a low-level grade three pull. It doesn't require surgery."

Surgery? No. Fucking. Way. "Grade three is worse than grade two?" This can't be right. My gaze sears into Luke's before returning to the doctor.

"Yes. For you to heal fully, you'll need three to six months to recover."

His statement hangs in the air.

"MONTHS?" I leap to my feet, instantly regretting my fast action as my *grade three* pull protests. I slump back down.

"I understand you need to get out on the road sooner."

"We leave in two weeks," Luke mutters. I can tell he's calculating how to reorder the tour to accommodate my stupid injury.

The doctor places his clipboard onto the desk. "The timeframe I gave you is to be back to full capability. However, you don't need to be one hundred percent to perform so long as you take extra precautions, modify your choreography, and don't aggravate the injury any further."

I sit up. "I'll do anything. How long?"

"I'm not going to say you won't have pain, but I predict you'll not have to move any tour dates so long as you work harder than you've ever worked before to rehab your injury."

Next to me, Luke exhales a long breath.

My fingers flex. I can do this. "What do I have to do?"

The doctor stares at me. "I'm not saying this will be easy. In fact, you're going to curse every second of your rehab, but if you want to meet your deadline, this is what you have to do. Put ice on your inner thigh for thirty minutes every three to four hours for the next two or three days."

He hands me a packet of information. "Then, do these exercises at least twice a day, more if you can handle it."

I open the folder and flip through a few pages. They don't seem too difficult. I nod.

Without waiting for me to speak, the doctor continues, "Many of the exercises require someone to spot you. For best results, and by 'best' I mean fastest, I suggest you work with a licensed physical therapist. You mentioned this Jenna who diagnosed you last night."

My stomach cramps and displaces the pain from my groin pull.

"No," I respond at the same time Luke says, "Good idea."

My hand goes to my good thigh and squeezes. Through clenched teeth, I mutter, "Not her."

Luke lowers his head. "We'll discuss this later, B."

Then he returns his attention to the doctor, who has a blue pad in his hand. My neck snaps. "What are you doing?"

"I'm writing you a prescription for a muscle relaxant. If you're going to be working as hard as I think you will, you're going to need them."

The doctor rips off a sheet of paper and extends it toward me. I remain immobile. I'd rather writhe in pain than get addicted like Darren did. Luke takes the prescription and pockets it.

The rest of the appointment continues, but two things play on repeat. One, no way am I taking any pills. And two, and equally as unshakeable, no *fucking* way is Jenna going to be involved with my recovery.

When we're in the car being driven back to the hotel, with my next doctor's appointment scheduled for two days before our tour starts, I express my absolute no-gos to Luke. Tapping the armrest, he says, "I get it about the pain meds. We don't have to fill the prescription, it'll just be in my back pocket if you need it."

"I won't."

"Fine. We'll stick with over-the-counter meds."

"Damn straight." I stare out the side window.

"As for Jenna—"

"Listen, Luke. I let her check me out last night because I didn't have any other options."

"The doctor did recommend you work with a physical therapist, and she's the only one we know." He pauses. "She did a great job on Darren's wrist."

"Before he died."

Boom. No arguing with me here.

Luke clears his throat. "Yes. Before he overdosed, B. He *overdosed*. That wasn't anyone's fault but his own. Certainly not Jenna's. She wasn't even in the state."

The sunroof provides a much-needed glimpse of the sky. "Fine. I agree Jenna had nothing to do with his death."

We ride in silence for a full minute. The vehicle turns right, and he asks, "Do you know another physical therapist? Cause I don't."

My mind races. "No, but there has to be some website we can check out." I fumble with my phone. "Here's one: At Your Service PT. It has great reviews. Sounds good to me." I flip through the website, clicking on About Us. "Fuck. This is Jenna's company." I toss my phone.

"It's the universe telling us something."

A factoid niggles in the back of my mind. "Didn't Jenna say she's an administrator now?" I retrieve my phone and read, "'Founded by Jenna Westfield, At Your Service PT aims to help you recover from surgery or injury . . .' Blah, blah, blah. Here it is: 'Ms. Westfield is the administrator for the company, now in two locations.' See, I was right. She doesn't do therapy anymore."

Luke shakes his head, causing his hair to brush against his shoulders. "How about this. We call"—he notices my stiffening posture—"*I* call Jenna and tell her your diagnosis. Perhaps she can recommend one of her therapists to work with you?"

My cheeks pull inward. "I don't think we should have anything to do with her, out of respect for Darren."

Now my manager's cheeks suck inward. "Do you really think Darren wouldn't want UC to associate with his girlfriend?"

My eyes slam shut. "No," I whisper. "He was proud of her, both as his girlfriend and as a professional. My guess is he'd be super pissed at us for *not* wanting to use her services." I watch featureless scenery pass.

Silence rings out for the remainder of our trip back to the hotel. I consider various pros and cons of working with Jenna. Pros: she's damn good at what she does, witnessed by the undeniable fact she rehabbed Darren in record time. Cons: she's local to New York City and my main base is in LA; she's now an administrator and doesn't practice anymore; she was Darren's girlfriend. Perhaps overriding everything, she was the first—and only—woman to make me rethink my no girlfriend policy, instituted after Lissa's betrayal in high school.

Somewhere deep inside, Darren gives me the stink eye.

Walking toward the elevators, I stop, causing Luke to halt his progress too. I take a deep breath. "If Jenna agrees to work with me herself, I'll do it."

Please, let her say no.

Chapter Five

We enter the hotel and Río's boisterous voice floats from the lobby bar. Luke taps me on my shoulder with his cell. "You go ahead. I have a phone call to make."

I lift my hand and enter the bar. "Bennett!" As if on an ancient episode of "Cheers," the entire clientele greets me. I wave and join the band at a table, where a Manhattan is placed in front of me.

As I swirl the cherry, I remark, "Kinda early to get your drink on, guys."

Río holds up a Gold Rush, a bourbon whiskey sour, his drink of choice ever since we discovered it a few years ago. "Hey, it's five o'clock somewhere." He starts singing the Jimmy Buffet song, getting everyone singing the refrain. I even join his craziness.

Coop moves next to me. "What did the doctor say? Was Jenna right?"

I sip my drink, my stomach starting to churn. Perhaps it's the fact I missed breakfast and spent the past few hours being poked and prodded. "Sort of." I point at a menu sitting on the table. "Can you hand me that?"

Distracted for a moment, Coop passes it to me. Río, 007, and Tris crowd in the table. After I place my order for a cheeseburger and fries, sparked by Río's choice of song, I explain, "Jenna hit it on the head. I do have a groin pull. She was wrong, though, about the grade level. It's a three and not a two."

Shit. The doctor said I need to ice it. When the server returns with a bottle of ketchup, I ask for an ice pack. All the while, the guys have been dissecting my proper diagnosis, and have learned about the recovery time, thanks to the internet and their cell phones.

"Yeah, so the doc said I can be on tour with UC as planned, so long as I ice it for a few days and then do these exercises." I hold up the folder he gave me.

"Dude, there's some serious exercises in here," Coop pronounces after flipping through the pages.

Río elbows 007 in the stomach. "We can set up visitation rights to you in the gym."

I rub two fingers across my nose. "Not exactly." When I have eight eyes on me, I continue, "He prescribed PT."

"As in physical therapy?" 007 shifts in his seat.

"Yeah." I don't want to share who Luke's calling right now.

Tris wades forward. "Who are you going to use?"

The weight of their stares breaks me. "Jenna, all right? Jenna is the only physical therapist we know, so of course Luke suggested her." The server brings my burger, and I busy myself preparing it while avoiding the band. My own recriminations are enough.

After I take a big bite of the greasy goodness, I chance a glance at them. Tris leans against his chair. Coop and even Río study the table. My gaze alights on the one person who I wish I didn't have to confront: 007, whose eyes bore a hole into my chest.

My hand flips palm side up, motioning for him to speak. He takes another moment, then says, "She is good at her job. If anyone can make this happen for you on our tight schedule, she can." Relief floods my system. "Just don't do it in front of me, okay?"

I shake my head. "I'm sure we'll spend our time in the gym. Let me know your schedule, and we'll work around it."

"Thanks," 007 blows out a breath. "I never thought I'd have to see her again, so keep her away from the band and we'll be good. You need to get better."

"Appreciate it. Besides, who knows if she'll even take me as a client. She's an administrator for her company, not a therapist anymore." This is my last hook to hang my hope she'll refuse the gig. She stirs too much inside me. Not to mention every time I look at her, I see Darren.

"Do you really think you'll be up for touring? You only have two weeks." Tris's question brings me out of my head.

"I was the one who jumped like a crazy person, landing hard on my leg. I'll make sure I'm ready to perform, even if it means I need to sit and rest when we're offstage."

Tris and Coop appear satisfied with my answer. 007's lips form a straight line, while Río jokes, "You did leap like you were gonna set a new high jump record." He laughs and looks around, holding up his glass. "What? Too soon? Bennett did bring this on himself. Gotta have faith he'll recuperate in time."

Sick and tired of this topic of conversation, I spout, "The after-party last night was off the chain."

Like with interviews, my diversion works. The band starts discussing all the people who attended, the positive buzz over the movie, and the hot chicks in attendance. Laughter rings instead of worried conversation about whether Jenna is going to be my physical therapist. Given the fact Luke has yet to reappear, I guess she turned him down. Good.

I remove the ice pack and toss it onto the table. *Especially* given where the pull is located. Sex is going to have to be limited too. *Guess I'll have to get more creative.*

The remnants of my cheeseburger remain on my plate, given my appetite has disappeared. Who the fuck jumps and lands in physical therapy? "I'm disgusted with you." My mother's voice echoes in my head.

Tossing back my Manhattan, I force her out of my mind. Among other things, I certainly don't need *her* riding me.

I reach for the packet of information provided by the doctor and read through the exercises. Some require a partner, but most do not. I don't need Jenna or anyone to work with me. I can do this alone. Like most things.

A pretty redheaded woman in a short skirt and tight top walks up to me. Perhaps she can help me work through my injury. "Hi," I greet her.

"Hello. You're Bennett Hardy, aren't you?"

Her eyes undress me, indicating she knows the answer. "I am." I lean forward and cup her cheek. "Who might you be?" Not that I care. Names don't suck me off.

She replies, but I don't pay attention. Her pink tongue licks her collagen-enhanced lips, stained red. I bet they'd look nice around my cock. This facet of being a rock star doesn't get old. I catch the end of her sentence, but it doesn't make too much sense. What does she need help with?

"Excuse me?"

She approaches my ear. "I said," she whispers. "I'm feeling naughty right now. Can you help?"

Hell yes. "You have a room here?"

"Sure do." A room key appears in her hand. "Ready to blow this stand?"

I certainly have a better idea of what she can blow. With a kiss to her cheek, I get to my feet and sling my arm around her. This chick will help clear my head. We take two steps and the pain radiating from my thigh makes me rethink her offer. Shit.

"Hey, darling, change of plans." Knowing his preference, I stop in front of Tris. Placing my hand on his shoulder, I say, "I think you'll have a better time with our keyboardist."

The two look at each other. She turns and puts her hand on my chest. "Are you sure?"

Miss Naughty doesn't care which rock star she's with, which works for me. "Yeah." I lean over to Tris and say, "You're welcome."

A grin spreads across his face. He bites his lower lip, a move that seems to work for him. It does this time as well. The two disappear from the bar.

I retake my chair and play with a French fry, not having the energy to chat with the band. Across the way, Luke enters and strides toward me. A gleam's in his eye I don't like.

Our manager makes a pit stop at the bar and sidles up next to me, sipping a beer. He plants his ass in the empty seat next to me. "Talked with Jenna."

"Figured you had."

"She said maybe."

My eyebrows rise. "Can't imagine why she wouldn't jump at the chance to be with UC again."

He chuckles at my sarcasm. "Have to admit, I was surprised she didn't say yes. She was, however, shocked she got the grade wrong but at least she had the right diagnosis." He raises his hand to order me another Manhattan, but I decline. Something tells me I'll need all my wits. "The money seemed to interest her."

"Money?"

"Yeah. It's not like I'd expect her to do your therapy for free."

I hold up the exercise packet. "Whatever. I bet I can do this on my own."

Luke laughs. "You do you. But if Jenna agrees, promise me you'll work with her."

"I'd rather have anyone else." Taking my time, I get to my feet. "On that note, I'm outta here. Going to put more ice on this in my room and rest my leg." With careful footsteps, I leave the bar to the strains of "On My Own."

I don't need anybody else.

I can't do this alone.

After watching a movie, icing my thigh, and sleeping ten hours straight, I got up and iced my thigh again. Then I took out a sheet from the packet and tried to do the first exercise. No way can I do these.

I grab the breakfast plate and go to throw it across the room, stopping myself at the last possible moment. It's not fair to take out my frustrations on eggs and bacon. With a growl, I pick up the compression bandage and roll it up my leg, tugging my shorts over my not-gorgeous new accessory.

Tea. I need some tea to calm the fuck down. I pour the hot water into a mug and dunk a berry fusion bag into it. If I'm going to be able to start the tour on time, I have to do these exercises. If I have to do these exercises, I need help. Full stop.

But does that help have to be in the form of a pretty woman with long, sandy blonde hair, connected to Darren? Only one thing wrong with this thought. She's not only pretty, she's insightful and sweet and . . . fragile. I grunt.

She said *maybe*.

It will be better for all concerned if we hire a different physical therapist. A dude. One with zero connection with UC. I pick up my phone to text Luke and tell him to end his quest for Jenna when someone knocks on my door.

"Be right there!" If only my hotel room door would stay unlocked so I didn't have to hobble over and open it, but what choice do I have? From halfway across the room, I yell, "Another minute."

When I reach the door, I use the bottom of my T-shirt to wipe the sweat off my forehead before opening it. Luke, holding a cup of coffee, passes by me with a quick hello. I offer him a seat in the living room and make my way there.

Grateful my ass is once again on the plush cushion, I sip my tea and wait. I hope he doesn't bring news that Jenna agreed. She's a complication I don't need in my life.

He sets his coffee onto the table. "Good news. Jenna agreed."

Of course she did. Because the universe enjoys a good laugh. I blow air through my mouth. "Yippee."

"C'mon, B. You know she worked wonders on Darren's wrist. You even remarked about his recovery at the time."

I reach for my tea but leave it on the table. "Well, that was then and about him. A lot's happened since. And this is *my* injury we're talking about now."

"I get it." Luke looks me straight in the eye. "I do. Things are different with you." When I open my mouth to speak, he holds up his hand. "One, you're not looking for a girlfriend like Darren was."

I rear back. "He was on the hunt for his next conquest, never a girlfriend."

Luke shakes his head. "He always hoped the next woman would be 'the one.' Then he met Jenna, and she *was* the one. Until the fog of drugs fueled his mind. He's been gone a long time, B. Any hold he had over this woman no longer applies. Besides, you're not dating her, she's just going to be your therapist. Nothing more."

I ponder what our manager said. "She was Darren's girlfriend."

Luke's head moves up and down in slow motion. "She was. Was. Past tense."

My eyes shut. "She agreed? To help me?"

"She did. Took a long while, I have to admit. Her agreement does come with stipulations, though."

"She's dictating to us?"

"I wouldn't call it 'dictating.'" He takes a sip of his coffee. "More like she has some conditions."

I run my fingers through my hair. "Can't wait to hear them. Isn't it bad enough I need her services?"

Luke chuckles. "The first stipulation doesn't matter to you. It was business."

My head tilts. "Like what?"

"She negotiated a bigger payout for her services. Necessitated by her second stipulation." He tips his cardboard coffee cup up to the ceiling, making sure to get every drop.

"Can't wait to hear this." I count the ceiling tiles as he switches his position in the chair.

"She's building a business out on Long Island, as you know. She has two locations, both of which require her attention. She can't afford to be away from them for any length of time."

Dread washes over me. "What exactly are you saying?"

Luke straightens his shoulders. "She wants to work with you in her clinic out there."

I swing forward, aggravating my inner thigh. I manage to contain my yelp of pain but not my grimace. For his part, our manager waits for me to get the pain under control. When it's subsided, I say, "What if I don't want to go?"

"C'mon, B. She's out in Aroostook, which is in the Hamptons. Playground of the rich and famous."

I let this sink into my brain. "I guess the party scene is hot out there."

"In season it is."

"Which won't begin for months."

We sit in silence until Luke adds, "King and Angie Hunte live out there year-round. I bet they can hook you up with a sweet rental."

King is Braxton Hunte's son, the lead singer of the Rock 'n Roll Hall of Fame band Hunte. I've met the band a few times and would loosely call them slight acquaintances. Also have jammed a couple of times with Braxton's other son, Trent, of The Light Rail fame. Because we had nothing else to do between tour stops, UC watched "Battle of the Real Estate Matchmakers," which featured both King and Angie. They seem like the real deal although I'm well aware of how the press can manipulate a story.

I shrug. "I've never met them."

"His father and brother are with Apex Hits. I have friends over there who can introduce you to King, I'm sure."

A slight grin touches my lips. "Imagine what Kenneth Dumont would say to such blasphemy." Apex and my label Platinum compete for top spots on the regular. We have Cole Manchester, Ozzy

Martinez, and Adam Baret, so I think we're on the winning side. But it's close.

Luke spreads his hands wide. "Let's keep this between us."

Despite the levity, if I agree to this plan, I'm brought back to the fact I'd be working with Jenna. One-on-one. On her home turf. "How long?"

"Right now, we have twelve days until the UC tour starts. So, eleven days. Think you can handle it?"

The gauntlet has been thrown. Eleven days. Less than two weeks. I can do anything for such a short amount of time. Our manager sees my capitulation before I even utter a word. He leaps to his feet—show-off.

Rubbing his hands together, he says, "Pack your bags. You're going on a short trip."

I hope this decision doesn't come back to bite me.

Chapter Six

All of my belongings are packed into the two suitcases I use for the tour. Since my wardrobe on stage is provided by the label, I don't need too much. Plus, if I want anything, I can simply buy it in whatever town we're in or have it delivered to the hotel *du jour*.

The band crowds into my suite. "It sucks you have to go away for PT," Coop moans.

I pause. "It's similar to when we're on a break from touring. We all go our own ways for a couple of weeks. Nothing different." Truly. We hang when we're on tour, then I usually go to some nice beach for the break. Alone. Well, I start off alone until some obliging chick realizes I'm there.

"I guess," Coop replies, tucking his sunglasses into the top of his shirt. "We've been together so long; you and the other guys are family."

Family. No, thank you. Instead of getting into it with our guitarist, I slap his back. "I'm sure you'll get along just fine without me."

Río joins us. "Don't tell me you're giving each other tearful good-byes."

Coop gives him a dirty look and replies, "Dick."

I appreciate both his timing and the reminder to keep my distance. "You wish." I limp over to my backpack and shove my lyric notebook in it. "Hoping I'll get some writing done out in the Hamptons."

"Sounds good to me." Tris walks up to us. "I've got some new stuff in the works as well. I'll email you when it's in better shape."

"Cool." Writing with collaborators makes everything better. We don't need to write anything since our new album dropped and the tour will support it, but this is how we work. Always having new songs to perfect keeps us on our toes. I know this isn't how other bands do it, but UC has its own ways.

The only band member who hasn't come to wish me well is 007. It's hard for me to get help from Jenna, but for him . . . it's an impossibility. "Hey, can you please do me a favor? Keep an eye on 007 while I'm away. You know my seeing Jenna is bringing up all sorts of shit about Darren's death. This is tough on him." Me, too, but I don't share this with the band.

"You know we will," Coop replies. "We've been through it before, and we'll do it again."

Coop's right. The fallout after Darren died was terrible, especially for the keyboardist's best friend. Seeing 007 laugh again was a milestone we won't ever forget. Watching him accept Tris as Darren's replacement was an even bigger one. No, I never want to relive such dark times. None of us do.

I catch the guitarist's hazel eyes, which appear browner today. "Thanks."

The moment is broken when someone knocks at the door. Tris offers to get it and Luke strides through, with 007 at his side. Wow.

I extend my right hand. "Happy you were able to see me off."

We shake. "It's not every day our lead singer leaves for PT. You'll be back in no time, jumping around the stage like the madman you are." 007 smiles. It doesn't reach his eyes.

"Not sure about the latter, but I know you're right about the former. Eleven days is no time at all."

"That's right," Luke pipes up. "Are you ready for the helicopter ride out to the Hamptons?"

"No way!" Variations of this greet my ears.

I toss my head back. "All you have to do is pull your groin and you too can get a ride in a helicopter."

They laugh. It's been nice hanging with them, I won't lie. If I believed in friends, these guys would be them.

They help bring my luggage to the taxi, then Luke and I are off to the helipad. On the way, he tells me to focus on my recovery and he'll take care of the tour. He does, however, promise to keep me in the loop about staging so I can hit the ground running—no pun intended —when I return.

Luke brings my luggage to the helicopter, where it's loaded into the cargo hold. He looks me in the eye. "Take care of yourself, B. I want you healthy and whole when you get back."

"Sounds good to me."

With a pat on the back, I turn and face the chopper with its blades whirling. An attendant points me toward the open door— where there are no steps or ramp. Under normal circumstances, I would simply hop into the cabin and buckle my seatbelt. These are anything but normal conditions.

I approach the doorway and toss my backpack onto the empty seat. At least no one else is here to witness my embarrassing entry. My hand fists around the grab handle, and using my good leg, I step on the thin bar and bring my other to meet it. I repeat these awkward movements, stopping to absorb the piercing pain.

A hand lands on my back. "You okay, buddy?"

Through gritted teeth, I reply to the pilot, "Yeah."

"Alright, once you get settled, we'll be on our way." Two more pats on my back.

Easier said than done. I stare into the cabin and will myself to take the final step. When my ass lands in the seat, I hang my head. If I can't do something as simple as enter a helicopter, how will I perform in front of thousands in under two weeks?

The pilot points to his headset and I put mine over my ears. His voice comes through them. "Welcome to the Airborne Jitney, Mr. Hardy. It's a pleasure to transport you today. Please sit back and enjoy the quick ride."

"Thanks."

Enjoy? I wish I had an ice pack to soothe my angry thigh muscle. At least the pilot refrained from making fun of how I entered the chopper. I can hear my bandmates from here, and I'm glad I left them at the hotel.

A short eight-minute flight later, we land at an airfield in the Hamptons. I manage the exit much the same as my entrance. A couple stands near an SUV, waving at me.

A blond guy with amber eyes—like his father's—greets me. "Hi, I'm King Hunte. Your manager Luke called us. It's a pleasure to meet you. I'm a big fan."

His sentiment is shocking, considering his father's in the Rock & Roll Hall of Fame. "Thanks, I appreciate it. I've had the pleasure of hanging with your father and brother before, and they're cool. I'm very happy to finally get to meet you."

The helicopter attendant brings my luggage to me, for which I give him a big tip. Feeling like a douche but knowing I can't do this myself, I point to the car. "Can you please put them over there?"

"Sure thing, Mr. Hardy."

King and I follow him. When King realizes I'm not keeping up, he shortens his stride. I sigh. "Normally, I'm much faster. I pulled my groin muscle, and it hurts like a bitch."

"Got it." He tilts his head. "If you're hurt, may I ask why you're coming all the way out to Aroostook?"

"My physical therapist is out here."

If King thinks my answer is weird, he keeps his own counsel. We stow—rather he puts the luggage into the trunk while I stand help-lessly next to him—and his co-star wife Angie greets me. "Nice to meet you, Bennett."

While she seems perplexed at why I'm not helping with my bags, she doesn't ask. Which prompts me to tell her about my injury.

"Oh no. Who are you going to see?"

"Jenna Westfield of At Your Service PT."

"I've met her a few times," Angie supplies. "We both go to the same Chamber of Commerce. She's quiet but has a good reputation."

Her assessment of Jenna provides a bit of comfort. At least coming here was the right decision. After we get into the car, I redirect the conversation. "Luke mentioned you might have a short-term rental for me?"

Switching into professional mode, Angie rattles off the details of three, fully furnished places she wants to show me. I hold up my hand. "Thanks for all your research, but I'm not up to checking out different places. Can you pick one for me? I trust you."

Truth is, I don't really care. Eleven days will pass in the blink of an eye. Even if it were a year, I wouldn't be bothered. I'm not one to put down roots.

King replies. "Sure. We have one pretty close to where Jenna's clinic is located, so it might be the most convenient."

"Sounds perfect."

He pulls up to the front door of a one-story bungalow, where he unloads my luggage. Again. "Since I'm not usually such a prima donna, how about I take you guys out to dinner as a thank you?"

Angie's full lips tick upward. "I'd love to, but I need to get home to our kids." The two share a soft look. "Our baby is six months and starting to get into everything. Her older sister is three."

"Congrats." Kids are not something on my bucket list. Growing up in my dysfunctional household taught me never to repeat my parents' mistake.

King says, "How about this? I'll drop Angie off while you get settled in your new house. Then I'll come back and we can go out to dinner."

"I wouldn't want to deprive you of family time." I may not want rugrats running around, but I'm also not a total douchebag.

"That's a good idea," Angie replies. "It's total chaos at the house between feeding them and baths, and King had to do evening duty twice this week. It's my turn."

"If you're sure?" I don't want to intrude, but it might be nice to get the inside scoop about my temporary town.

"Definitely." King wheels my luggage into the house. "I'll be back in an hour. Will that be enough time?"

Seeing as all I need to do is unpack and ice my throbbing leg, I can be ready in forty-five minutes. "Perfect."

The couple drives away, and I fumble lugging my bags into the bedroom. Although I want to sit and take a breather, I decide unpacking is the better choice. Get it done, earn the ice pack. When I'm sitting on the plush sectional facing a big screen television hung above a modern fireplace, I put ice on my throbbing thigh. Guess I pushed a bit too hard.

"Get used to it. I'm going to rehab hard so everything can move forward without a hiccup." My thigh protests my resolution but I don't care. I deserve the pain for doing something so stupid.

The doorbell rings and I check the app to confirm it's King. Because I still have ten more minutes on my ice pack, I press the "talk" button and tell him to come on in. A minute later, he strolls into the living room. "Guess you're not worried about security?"

I shake my head. "Nah. I slipped out of the City and no one knows I'm here."

"Yet." King sits on the sectional a couple of cushions away. "Believe me, the paparazzi will find you. Since it's off-season here, they may be more rabid than ever to get a scoop."

My gaze drifts to the tray ceiling. "Great. All I want to do is recover in peace."

"I think if you keep a low profile, most of the full-time residents won't bother you." I pull the ice away from my leg and he takes it to the kitchen for me. "Maybe wear a disguise. It helps Dad sometimes."

"How about I use a cane? No one will recognize me then."

We both chuckle. King puts his hand on my shoulder. "C'mon, Charlie Chaplin. Let's go to a nearby restaurant, less than a ten-minute walk. Should I drive?"

"If we go slow, I can walk. The exercise should help me." I lock the door, and we lumber toward the restaurant. We stop in front of a store boasting the largest selection of arcade games in the world. Pinball machines, Pac-Man, Donkey Kong and more are on display. My gaze lights on my favorite.

Embarrassed but needing a break, I pant, "Can we check out this store?"

King notes, "This place is the bomb. If they don't have something you want, they'll get it for you."

I've been wanting to get an Asteroids Deluxe forever. Without a home to store it, though, my pipedream dissipates. "Can you play them in addition to purchasing?"

"Don't you know it."

I lick my lips. If I can't buy one, I can still play it here. Realizing the throbbing has died down, I motion to keep going, thrilled when I'm sitting in the restaurant.

"Which game?"

Unsure what King means, I ask, "You mean in the arcade store?" When he nods in the affirmative, I admit, "Asteroids Deluxe."

He sits taller. "I'm more of a Pac-Man guy myself. I hold the high record in there for that one. Although, I'd be open to learning a new skill."

We spend the next half-hour bonding over arcade games, discussing the role he played on TV as well as his love for real estate. I deposit the cherry from my Manhattan onto the table. "So you're not tempted to return to the small screen?"

"Nah. Angie and I make appearances on the show from time to time, but we have new agents whom the cameras follow. Angie and I have two daughters now, and we don't need the intrusion, you know?"

"Cameras sure can be. Although with the movie, we learned how to keep them at bay."

"We haven't had a chance to see your film yet, but it's gotten amazing buzz. UC seems to be back on top."

"Thanks. We're happy to be making music again. The movie Quinn Walker made is the bomb, if I do say so myself."

He raps his bourbon on the table. "A healthy ego must come with being a rock star. Dad and Trent both are never in short supply either."

I retort, "I don't think a reality TV actor is missing out."

"Touché."

Instead of our server, a woman appears at our table. She has glossy pink lips, long brown hair and eyes that match. She's wearing a skintight dress that doesn't leave anything to the imagination. Not that I blame her—her bod's rockin'.

"Hey, King," she sidles up to him. "How's the real estate biz treating you?"

His features tighten. "Great, Michelle. Been keeping us busy."

She trails a manicured fingernail up his arm. His lips purse. "Even in the off-season, you're still moving and shaking."

"Angie and I like to keep things interesting."

She fluffs her hair, tucking it behind her ear. Next, her fingers play with a large hoop earring. "I bet you do."

King's gaze meets mine and speaks a silent question. I shrug. "In fact, this is our newest client. He just rented the bungalow a few doors down."

Michelle turns her attention to me. If I were in the market for a hot chick to while away the hours, she would be a good candidate. Right now, though, I'm not feeling her. Mostly I'm feeling my freaking groin pull, and don't want to do anything to delay my progress.

"I swear, do you only associate with beautiful people or what, King?"

"I do my best."

His tone and demeanor suggest he's ready for her to move on. Given my situation, I am too. Before I can open my mouth, she stares at me, tapping her finger on her lips. "You look familiar."

Crap. At least King didn't introduce me—I don't want to deal with her attention, or potential paparazzi. "I'm only in town to get some physical therapy." My statement should make her leave us alone.

"Really? I work for the number one doctor here in Aroostook. Who sent you here?" King long-forgotten, I've now captured her imagination.

"A doc from New York City. He didn't recommend the therapist, and we already knew her."

Michelle moves to my other side. "Interesting. I can give you the scoop on everyone here. Who's the therapist?"

What harm can this do? Maybe I'll learn a little more dirt about Darren's girlfriend, so I know what I'm walking into tomorrow. "Jenna Westfield."

Michelle's nose scrunches as if she smelled a rancid lemon. "You can do much better than her, handsome. What about—"

On second thought, I don't let her finish her recommendation. "I'm afraid this is a done deal. Contract signed and everything." Was there a contract? I consider this question for a moment and decide I don't care. "I start tomorrow."

"There's still time to change your mind." She flips her long, brown hair. "Right, King?"

"I think Bennett here has everything well in hand."

Michelle rises on the balls of her feet. "Bennett? Unusual name. Not Ben or En?"

God no. I shake my head, ready for the inquisitive—although sexy—woman to disappear. Across from me, King stands. "If you'll excuse me, I need to use the restroom. I'll be right back."

The able-bodied guy strides toward the bathrooms in the back of the restaurant. He looks as if he never even had a hangnail. I hit the top of my thigh, causing a ripple effect throughout my leg. Fuck.

Go for deflection. "I take it you're not a fan of Jenna's?"

Michelle rolls her eyes. "You could say that, *Bennett*." I ignore how she stresses my name. "I've known her forever. She's sort of a," she pauses. "A holier-than-thou type of person."

I consider her assessment and find it lacking. "She's always seemed down-to-earth to me." Darren never could've been with someone with a chip on her shoulder.

"She can play nice if the situation calls for it." Michelle leans in. "But don't be fooled. The woman's a snake."

Smart. Skilled. Sweet. Not any of the s-words Michelle used to describe her. I lean back in my chair.

"So, *Bennett*, enough about your therapist. You look familiar. Tell me where I know you from—do you party in the Hamptons often?"

Michelle's question takes me to summer parties on this glitzy East Coast. "I have been to some events out here. Maybe that's where you saw me." Please don't dig.

Fingering her earring again, she says, "Maybe." After a moment, she points at me. Her voice raises, "You're Bennett Hardy of Untamed Coaster fame. I *knew* you looked familiar."

"Shh," I hush her. "Please keep your voice down. I really am in town for rehab and need to lay low."

In a sultry move, Michelle checks me out. "No one knows you're here?"

"Outside the band and Jenna, no." I'm sure the doctor doesn't even remember Jenna's name.

"Didn't you have a big movie opening recently?"

Damn. I'm not getting a good feeling. Better flirt and try to rile her up rather than use logic. I lean my arm against the table and drop my voice to a sultry tenor. "We did. Too bad I didn't know you then, or you could've been my plus one." If nothing else, she would've looked hot on my arm.

"I like the sound of that." She giggles and pushes her tits toward me. "Untamed Coaster's music is amazing."

I let my gaze drop down to appreciate her assets. Seen better, seen worse. "Appreciate it." Where is King? He should be back by now.

Our server approaches, causing Michelle to jump to the side. While he's clearing the table, King finally reappears. I address the woman ogling me. "It's been a pleasure meeting you, Michelle. Maybe I'll see you around town while I'm here." Please don't rat me out to the media.

"I'd like it." Her hand drops to my forearm. "How long are you in town?"

I school my features to appear disappointed. "Only a couple of weeks."

"Could be enough time for what I have in mind."

Not with my injury.

King steps into our conversation. "Michelle, he's here to lay low and concentrate on rehab. I'm sure he'll get in touch once he's in better shape."

I nod. "Give me your phone number and I'll give you a call."

I pass her my phone and she types. "I'm under Michelle in Aroostook."

Retrieving my phone, I smile. "Thanks."

She walks away, and I allow myself to admire her ass for a moment. My gaze returns to King. "No way was I giving her my digits."

King chuckles. "Smart man."

Our server comes back and drops off the tab, which I insist on paying. After I sign the credit card slip, I note, "Your Michelle was a bit pushy."

"First of all, she's *not* 'my' anything. Second, from where I sat, she seemed pretty interested in you and your situation." King takes a deep breath. "Third, but most important, please don't tell Angie I was talking with her."

"It's like that, is it?"

"She's nice enough, but Angie has a definite opinion about her." He chuckles. "I, for one, don't want to cross my wife."

"Your secret's safe with me." I stretch my leg, ignoring the ripple of pain. "I better get back to the house and ice this again."

When we're outside, I sag against the wall, getting my breathing back under control. Hard to believe such an easy task causes me to pant now. Sucks.

King waits next to me. "My advice, man? Steer clear of all women, especially Michelle, and focus on your rehab."

"Without a doubt."

Chapter Seven

The next morning I report to At Your Service PT at eight on the dot, my head full of steam. I'm ready to get to work and put this injury behind me. Jenna better fix me. Fast.

No one is in the waiting area, so I enter the main physical therapy room. Machines, equipment, weights, exam tables, and much more await. No stranger to hard work in the gym, a small thrill ripples at the prospect of working on new muscle groups.

Jenna walks out of a corner office carrying a clipboard. Unlike at the movie premiere, she's wearing a pair of dark navy scrubs. Her hair's pulled back into another ponytail.

"Glad to see you're punctual." Bet she wasn't used to that with Darren, who always ran at least fifteen minutes late. On a good day.

I mumble, "It's one of my talents."

"Did you bring workout clothes?"

"I did." I hold up my duffle.

"Great. I'll show you where you can change. If it were warmer out, I'd say you could come already dressed, but Mother Nature's being a tad picky lately."

Dang. Has to be a record for her stringing the most words

together. Since no response is required, I slip into the changing room. I soon return to the main area in my grey sweats and a Hunte T-shirt. Felt it was appropriate, given my dinner companion last night.

Jenna begins, "I got your doctor's report. Have to say I was shocked at the stage three diagnosis, but we'll get you fixed up in no time." *Damn well better.*

She asks me some questions about how much I iced it, my general fitness level, and current pain level. "It doesn't hurt all the time," I reply. "When I move a certain way or put too much weight on it, I'd say I'm around an eight. If I'm resting, I'd give it a three or four."

She nods and takes notes. "All right, we're going to start off today with an objective movement exam that will test the strength and range of motion of your groin muscles so I can develop the best protocol for your recovery."

"Sounds wonderful."

Jenna doesn't react to my dry tone, merely points to the examination table. "Lie down on this and we'll get started."

With precise movements, I sit on the table, my legs dangling. "I'm usually the one putting a lady in this position."

She steps back and rubs her arms. "Lie down."

Geez. I thought Darren said she had a sense of humor? I remember enjoying our first—and only in-depth—conversation. Seems like the *Godfather* movies are no longer on her radar. My back contacts the table.

"Good. Now put the ankle of your good leg against your knee." When I follow her instructions, she continues, "I'm going to stabilize your hip and push down on your knee. Since this is your good leg, I'm hoping you don't have any pain or strain. Let me know if you do."

What does she mean by *stabilize?*

Instead of asking, I follow her instructions. One of her hands holds onto my hip. Her other hand pushes against my knee, which moves quite far. She releases my legs. "Any pain?"

"Nope. All good." I catch my bottom lip between my teeth, willing my body not to respond to her touch. The fact she's about to inflict pain—and gave me a wrong diagnosis to start—are all the deterrents I need. "Are you going to push as hard against my bad leg?"

She shakes her head. "No. I wanted to get a baseline. I'll go easy on your injured leg."

Relieved by her words, I position the ankle of my bad leg against the opposite knee. Her hand lands on my other hip bone while she takes her time in lightly pressing against my knee. She doesn't have to go far before I'm sucking in air like a guppy.

"How bad?" She returns my leg to a straight position.

My heartrate beats faster than if I were running a 5k. "Ten."

Her ponytail swings. "I'm sorry, Bennett. I wasn't trying to hurt you. I need to know what I'm working with here."

She seems to really mean what she's saying. "I get it. I'll deal with whatever pain you inflict if it means I'll be ready for our opening date."

"It's not going to be easy, and I'm not making any promises. But I will work hard to get you there."

I can welcome pain if it equals getting over this injury. Plus, it'll keep my mind on recovery rather than the woman in charge of my physical therapy, who's been touching my hips and knees with strong yet surprisingly supple hands. Ones that would feel amazing on other parts of my anatomy. *Stop it, Bennett! You're only here to get therapy.*

Jenna pulls my Hunte T-shirt up. *Whoa.* All the time at the gym was worth it for my cut abs, which she doesn't appear to notice at all. Instead, she positions my good leg at a ninety-degree angle and puts her hand on my knee. "Now, push hard against my hand. Again, I'm going to compare your two legs."

I push against her hand without any problem, already knowing the other side is going to hurt like a bitch. When she tells me to do it again on my bad side, I clench my teeth and push. Tears spring to my eyes as pain floods my system. Within seconds, she jumps backward and writes something on the paper on her clipboard as I concentrate on breathing through my nose and out my mouth.

When my breath evens, she explains, "I'm going to do what is known as 'palpation.' All it means is I'm going to press on various areas in each of your legs and compare them."

Let this be over soon so I can crawl into a corner and cry like a little girl. "Go ahead."

"All you need to do is lie still." Keeping my shirt lifted, her hand touches my good leg, digging deep into the tendons and muscles in my thigh. I focus on anything to keep my lower appendage well, low. She moves to my bad side.

"If you wanted to get in my pants, there are much easier ways," I joke.

"Bennett, I'm not a groupie. I'm a trained physical therapist trying to do a job. Now lie still."

She repeats her exploration, touching the pull and causing me to cry out. Her hands spring from my legs. After a minute, they return to complete her palpation. What a word. Palpation. Should be *palpitation* because when she touched the pull, it sent me into one. I focus on the throbbing centered around my injury rather than the woman who caused it.

She tugs my T-shirt down, skimming her fingers over my abs. I would make a crude comment about this, but my leg hurts too damn much. The sound of her pen scribbling provides background noise while I calm the fuck down.

"You can sit up now. I only have one more test I'd like to do if you're up to it?"

Like I have a choice. I come to a sitting position and my legs, once again, dangle over the side of the table. At least there's no pain in this position.

She points to the floor. "For this load test, I need you to get off the table and lie down on the floor on your left side, with your right leg stretched out. Place your left foot in front of you."

I try to get into the proper position, but her head tilt indicates something's off. The next thing I know, she moves my legs to her liking. Good thing I'm wearing sweats.

"Everything good?"

I query my body. "Yeah. No pain."

"Good." She offers a small smile. "What's going to happen is I'll ask you to hold your right leg up, then I'm going to press down. Your job is to use your inner thigh muscle and not to let me move your leg. Got it?"

My lips purse. "You want me to hold up my bad leg?"

"Yes."

With reluctance, I lift my leg. The pull reminds me it's there.

"How's the pain level?"

"I'd give it about a three."

"Alright. Now I'm pressing down. Don't let me move your leg."

Pressure is applied to my leg, to which I counteract for a moment. Then the injury roars to life loud and clear, and I let my leg drop. I turn onto my stomach and will the pain to stop.

A hand smooths my T-shirt, which I didn't realize had ridden up. "You did it. Good job."

I lifted my leg for maybe five seconds. Without moving my head, I murmur, "You need to hang out with other people. Your bar for what constitutes a good job is so low a worm could get a trophy."

"Your injury is a low level grade three pull, which means we have a lot of work ahead of us to get you performance-worthy." She helps me sit up on the floor and joins me with her clipboard.

For the first time, doubt creeps in. If I can't take the stage, will UC replace me with a new lead singer? *Not. An. Option.* "I'm willing to do whatever it takes."

"Good." She reaches behind her head and tightens her ponytail. "Here's the plan. You need to come here twice a day for a couple of hours, at eight and again at six or so."

I swallow. This is no joke. Will she be able to fix me?

Unaware of my inner turmoil—or ignoring it—she continues, "We'll work on exercises, sometimes using weights, but also give you massages, heat, and ice. When you're not here, I'll need you to rest and elevate your leg, and ice it at least once a day."

"Gotcha." I crack my knuckles like Luke does. Gotta drop the pussy act. "I'm ready."

"I see your doctor prescribed pain medication." Her grey eyes shift from the papers to me. *How did I not realize before how expressive they are?*

I blink. "Which I refused. Luke has the script. Over-the-counter stuff is fine."

Her breathing shallows. "I understand."

I know she does, probably more than any other person on earth. Still, I feel the need to explain. "After what happened with Darren, the band agreed never to be tempted with that stuff again. I'm not going back on my word."

"Thank you."

I almost don't hear her, given how quiet her voice has fallen. "We didn't know he was addicted, Jenna. He hid it from us. From all of us." I pick at my sweats.

We remain silent for a full minute. Jenna clears her throat. "One more condition to go over. No sex until you're healed."

My hands fly above my shoulders as if I were surrendering. "What? I wasn't told that before."

Her pen taps against the clipboard. "It's right here. With a groin pull being so close to, well, you know, you can't risk reinjuring it. Sex would be a primary culprit."

I've never heard the words "sex" and "culprit" in the same sentence. I don't think I ever want to again. "There are ways—"

She cuts me off. "No sex until you're healed. It's for your own good."

"Months? You're really telling me I can't have sex until I'm one hundred percent again? Are you crazy?" I'm now mentally stomping all over the idiot Bennett who did the crazy jump. What the hell was he thinking?

"I'm sure you can, ehm, get busy before the full six months are up, Bennett. The doctor wants you to be generally pain-free before jumping into bed with your girlfriend, that's all."

"I don't do girlfriends." A vision of Lissa flits through my brain, and I repeat. "Never again." I'm not down with this "no sex" news, though, so I repeat, "I don't remember this instruction from the doctor."

She turns her back to me, gets up, and walks to the counter. Leaning her hip against it, she points to a paper. "Want to read it?"

I rise—albeit awkwardly—and reach out my hand for the clipboard. "No offense." She passes it to me and damn, that's exactly what it says. I rub two fingers over my nose. "To be revisited."

She retakes the clipboard and scribbles something. "Duly noted."

We stare at each other. Her high cheekbones are made more prominent by having her hair pulled back. She's definitely lost weight since she was with Darren, but also has gained an air of . . . confidence. The biggest difference I've noticed, though, is her demeanor. She always was quiet, but had a ready laugh and quick wit. The wit's still there, but the laugh? Not so much.

I know what it did to UC, but what has Darren's death done to *her*?

Chapter Eight

"You did great this morning," Jenna notes. "Normally, I'd have the patient come back in a couple of days, with instructions to take it easy until then. But I'll see you in a few hours so we can work against your tour deadline. I'd like to end this session with a quiet rest, though, so your muscles can calm down after all this work."

Jenna directs me to a massage table, where I relax. My body's shot. My eyes close.

"Bennett," Jenna touches my shoulder. My eyes fling open and the wall clock shows I was out for twenty minutes. "Sorry to startle you. I wanted to let you know you can go home for a while. I'll see you again at six."

I blink several times. My body feels as if a dozen rollerbladers skated over it and left me on the sidewalk. I get to do this all over again in only a few hours? Seems like I have no choice.

Using my core muscles, I sit up and shove all my weariness behind me. Rather, I don the mask I've worn whenever I was at a crossroads. Before UC was discovered. When UC started the first tour as the headliner. Upon UC's return to the stage following Darren's death.

My cheek quirks. "Thanks, Jenna."

Her gaze drops to the floor. "Do you want me to loan you some crutches? It'll help relieve the strain you've put your leg through during the past two hours."

"No. I can't afford to be out in public with them. It'll hurt UC's reputation."

"You *are* hurt," she insists.

The need to keep my dumb jump on the downlow rears its ugly head. *Never show weakness.* "Not if people don't know."

It seems as if she wants to say something else, but she doesn't. I hop off the table, careful to land on my good leg. With a cheery wave, I maintain a normal gait as I walk out of the clinic.

Two seconds later, my body demands I duck into a side alley and gulp air. My head leans against the brick as I struggle to contain my breathing. PT is fucking hard. Not letting others see my pain is harder. *Enough with the pity-party.* Not getting a rental car due to my injury was the smart thing, so suck it up. I force my feet to continue homeward bound.

Shortly, I punch in the security code to open the door and enter my rental. It's still and quiet, the way I like things. I swipe a bottle of water out of the fridge and collapse onto the sofa. The bed is too far away.

I close my eyes, telling myself I'll order lunch in a minute. An hour later, my ringing phone wakes me. The ringtone—"Cleanin' Out My Closet" by Eminem—taunts me to accept the call. In the end, guilt forces me to do so.

"Hi, Mom."

"Bennett, I heard about your movie. Seems like your band has done something worthwhile for a change."

My blood pressure rises, this time not from physical therapy. "UC's done a lot of good things throughout the years. The movie was fantastic, though."

"That girl, Quinn, seems to be getting lots of good press. She must be a bloody magician, considering what she had to work with."

This is why I shouldn't have picked up her call. Unfortunately, the memory of Dad pleading for me to take care of her always wins. Always. I change the subject. "How are you doing? Everything all right in New Jersey?"

"Oh, it's okay here. Ramona is a bit of a nudge, but tolerable."

At least this is good news. She needs to get along with the people around her. "Good to hear it. Try any new recipes lately?" The only thing Mom ever enjoyed is cooking. Dad used to give her a new recipe every morning, which usually made her smile. My tactic is rewarded when she goes off about three new dishes she prepared.

"All your talk about food has my stomach rumbling." No joke. I need to get food STAT.

"I would give you some of these delicious potato pancakes if you were even in my state." She pauses. "What state *are* you in, Bennett?"

"New York. I'm out in the Hamptons."

"Oh," she scoffs. "La-di-da."

"It's off-season, Mom. Not many people are out here."

"Which means you have a mansion all to yourself. Plus the two, three, or five scantily dressed women waiting on you hand and foot."

I suck in the air of my cozy rental. Not a single other person here with me, but I don't correct her. Why bother? "It's quiet out here. Relaxing. Good for my recovery." *Shit.* Why the hell did I say that? I jump in, "I mean, it's good for me to rest before the UC tour starts in a couple of weeks."

"Recovery?" Of course she picked up on that word. "Are you in rehab for drugs? Alcohol?"

Fuck. Amazing how her mind would go *there.* "Mom, I'm clean."

"Ramona won't let me live this down. My son is addicted to illegal substances. How could you do this to me?"

Ramona won't believe her. Probably not. Will she? *Fuck me.* There's no way out of this but to come clean. "Mom, calm down."

"'Calm down?' How dare you tell me to 'calm down?'"

I need to divert her attention before she gains a full head of steam. "I pulled a muscle and need physical therapy."

Her tirade stops. I let her process what I told her. "You're in therapy?"

My shoulders slump. "Physical therapy. We've kept it out of the press, so please don't share this information."

"If your sister were here, she wouldn't have done something so stupid as to pull a muscle. Then go off to the sticks for therapy."

I sigh. Here we go again. "The Hamptons are anything but 'the sticks.'" I correct the only part of her statement I can. I don't have the energy to deal with the rest. My stomach protests and provides me an excuse to end this farce of a conversation. "I need to eat, Mom. Remember, don't tell anyone where I am. Or what I'm doing."

"Your secret's with me." She disconnects the call.

I pick up the fact she didn't add the word "safe." I send up a prayer my injury will remain under the press's radar. To divert my thoughts, I order food delivery and finish my bottle of water. My body lets me know I also need to use the bathroom.

Under my breath, I mutter, "Please don't let this be as painful as talking with Mom," and I stand. My steps are easier than before, and I make quicker work of this task. When I emerge from the bathroom, the front doorbell rings with my food delivery. At least it wasn't left on the stoop. Picking up a baseball cap, I keep the bill plastered to the floor while the money-for-food exchange is made. My identity remains unknown.

At the island, I scarf down two slices of pizza before taking a swig of soda. With deliberate steps, I sit on a stool and eat a third slice. My mind wanders to Jenna this morning.

How determined she was to help me.

How well she explained each exercise.

How gorgeous she is.

Whoa. Stop right there, buddy. She was Darren's and always will be. Plus, she's only doing her job and fixing me—given she got it wrong at the start and all that.

I push away from the island, go into the living room, and flick on the television. Changing the channels, I stop on a college basketball game, but it doesn't hold my interest. I want to be playing the game rather than watching it. My fist connects with my thigh. *Hurry up and heal.*

Toward the end of the first half, I check the time. Thirty more minutes before my next PT session. I swap out my T-shirt and toss another sweatshirt over my head. Might as well head over there now. Don't want to be late.

Unlike this morning, the reception area is filled with people. Patients stare at me, some with their mouths open. Great. So much for keeping my whereabouts on the down low.

I force a smile. "Hi, folks. Great day for some PT, huh?"

A couple of women in their mid-twenties use their hands to fan their faces. Older men appear not to know who I am. I give my name to the receptionist and take a seat next to the gentlemen.

One man asks me, "What'cha here for?"

I point to my thigh. "Pulled my muscle. You?"

"I got a hip replacement two months ago." He indicates the man next to him. "He's working out a rotator cuff injury he got while skiing."

Both of which are better than doing a crazy-ass jump onstage. Figure I can do a little digging. "Has Jenna helped you?" I indicate his hip.

"Not Jenna, my therapist is Austin. He's pretty good, but always seems to be focusing on the next thing rather than giving me his full attention."

The other guy rolls his shoulder. "I'm with Courtney. She's really good."

I guess Jenna was right in that she's not taking any more patients. Given how attentive she was to me this morning, I find it hard to believe she's not doing it full time.

The women across the way point at me, and I shift in my seat. The man next to me says, "Are you somebody?"

I ask myself this question on the daily.

"He's only the lead singer with one of the hottest bands in the country," one of the ladies supplies.

The other corrects, "In the world!"

After offering them my rock star smile, I mutter, "They're overstating things."

The guy with the hip replacement nods, but his brows furrow. The rotator cuff man asks, "What's your name again?"

A genuine smile crosses my face. They have no clue. "I'm Bennett Hardy. I'm with a band called Untamed Coaster and we're going on tour in a couple of weeks."

"Hence you're here to rehab that pull."

My hand claps hip guy on the shoulder. "Exactly."

"We won't tell anyone about you." A devious glint enters his eyes. "Not even our granddaughters."

I offer him my fist, which he bumps. These guys are all right. "Want a photo? For your granddaughters, I mean." They agree and I take the selfie using the rotator cuff guy's camera.

Soon, Jenna comes to the door. I wave at my two fellow patients and follow her to the back. I have to address this situation before we begin. Alone in the back area, I say, "We need to come up with a better system. While I enjoyed talking with a couple of your male patients, the ladies could've been a problem."

Jenna's cheeks pinken. "Bennett, I didn't think of that. I'm so sorry." She fiddles with her ponytail. "How about you text me when you're five minutes away, and I'll meet you at the back elevator?"

"Yeah. Makes sense. Appreciate it, Jenna."

Problem solved, she has me lie down on the floor and repeat the exercises I did this morning. Knowing what to expect, things are a bit smoother. Not easier, as my thigh muscle protests. Simply smoother.

While I'm concentrating on a particularly difficult exercise involving a small medicine ball, Jenna says, "If I didn't say this before, congratulations on the movie. It was," she takes a breath. "Informative."

I force my thighs to hold the ball. She wasn't with the band after Darren's funeral. Trying to lighten the mood, I ask, "What did you learn?"

"Oh, a lot. Quinn really captured you guys. Gave people an insight into how you came back."

"Quinn's amazing. We owe her a lot for how she put the film together." She captured us on tape while UC put in the work. "It was tough. After Darren's funeral, UC sort of fell apart. Until we realized we needed to keep performing. It's in our blood, and Darren wouldn't have wanted us to quit because he's not around."

She walks around me, adjusting my leg. I anticipate pain, but none comes. At least not from my thigh. "I agree. He spoke of you and the band all the time. He was so proud to be part of UC. He loved being with you guys."

Until he got hooked on painkillers. "That he did. This one time, Darren was onstage performing one of our hits, 'Make Me Feel It,' I think, when someone in the crowd screamed his name. He zeroed in on the boy, maybe fifteen years old, and motioned for our security to invite him to the meet and greet. Turns out the kid was learning keyboards and Darren was his idol."

Jenna completes the story. "Darren paid for his lessons and now he's a member of one of your opening acts."

Our gazes lock. Her grey ones hold pride with an overlay of sadness. I'm sure my green ones look the same.

"He's good on the keys," I note. "Hey, I'm not feeling any pain. Can I try something new?"

Jenna seems to have an entire inner dialogue with herself before taking the medicine ball from me and asking me to stand on a mat. She folds a towel and places it on the floor. "I don't usually move on to this exercise until I've been working with someone for at least five days. You can try it, but only one repetition."

I nod and she shows me the exercise. "Bet I can do five." As she demonstrated, I stand on my left leg with my right foot on the towel. Then slide it out and bring it back into the mat.

My pulled muscle screams.

My hand flies to my inner thigh. "Oww!"

"I knew it was too soon," Jenna mutters. She grasps me by the arm and brings me to the table. "Lie down."

I manage to man up and follow her direction. She immediately begins to massage my thigh, getting way too close to my junk for my—or Darren's—comfort. "Whoa there. I can do that."

"Stop it, Bennett. You're always so reckless and over the top. Exactly what landed you here in the first place. Let me do my job."

Holy. Shit. I'm not going to take her criticism lying down, despite the fact I am flat on my back. "I'm neither reckless nor over the top."

Jenna continues to massage my angry tendon, unclenching it bit by bit. She pulls away from me for enough time to rub her thumb and pinky together, then she's back giving me the massage. In a clipped tone, she says, "Fine. Then explain why you're here."

"Because I did a stupid jump. I was amped up after the movie and our performance. Sue me." I count the ceiling tiles above my body.

The massage continues in silence. Little by little, the pain in my inner thigh decreases. Frowning, she asks, "How's your pain level?"

"Two."

My petulant response is received without any fanfare. "Good. We're not going to add more exercises until I know you're ready. We don't want a repeat of this fiasco that could jeopardize your recovery."

Her assessment shuts me down. She's right. I need this to go smoothly from now on. "Fine," I grumble.

She walks to the other side of the room and pulls something out of what I believe to be a freezer. "Here's an ice pack. I want you to ice this for twenty minutes." She puts it on my leg.

The icy cold numbs my pull within moments. I take a deep breath and relax.

"Seems like I found something to calm you down."

Just like that, my need to move returns. My hand lands on the ice pack and I'm about to throw it across the room when Jenna reappears at my side. Her fingers press the ice pack down. "It needs time to do its job."

Knowing she's right, I remove my hand. This is the second time this session she's offended me. "Do you always insult your patients or am I special?"

Jenna fiddles with some papers. "I haven't worked with patients in over eighteen months. I'm rusty."

Since Darren died. "I'd say." My mind churns. "I don't need to calm down."

The inside of her cheek clenches. "Bennett, you're in perpetual motion. You never sit still for longer than a meal, and even then, you're twisting in your seat."

Because I'm always on the lookout for the next thing. A new place to visit, a new song to write, a new experience. Sitting still isn't my forte. I refuse to dig any deeper into this. Not going to get lost in the morass that is my psyche.

"Darren was no better," I challenge.

"You're right. He certainly was the joker of your band, ready to lead the next prank." A wistful smile crosses her face. Then her shoulders straighten. "He was the complete opposite of me."

Her observation seems spot-on. Opposites attract and all. Still. She's more akin to me, although we show it in different ways. No need to share this nugget with my physical therapist. "Darren was the life of any party."

She tidies up the room. "Well, I think we're done for today. Feel ready to go home?"

I follow the whirlwind change in conversation and agree.

"If you wait here for a few minutes, I'll collect my things and show you the back elevator, so you'll know where to meet me tomorrow morning."

Coming to a sitting position, I say, "Thanks."

We take the back elevator down to the street level, then exit the building. The privacy here is exactly what I need. I appreciate her thoughtfulness. "This will be perfect. I'll give you a five-minute heads up before I arrive."

We walk a few steps. "How's the leg?"

I query my limb. "It's not hurting too much." *I'd give it about a six.*

"Want me to drive you to your house?"

Because her tone is open and not sympathetic, I agree. We get into her Lexus SUV—grab bars are my friends—and I direct her toward my rental, to which we pull up minutes later.

"I'm happy you found something nearby." She puts her vehicle into park.

"Me too. I let King and Angie pick the one nearest your clinic."

"As in the Huntes?"

"Yeah. I've met his father and brother, but I hadn't met King until now. Angie said you two are in the same Chamber of Commerce?"

"We are. They seem nice, but I haven't had too much interaction with them."

My fingers curl around the door handle, not excited at the prospect of eating all alone. Being by myself allows too many thoughts to swirl—ones I don't want to revisit. "Want to join me for dinner?" I replay my ask, realizing I sounded desperate. What would Darren say? *Do Not Fuck list, remember?* I force the mask over my face again. "I'll be going out, not cooking. But you don't have to join me, if you have other plans."

"I actually do." She bites her lower lip. "I usually get together with Ma once a week, and tonight's her night."

"I get it." Although I don't. Her connection to her mother is foreign to me. However, I do need to come clean to her about one thing. "Darren was blown away by you, you know. He couldn't believe his luck when you agreed to go out with him. Even on the night he, well, you know, he was proud you were on his arm. I wanted to be sure you knew this."

She stares at the steering wheel. "As I said before, Darren was my total opposite, with his big personality and oversized thirst for adven-

ture. I'm a homebody, Bennett, an introverted one at that. I think I
was caught up in his aura. He made me feel special."

Because you are. I keep this errant thought to myself. "He had a
way about him, for sure." He was the first guy to cheer from the sidelines. When I got my GED, he led the charge to celebrate my accom-
plishment. He saw life as a big adventure to be enjoyed to the fullest.

"He did," Jenna agrees. "Those days are long over for me. I need
someone safe, who doesn't rock the boat." She sighs. "Who follows
instructions."

This last statement makes me think she somehow blames herself
for Darren's actions. I turn in my seat. "I'm sure Darren forgot he
took pills before he went drinking that night." He never seemed like
he was addicted to them, although looking back, his behavior did
become erratic following his injury.

She smacks the steering wheel. "I told him not to drink. He was
on oxy, which you shouldn't mix with alcohol. Why couldn't he listen
to me?"

Her anger speaks to me. "Don't blame yourself. We were touring
with him and should've picked up the signals. In the end, it was his
decision." Shitty one, but his.

"He made me believe in more, you know? Truth is, someone like
me needs to stay in my lane and not try to be part of a worldwide
phenomenon." She shakes her head. "This is where I belong. I've
carved a nice life for myself in Aroostook. I have two clinics now, you
know. With a third one in the works."

"I think we all can be whatever we want to be. It seems to me you
enjoy physical therapy and working with patients, so that's a great
reason for you to stay here."

"Exactly."

Is she trying to convince herself? Not going there. "Well, I better
go. Enjoy dinner with your mother. See you in the morning?" I open
the car door.

"Sounds good. Have a good night, Bennett."

I stand on the sidewalk and watch as she drives down the street.

Our conversation lodges deep into my soul. She tried to help Darren, and when she failed, it changed her life so much that she's barely recognizable. Not for the first time, I wonder how far and wide the ripples of his death go.

If it were me instead of him, I'm sure the ripple would be more of a trickle. If that.

Chapter Nine

I'm awakened by a throbbing in my lower half. My thigh, to be precise. I pound the bedding—why is this groin pull following me, even in my sleep?

I flip over, punch the pillow, and close my eyes. Two hours later, my phone's alarm goes off. Another "restful" night's sleep is in the books.

As I sit up, I peek through the blackout shades. At least it's not grey outside. My feet hit the wood floor and I make an effort to walk in my usual gait toward the bathroom. Within three steps, I'm rubbing my thigh. I need to get back to normal fast.

After brushing my teeth, I allow the shower to heat up. If rehab fails, I better come up with another way to perform. No running around the stage, certainly no jumps. I might be able to walk down the stage to get closer to the fans, as long as I keep my pace slow. Maybe I need to forget healing this pull faster, and think of alternative ways to rock the house?

This sucks.

My boxer briefs hit the floor and I stand under the spray. I flip the showerhead to the massage function. Water rolls down my face and neck, over my torso and down my legs. I let it soothe my tired muscles. My cock, still with its morning wood, demands attention, so I give it a long stroke.

Which leads to another.

And another.

Soon, all my attention is focused on getting myself off as my hand slides up and down. My balls pull up and I stand wider, shooting onto the shower floor. My groan, "Jenna," catches me by surprise at the same moment my angry groin pull makes its *dis*pleasure known. I stumble backward, landing on the stone bench with a thud.

I rub my thigh while the pulsing shower provides background white noise. Why on earth did Jenna's name come out of my mouth? She's Darren's. He put this woman on UC's *Do Not Fuck* list in permanent marker. Never to be erased.

With care, I stand and finish my shower. After I dress, I check the time. Since I still have nearly two hours before PT, I don my handy disguise of sunglasses and a baseball cap and decide to take a short walk around Aroostook to find another place for breakfast.

Instead of turning right out my front door, I go left and come up to a commercial street. At least this one has more shops than the other streets I've noticed. A florist, toy store, several restaurants. Too bad they're all closed at this time of the morning. This town must have a diner, though. Even though we're out of my home state of New Jersey, the diner capital of the world, New York is only one state over.

The next storefront is for Russo Real Estate, which is King and Angie's place. I stop and check out their many listings. A few on the waterfront are gorgeous. One, in particular, captures my attention.

"I can arrange a showing, if you'd like."

I turn my head and diminutive brunette smiles up at me. "Hi, Angie. Didn't hear you come over." I glance behind her. "Is King with you?"

She shakes her head. "No. He has a showing this morning. Want to come in? I can give you more information about this listing." She points to the waterfront house at which I was staring.

My hand steals across my stomach. "Maybe some other time. I need to get breakfast and then go to physical therapy."

"How's it going?"

My shoulders lower. "It's going."

"I hear you." Her fingers twirl the ends of her hair. "I don't have to open the office for an hour or so. C'mon," she motions for me to join her. "I'll take you out for a real Hamptons breakfast."

What have I got to lose? Plus, I need to eat. "Sounds good to me."

We approach a convertible, which doesn't seem to be her style. Especially without room for car seats in the back. "King's?"

She grins. "Sure is. Since he has the showing, I get to drive it today, though." She tosses her bags into the small backseat. "Get in."

Ten minutes later we're parked on Ocean Avenue, which faces the water. I inhale, savoring the salty air. Bundled-up joggers pass us on the wooden boardwalk. My heart pangs at not being able to join them.

As if reading my mind, she says, "You'll soon be out there. Let's go get some fuel."

Fuel. Good word for the three-egg omelet, toast, and side of bacon I devour. I'm going to need all this fuel to get through PT today. Throughout our meal, Angie's been a delight. I can see what drew King to her.

"I don't know too much about Jenna, other than she has a great reputation for physical therapy around here. She runs two clinics." Her voice drops. "I understand her boyfriend's death hit her hard."

"It did for all of us." I swallow the last bit of my tea, which has turned bitter.

Angie's hand goes over her heart. "I'm sorry. For a moment, I forgot he was your bandmate, too. My condolences." Her left wrist falls to the table, with the name Dante visible along with King and those of their two daughters. Her chest expands on a breath, and she points to the tattoo. "I know what it means to lose someone you love. My first husband, Dante, is always with me. He brought King into my life."

Her honesty washes over me like one of our encores. "That's what Luke said about Tris. Darren brought him to the band for a reason."

Her left hand covers mine. "Believe him."

Our moment is broken when Michelle walks to our table. "Bennett, I thought that was you! How are you doing?" She leans closer. "How's the leg?" She flips her long, brown hair, a couple of shades darker than Angie's. "Hi there, Angie. How's the real estate business coming along?"

I glance between the two women, one an overeager botoxed puppy while the other has a fake smile plastered across her surgically untouched face. I lean back in my chair and wait for Angie's reply. "Hi there, Michelle. I didn't realize you knew my new client, Mr. Hardy."

I tip the hat sitting on the seat next to me toward her. Client relationship. Nice way to keep it professional, Mrs. Hunte. Michelle, however, doesn't take up the mantle. "We met a couple of days ago, when he was out to dinner—"

Not knowing whether King shared our meeting with his wife, I speak over the rather annoying woman. "Yes, Angie. I met Michelle here when I arrived in town." I focus my gaze on the woman, wearing a pair of very tight jeans. I wonder if she was sewed into them like they did Olivia Newton-John in *Grease*? "I want to thank you for not spilling the beans of my whereabouts to the media. I'm enjoying my anonymity."

Michelle reaches out to me, running her fingertips over my forearm. "Of course. How's rehab going?"

"I've only been at it for a day. Too soon to pass judgment."

Her arms cross her ample chest. "There's still time to switch physical therapists, you know. I'm sure you'd already be seeing results with someone else."

"I'm good." While I want faster results, I'm not going to jeopardize my recovery by pushing too hard like I tried to do yesterday.

Jenna knew the probable outcome but still let me try. Lesson learned she has my best interests at heart.

Michelle opens her mouth, but the alert from my cellphone indicates I have fifteen minutes to get to my appointment. I rush a quick good-bye to Michelle, drop a hundred-dollar bill onto the table, and escort Angie to her car—who graciously agrees to drive me to PT.

On our way to the clinic, I text Jenna to let her know my ETA and direct Angie to the back of the building. "What do you know about Michelle?"

From the driver's seat, she slants a glance toward me. "She's a bitch."

Well then. Guess Angie doesn't mince words. "I can see that." I chuckle. "She's banging hot." Not that I'd tap her even if it wasn't against doctor's orders, though. She seems too . . . high maintenance. With all her negativity toward Jenna, I don't get the feeling she's trustworthy.

Angie's shoulder lifts. "If you like the plastic look, by all means."

Like all the influencers and models who run in my orbit. "Plastic can be fun." The last time someone *not* of that ilk caught my attention, it was Jenna. Before her, Lissa in high school. Fuck. I glance at the woman behind the steering wheel, who's nothing if not real. "So long as you don't need to look under the hood." When do I *ever* do that?

We arrive at the back of the clinic where Jenna's standing by the door. I unbuckle my seatbelt and open the door while Angie does the same. Because she's more agile at the moment, Angie beats me to Jenna, arms extended.

"Jenna. So great to see you again." Angie brings Jenna in for a hug.

"Hi, Angie." Jenna steps back, a bit awkwardly. "Bennett told me you and King got him his rental."

Angie nods. "Everything going well for you? I understand you opened a second location."

Jenna tucks her ever-present clipboard under her arm. "We did, six months ago. Looking for another spot for a third location now."

"Great. Please reach out if we can be of any help." Angie passes her a business card. Smart business move.

"Will do." Angie gives me a hug and hops back into King's convertible. Not jealous of her mobility. At. All.

Jenna brings me out of my musings. "Are you ready for today?"

"As I'll ever be." I open the clinic's door and indicate she should precede me. Even though I'm injured, I still have some gentlemanly courtesies in me. I try not to concentrate on her ass—*off limits*—as she leads me toward the elevator. Since the clinic's situated on the second floor, I'd normally take the stairs. Being injured sucks.

In the back room, we begin my exercises. When Jenna's adjusting my leg, I remember my shower this morning. How I yelled her name as I came. Since her hands are on me now, I mess up again on purpose. She corrects me once more.

This time, instead of moving my leg as she's directing, I grab her hand. Her skin's so soft. I rub my thumb over her palm.

She's capable. Caring. Devoted. Sweet. Kind. Sexy.

The type of woman who belongs in a couple. Where I'm the other half.

For the first time, I don't feel like bolting at this thought. Darren's *Do Not Fuck* list doesn't seem as insurmountable as before.

Jenna's grey eyes widen. Not trying to pull away from me, she verbalizes the question running through my own mind, "What are you doing?"

I gaze into her expressive eyes. I can use a little distraction from all this hard work. "I can think of some more fun exercises we can do." For some reason, I channel Tris and bite my lower lip.

She yanks against my hand and frees herself. "No sex. Doctor's orders."

Her leap to sex makes my head spin. Is she thinking about me like I've been fantasizing about her? My voice lowers, beneath its normal tenor. "There's plenty of other things we can do."

"Are you high, Bennett?" She snaps her fingers in front of my face. "Did you take the pain meds?"

"What? No. You think, after Darren—"

My use of her ex-boyfriend's name causes her to stumble backward. In a strangled voice, she says, "We're done here." She flees the room.

Crap. This situation's fucked up.

I'm fucked up.

Chapter Ten

I adjust my regular clothes and stand, walking around the room. When Jenna doesn't appear after a couple of minutes, I throw my shoulders back and saunter toward the connecting office. Well, saunter would be the accurate term if I didn't have this big fucking knot on my thigh that refuses to let me walk like normal.

My knuckles rap on her door. A discombobulated voice says, "Come in." I take note of the undercurrent of resignation, but it doesn't stop me.

Opening the door, I throw her the smile I use during all our concerts. One that ends up with roadies clearing the stage of bras and panties. Jenna, however, doesn't appear moved. "Hey, thanks for a good session earlier. I think I made progress this morning."

Her brow quirks, questioning whether my normal tone now is the real Bennett, or the earlier, flirty one was. I'll never tell.

"Yeah," she clears her throat. "Yes, you did well."

I nod, resting my good hip against a bookcase. "I did learn my lesson from yesterday. I can't leapfrog ahead in my recovery or else I'll suffer the consequences."

"I tried to warn you."

"Yes, I know. At least I learned quickly—only one try."

An unwilling laugh comes out of her mouth, which makes me relax against the bookcase. No lasting harm done. "I thought you were going to do five reps."

"I'm man enough to admit I would've been on the floor."

She walks around her desk and leans against it, mirroring my posture. "Any plans for your afternoon off?"

"I was thinking of checking out the arcade game store. Want to see if I can beat some of the people on the leaderboard."

Her eyes turn a lighter shade of grey. "I used to spend hours in that place playing Donkey Kong. My sister knew to pick me up from there before dinner."

"Sister?" This is the first I've heard her mention a sister. I thought she was an only child.

"Yeah. She's ten years older than me, so she's more like an aunt. Kara's married and lives in the City with her husband and two kids. We're not close."

I take in this new information. Tit for tat. "I'm an only child. Sounds like you were one as well, more or less."

"Aside from birthday and big holiday texts, we don't have much to do with each other. I like her though, even if we don't have much in common."

"I get it." I push away from the bookcase. "I don't want to take up more of your time. I'll hit the arcade and see you back here in a few hours."

"Enjoy."

I don't push my luck, rather slip out of her office, the workout room, and take the back elevator to the street. Jenna's filled with mysteries. The more I unpack, the more I enjoy spending time with her.

I stop at the arcade store and play a couple of games of Asteroids Deluxe. By a "couple," I mean like twenty. My name—rather, "Benjamin Howell"—now sits in the top nine. The scores ahead of me are fierce. I'll get there. I still have a good week before UC needs me.

At six, I return to the clinic where Jenna leads me through more exercises. She keeps adding repetitions or weights or seconds to holds, so my body continues to improve. If by improving it means not screaming in pain, that is.

She puts the medicine ball away. "You did good tonight. Hop up on the exam table and I'll get you an ice pack. You're going to need to elevate your leg as much as possible at home."

I salute her. "What's in store for me tomorrow?"

A devious grin crosses her face. "Remember the exercise you tried with the towel on the floor?"

I run my hand through my hair. "Yeah."

"You're going to do it for real tomorrow. If these were normal circumstances, I'd have you hold off for a good week but—"

"These are anything but 'normal circumstances,'" I finish for her, forcing my heartbeat to not explode from my chest. That exercise fucking hurt. If Jenna thinks I'm ready for it though, I'll do my best. *For her*.

Correction: For. Me.

"True. We need to work on your lateral movements. Onstage, you don't walk in a straight line when you're performing."

I extend my fist. "Thanks."

She bumps it, then retreats into her office. I force my attention to the ice pack, blanking my mind. I don't need to dwell on the interesting woman making the injury I brought on myself go away. At least, making it lessen.

Shortly, the whisper of a new song echoes in my mind. The lyrics are about seeking help from unlikely sources. I snort. This couldn't be any more unlikely.

I grab my phone and open the notes app, then put down my thoughts. Perhaps one of these lines will make it into a song I'll present to UC. Maybe.

The connecting door opens and Jenna reenters the room. "Let me take the ice, and you'll be free to go for the evening."

I pass her the pack and fix my grey sweats. I probably should

wear shorts tomorrow so the ice will have direct contact. I move my
hands next to my hips and swivel to get off the table. Not as painful
as the first time, for sure.

"Are you leaving too?"

She nods in agreement. "Let me get my bag and I'll walk you
out."

"Take your time." My words are to her retreating back, and by the
time I make it to the elevator, she's already there.

"You may not feel it, but I can see your progress, Bennett. Keep
focusing on your recovery."

"Not like I have much else to keep me occupied."

"Well, you're not wrong. Aroostook in the late winter is anything
but a bustling metropolis. Focus, and you'll be ready to go in no
time."

"Meaning a little over a week." The kickoff of UC's tour looms
above us both. "Do you think," I cough. "Are there any moves you
could teach me to hide my injury from the public when I'm
performing?"

"Why don't you want people to know? It's not like a major injury
or anything."

"I know. It's a stupid one. And after we lost Darren, I don't want
to cast a shadow over the band."

She's quiet as she takes in my words. "Want a lift?" She stands
next to her white Lexus SUV.

"I'd love one, thanks."

A short time later, she stops at my rental. "Good job today,
Bennett," she praises. "See you tomorrow at eight."

I don't want our evening to end, so I think fast. "Do you still think
The Godfather part two is better than the original?"

Her hand goes to the back of her ponytail. "It is."

I sigh. "Too bad. I was going to invite you out for dinner, but I
can't be seen with someone with such bad movie taste." I hold back
my grin.

"Oh well. I'm sure you can find someone who agrees with you."

As soon as I shut the car door, she locks it. "See you in the morning." The car drives away.

I enter my rental and grab a bottle of water, downing it in a few long swallows. I wish she had taken me up on my dinner invitation. Again, Darren's face makes an appearance. *I get it.*

My phone rings with "Cleanin' Out My Closet." I can't bring myself to talk with Mom now. She doesn't get to stomp all over me twice in one week. Someone else will call if there's a true emergency.

After a quick change, I walk around the block which, thankfully, is well lit. About three-quarters of the way through the impromptu workout, my groin pull starts to act up. First Jenna, then Mom, and now the injury. *Why won't all this shit go away?* I limp to the same restaurant that King and I enjoyed on my first night in town.

At a table for one, I order a hangar steak with garlic mashed potatoes. When the server disappears, Michelle takes her place. "Wow. Twice in one day, I should play the lottery." She giggles.

The chick's not too terrible. Her long, brown hair is nice. Her glossy, pink lips look suckable enough. Or they would look nice wrapped around my cock. Still, there's something off-putting about her. Maybe Angie's assessment?

Michelle points to the empty chair at my table. "May I join you?"

I guess she's better than no company. Even if I did want to work more on the new song. "Sure. It's your death warrant."

She slinks into the chair. Leaning toward me, she asks, "Are you making progress with your PT?"

Warning signals go up. While she hasn't said anything to the press—yet—she's a wild card. I wave my hand. "I am. I'm sure I'll be back to normal in no time." I keep my hands on the table instead of rubbing my thigh.

She licks her glossy lips. "My offer still stands. I can get you with a much more reputable physical therapist."

What does she have against Jenna? My back straightens. "I don't think it would be good to switch therapists now. I have a program all set, and things are in place."

Michelle's chest juts forward, highlighting her ample rack. "What are your plans when you leave Aroostook?"

This I can answer. "Going on tour with UC. We'll be on the road for months." Where I love to be. Performing is amazing, not to mention the adoration of our many fans. Being on tour also means we don't stay in one place for more than a couple of nights, so anyone who gets too clingy is left in the dust.

Her pointer finger traces her lips. "I bet you do lots of damage to ladies' hearts."

I offer her a lopsided grin. "I think we all get what we want."

She places her forearm on the table. "Sounds intriguing."

My server chooses this moment to appear, delivering my Manhattan and taking Michelle's order. A moment later, she reappears with a glass of bubbly.

I lift my glass toward her. "To an entertaining evening."

"I'll drink to that," she giggles.

Michelle and I flirt throughout the night, eating bites off each other's plates. To be fair, she eats more of my hangar steak than I steal from her Waldorf salad. Why must women always order rabbit food?

After the dirty dishes are taken away, Michelle's hands land on her flat stomach. "I'm stuffed." She pauses. "At least my stomach is full."

This is where I should invite myself into her room and panties. She's gorgeous and knows how to use that mouth of hers, judging by the way she handled the cherry garnish from my drink.

Several facts counsel against this plan of action. One, the doctor prescribed no sex until I'm healed. Two, I have an early wake-up call for PT tomorrow. Three, Michelle's not real. Like all the rest, her plastic looks good on camera and is about as deep as her profile pic.

For the first time, I realize I want a true connection with someone rather than a fleeting moment of pleasure. To be with someone who sees beyond my rock star persona. I freeze. Why on earth would anyone want to see the real me? There's nothing but disappointment and failure lurking beneath this well-groomed surface.

I guess I'm doomed to be with chicks like Michelle forever. Jenna pops into my mind, and I dismiss her—such a multi-faceted brilliant woman would have nothing to do with me, even if Darren weren't floating between us.

I gaze at the chick sitting across from me but can't muster any passion for her. I need to let her down with care, so she doesn't blab to the world about my whereabouts and why I'm here.

"I had a great time with you, Michelle. I wish this evening could continue, but I'm under strict doctor's orders to remain celibate until my injury is healed. I hope you understand."

Her plump lips purse. "Jenna imposed a no-sex rule on you? Seriously?"

I shake my head. "The order came from my doctor in New York City." Not a lie.

"Well," she coos. "There are plenty of other activities we could enjoy without going all the way. I could lick your six-pack." Her eyes skim down my torso. "You could lick my . . ." She cups her tits.

"As enticing as your offer is, Michelle, I think I'm going to have to pass tonight." I reach into my wallet and leave a wad of cash on the table. Standing, I walk to her chair and pull it back. "Who knows? Perhaps another time?"

She scrambles to her feet. "Watch and drool."

Hips swaying, she walks out of the restaurant. Not a drop of saliva enters my mouth. Under my breath, I mutter. "Or not."

Chapter Eleven

My eyes spring open, greeting a day drenched in sunshine, if not heat. At least the blue skies amp up my mood. With tentative movements, I push the sheet down my body and move my legs. The pain is still there, but less pronounced.

Once my morning rituals are complete, I slide a pair of shorts up my legs and then cover them with navy blue sweats. I'll fit right in as I've noticed guys at the clinic working out in shorts. I toss on an Ozzy Martinez T-shirt and sweatshirt.

The walk to the clinic takes me only three-quarters of the time today. I bet I'll get it down to under half before I leave. Standing outside the back entrance, I call Jenna.

"Hi, Bennett. Five minutes?"

The sound of her voice causes a thrill to zip through my body. I quash that shit. "Nah. I forgot to text you, and I'm downstairs now."

"Okay. I'll be down right away." She disconnects our call.

Why am I even thinking about Darren's girl like this? If he were here, he'd whack me upside the head and tell me to get my own chick, before kissing the fuck out of her. The visual is strong when Jenna opens the door for me. I raise my hand. "Thanks."

When we're inside the elevator, she pulls a hair tie off her wrist and gathers her lush blonde hair together into a ponytail. Damn. I much prefer her hair down.

"Why do you always wear it in a ponytail?" The question's out of my mouth before I realize I've said it aloud.

"Because it gets in the way when I'm working." She does a ninja maneuver and *voilà*, she sports a ponytail.

Once inside, I take off my sweatshirt and shoes. Jenna sucks in her breath when my hands go to my waistband, causing me to glance up. "I figured shorts might make this easier."

"Oh, right." She plays with her ponytail. "Very smart."

I force myself not to smirk as I slide my sweats down my hips. "What should I do first?"

She nods. "Go ahead and do the exercises from yesterday, only add another ten seconds to each hold and do another round. When you get on the mat, I want to add something to that one."

I nod and begin the exercises. They're not as hard as the first day, even when I add in the additional time and reps. My thigh's still complaining, perhaps not as loudly. I walk over to the mat.

"You did very well with those. How's the pull feeling?"

"Around a four."

She folds the towel and places it on the floor. "Great. You're moving along nicely." Jenna positions me on the mat and I put my foot onto the towel. "Now this time, after you slide out to the side, I want you to end with a squat." She demonstrates.

Piece. Of. Cake. "I've done a million squats at the gym," I boast.

"Then you should have no issue adding them to this exercise."

I got this. My foot slides out to the side, I do a textbook squat, stand up. "Holy Hell!" My hand grabs around my thigh where the muscle throbs.

"How bad?"

Through gritted teeth, I reply, "Ten."

She rubs my back, which—shockingly—diverts my attention. Once the throbbing subsides, my breathing returns to normal.

"Better?"

I query my body. "I think so."

"Great. Do it again."

My eyes pop wide open. "Are you serious right now?"

She nods. "You have to work through this lateral pain. I know it hurts—"

"Like a mother effer," I supply, rubbing my thigh.

As if I hadn't interrupted her, Jenna continues, "The only way you're going to be able to get on the stage with a minimal amount of pain is to work through it now. Take it much more slowly this time. Don't try to win a squat contest, but I need you to push yourself a little."

Damn. The woman makes sense. Frowning, I rub my thigh. "No pain, no gain."

"I wouldn't exactly say it like that," she corrects. "More like 'no pain, no success.'"

I suck in my breath and focus on the task at hand. I can do this. I already know how bad it can be and I'm not revisiting. My leg slides out to the side. When I'm in position, I take my time in lowering toward the floor, moving my arms into a prayer posture at my chest. I raise to my full height with my arms sailing behind me, then use my leg to bring the towel to my other foot.

"How'd that feel?"

Through clenched teeth, I reply, "It hurt." I exhale. "But not as badly."

"Great. Think you can do it again?"

I concentrate and replicate the movements. "Pain's about a seven," I say without her asking.

"Much lower than the first time. I promise it'll get less painful the more times you do it."

"We'll see," I reply, heavy skepticism intended. My disbelief is disproven by the fifth time I do the squat. "I'm at a five pain level," I admit when I stand.

She blesses me with a gorgeous smile, causing my heart to do a somersault. Unaware of her effect on me, Jenna says, "Think you can finish up a set of ten?"

"I'll try." I take the slide and squats carefully, nothing like the first time I attempted to do it, and feel like a million bucks when I complete them all.

Jenna claps. "Fantastic, Bennett. Want to take a short break before doing this all over again?"

My ears must be clogged. "Again?"

She walks over to the fridge and retrieves a bottle of water. "Two sets."

"Fuck me." I accept the bottle of water and drink half of it down in one gulp. "Who knew doing a squat could be this difficult?"

She remains quiet, although the slight smirk on her face tells me all I need to know. I raise my eyebrow. "Enjoying my pain?"

"Not at all." She sips her own water. "I'm thrilled at how much energy you're putting into PT. I understand how difficult this can be, but know when you're up on stage, you'll thank yourself for doing it now."

I finish the water and toss it into the garbage can. "I'm ready for round two." Heart pounding, I step onto the mat and place my foot onto the towel. Exhaling, I begin the exercise again, and before I know it, I've reached ten repetitions. My pull is growling and grumbling, but I still made all the reps without stopping.

"I did it!" Arms high in the air, I pick up Jenna in my exuberance and spin around. For her part, my physical therapist throws her head back and laughs.

A knock sounds. "Excuse me, Miss Westfield?"

The male voice penetrates my mind and I let her slip down to the floor. Jenna adjusts her scrubs. "Austin." Her hands fly to the back of her head and she yanks on her ponytail, which loosened when I picked her up. "I've told you several times to call me Jenna."

I focus on the new guy. He's almost as tall as me, with short, light brown hair and brown eyes. A few years younger than me. He smiles at Jenna and a dimple appears. Dude.

"Jenna," he repeats as instructed, although his gaze bounces between the two of us. "Did I interrupt?"

"Of course not," she responds. "Bennett here just completed a difficult exercise and I'm going to ice his leg now. Do you have something you want to discuss with me?"

He glances at me and flexes. *Seriously?* "I do."

Not responding to his dick move, Jenna tilts her head. "Go into my office and I'll be there once I get Bennett set up."

"Sure thing." He brushes way too close to her than he needs to.

Jenna walks over to the freezer and pulls out an ice pack. "Here you go." She places it on my bare thigh, causing me to hiss. Without waiting for me to say anything, she sets the timer and vacates the exercise area into the office. At least she left the door open.

I lie on the exam table, keeping the ice in place while shamelessly eavesdropping on their conversation. If she had wanted it to be private, she would've closed the door, right? He discusses one of his patients with her, but I can see through his lines. He wants in her panties.

Heat surges through me.

What was that?

Austin—who my mind has nicknamed "Asshole"—chats her up about the protocol to help another patient. To me, though, he seems to have all the answers and is seeking affirmation. More like access. *Asshole.*

At the very least, I'm not hearing any giggles from her. Has to mean something. Perhaps these two are involved? No way. He's too apple-pie for her. She likes her men a bit rougher around the edges, if Darren is a good example.

Darren.

Shit.

I tune the two out and focus on reviewing the exercises from today. The squats sucked, but I managed to do them. I'm going to kick this groin pull's ass. Is that even a thing? Whatever, I'm going out on tour with UC as planned, and that's all there is to it.

The timer goes off and I remove the ice pack. I glance toward the doorway, but they're still talking. Getting off the table, I walk to the freezer to replace the pack, then put my sweats over my workout clothes. Instead of lingering in the exercise room, I enter her office. They're standing close to each other. Four eyes land on me.

I plaster a smile on my face. "Timer went off so I replaced the ice pack."

"Great, thanks." Jenna glances between me and the Asshole, landing back on me. "Good session this morning."

My head bobs. The two of them remain on the same side of her desk, and my chest tightens. I've never experienced such an annoying feeling. I rub my upper pecs.

Asshole—Austin—says, "It's lunchtime, Jenna. Want to grab a bite?"

No way am I letting some snot-nosed guy insert himself into Jenna's life. Not on my watch. "Sorry, dude. We've agreed to go out to celebrate my hard work." I extend my arm toward Jenna.

To his discredit, the Asshole squares his shoulders. "We don't mistake patients for friends, right, Jenna?"

Seriously? "Jenna and I go way back." I refrain from calling him pipsqueak. Barely.

Jenna's head bounces between the Asshole and me, and she adjusts her ponytail. "Austin, that's our usual rule. Bennett here is an exception given he was friends with Darren."

Austin's expression remains mutinous, although it's clear he knows who Darren was to her. For my part, I ignore the pang that comes with being tied to her dead boyfriend, UC's keyboardist. My good acquaintance. An unknown longing to be *her* friend rises up.

Deciding to end this odd standoff, I step forward and toss my arm around her shoulders. "Where should we go?" Dismissed, Asshole.

Jenna addresses her next comment not to me, but to him. "You're doing a great job here, Austin. I like your protocols. We can pick this up later."

He looks like he wants to protest, but Jenna shuts him down. I refrain from pumping my fist. When he leaves, she turns to me. "Seriously?"

I step back, hands in the air. "What?"

"I don't remember agreeing to go out to lunch with you."

I grin. She didn't tell that to the Asshole. "We need to eat."

"Well, true." Her shoulders lower.

"How about this? You drive, I pay." When she doesn't look convinced, I add, "Then we come back here and do it all over again."

"Guess I'll save the weights until later."

Weights? This woman has way too many tricks up her sleeve. "Should be interesting. Let's go eat."

Chapter Twelve

J enna takes a moment to change out of her scrubs. Now in a pair of black leggings and purple tunic top, she drives us to a tiny café about fifteen minutes from her clinic. It has a contemporary vibe. I open the menu and am surprised by the unique offerings. "I almost feel as if I'm back in California. This menu is rad."

"This place never disappoints." She plays with the silverware, switching the fork and knife, and depositing the white paper napkin onto her lap.

I follow suit, then we give our orders to the server. "I think I'm making progress. The pull still bothers me, don't get me wrong, but it's less pronounced." I consider. "Less growly."

"Exactly what your therapist wants to hear."

"Especially with less than a week to get me fully functional." I want to talk about something other than my rehab. I want to get to know *her*. "So, tell me Jenna, did you always plan on being such a business mogul?"

She chuckles. "Business mogul? Hardly."

The server drops off our drinks—a diet soda for Jenna and a bottle of water for me. When she doesn't continue, I say, "I think owning two physical therapy clinics—and opening one more—qualifies. Was that always your goal? To move on from working directly with patients to overseeing a number of clinics?" When she doesn't speak, I add, "I can attest to how awesome you are with patients."

Her hand goes to the back of her head, and she tightens her ponytail. "Well, no. I never thought I'd be an administrator. I love working with patients, one on one." She takes a sip of her drink. "Loved," she amends.

I tilt my head. "You don't enjoy working with me?"

Her head shakes. "I do. I really do." Her finger runs over the top of her glass. "Perhaps I should've listened to Austin when he reminded me it's best not to fraternize with patients."

I may only have my GED, but you don't have to be a rocket scientist to know where she's coming from. "Because of Darren."

"We didn't date until he was no longer a patient. But, yes, because of him."

An awkward silence descends. I remember how chuffed Darren was to have her on his arm. How he turned all the other chicks away and bragged about Jenna. Spending time with her now, I'm starting to understand his fascination.

The fact she treats me like a normal guy is a massive turn-on. She doesn't get caught up in the trappings around me. Maybe I should let her be, as I don't have anything other than my rock star status—and a GED—under the hood. On the other hand, she's a warm and wonderful human being who has advanced degrees and two clinics under her belt. What do I bring to the table?

Maybe I could help her loosen up a bit and enjoy her life? Because I can't control my imagination, I ask, "Do you miss working with patients? I mean, the threat of not going on tour as we planned is enough to make me do all sorts of weird exercises. Like standing on a towel and doing squats. I can't imagine not doing what I love." How else could I mask all my faults?

"Being an administrator is related to the field, you know. I advise therapists who work directly with patients. I'm still sort of hands-on."

"Once removed."

"Well, yeah."

The server chooses this moment to deliver our meals, so we dig in. I place the sweet potato fries into my meatloaf sandwich and cut it in half. The mere aroma makes my mouth water.

Glancing across the table, Jenna's picking up her tuna melt. She takes a big bite, and cheese oozes out of the side. I like the fact she's eating real food. Not a lettuce-fest in sight.

I taste my lunch and it's like heaven in between bread. After I swallow, I remark, "Damn. This is fantastic."

She grins. "I know. We were lucky to get a table, but a late lunch like this is usually okay. Dinner always requires a reservation."

"I can see why." I insert more of the sandwich into my mouth. When it's gone—and she still has a half to go—I drink my water and contemplate what she told me. My finger traces the condensation rolling down the bottle.

After Jenna wipes her hands and tosses the napkin onto her plate, I ask the question that's been running around my mind. "You do know Darren raved about you as his therapist, right? You got him back up and running in no time."

"Thanks. Except for the fact the pain meds did a lot of the heavy lifting." Her lips curl downward.

"Hey, your physical therapy got him back in the game. You can't blame yourself for his addiction." Hell, I've heard this platitude innumerable times.

"Kinda hard to avoid it."

"I understand. I really do." Her grey eyes zing into mine. "UC was with him every day and we didn't know the extent of his addiction."

She swallows. "I knew he had prescriptions. I always warned him not to mix them with alcohol. I never thought—" She stops talking.

"None of us did."

Once again, silence descends. This time, without the awkwardness. Only sadness.

Jenna picks up the conversation. "I told him, you know. I told him to take his meds before your concert that night. I also warned him not to drink."

For like the hundredth time, I think back to that night. I didn't know he took the oxy before our gig, but I did know he was drinking afterwards. Still, it's not what killed him. "The alcohol didn't cause his overdose."

Her head hangs. "I know. When we were on the phone that night, he was pretty wasted. Loud and funny, but wasted. He kept asking," she pauses, and her throat constricts as if she were trying to swallow over a boulder. "Darren asked me about three times if he took his meds that evening. I told him he had before the concert, and he'd feel better in the morning. We were on FaceTime, so we could see each other. It was late. He started taking off his clothes to go to sleep. When his hands landed on the waistband of his boxers, I told him not to take them off."

She swipes her palm across her eyes. "I was thinking he'd be more comfortable wearing them if he had to run to the bathroom to throw up."

"Mystery solved." My comment brings her gaze back to me. "You mentioned you told him to keep them on, but never gave an explanation. Makes total sense. Who wants to be butt naked on their knees in front of the porcelain god?"

"Exactly." A single tear floats down her cheek, which she swipes away. "I should've called you or someone else in the band. Pierce. Anyone. I should've asked you to check up on him."

I shake my head. "It wouldn't have mattered unless we caught him in the act of taking more oxy. You said it. He didn't remember if he took an earlier dose. He probably thought he was doing something good by taking another one." I fiddle with the fork on my empty plate. "And another."

"I bear the brunt of blame here. I knew oxy is highly addictive but still encouraged him to take them because of the pain." She turns her head and looks at the wall.

"Hey, Jenna." My hand lands on top of hers. "You can't blame yourself. Ultimately, it was Darren who took the pills. Don't forget, they helped him heal, too. They served their purpose. He abused them."

I needed to say this as much for her as for me. Only Darren is to blame for his decisions that evening. If only I could live this truth. From the looks of it, Jenna needs to embrace it as well.

She removes her hand and touches her cheek. "When did you get so smart?"

I shrug. "Born that way?" *As if.* Wanting to put the issue of Darren's death behind us for now, I press, "You decided to stop seeing patients after he—"

"Yup."

"It's a big loss to the public."

She tilts her head but conversation stops when the server appears and clears our dirty plates. We decline anything further, but compliment the chef. She tells us she'll be right back with our bill.

I press, "How do you manage to oversee two different locations?"

"Not alone." A small smile plays across her face. "Court— Courtney—and I went to physical therapy school together, and I trust her implicitly. I tapped her to run the clinic we meet at, while Felipe is in charge of the other one. At Darren's funeral, I promised him *and* myself I would open ten clinics in five years as my way to honor him." She bites her lip. "Ten was a special number to him."

Was it? Without remembering, I nod. "Already well on your way." What fraction is she at? One-third? One-quarter? Never was any good at math.

"Working on raising the capital for a third."

I connect the dots. "Which is where I come in and why you're back to seeing patients? Or at least me."

"Well, yeah." Her chin juts up. "My clinics are in the black, and

I'm turning a profit. We provide a much-needed service in the Hamptons." She crosses her arms.

Her determination is commendable. She has confidence in her therapists and clinics. "Is that why the Assh—I mean Austin, was asking for your opinion about his services this afternoon?"

"I have an open-door policy for all my physical therapists. It's as much for them as it is for me, you know. Keeps me involved."

Something tells me she knows more about physical therapy than the Asshole ever will. "Don't you miss it, though? Being hands-on?"

"Seems like I'm pretty hands on with you."

Other ways she could be hands on with me flit through my brain. *Whoa.* "Guess it falls on me to keep you on your toes. Can't rely on Austin for everything."

"I probably should see some patients now and then. To keep my skills sharp."

The server comes and I pay for our meal, as promised. This interlude has made me see Jenna as more than my physical therapist—or Darren's ex. She's quiet, yet vivacious when talking about something that stirs her soul. Outgoing in a reserved kind of way. Her inner strength is captivating.

And still on the *Do Not Fuck* list. Perhaps it's not as ironclad as I once believed?

I stand up from the table, only to have my bad leg hip checked. Pain shoots throughout my body. "Holy fuck!"

My yelp could be heard throughout the restaurant. The perpetrator—Michelle—caresses my mid-thigh. "Oh my God, Bennett. I didn't realize you were there."

Jenna rushes to my side. "Get your hand off him. You don't know what you're doing."

I'm ushered into my chair, stars tangoing before my eyes. The server returns to see if she can do anything, and Jenna orders an ice pack. Oh joy.

Hovering, Michelle now strokes my shoulder. "I'm so very sorry. What can I do to make you feel better?"

A frown mars Jenna's face. "Seriously, Michelle?" she snaps. "Haven't you done enough already?"

In a saccharine voice, the bitchy chick replies, "If he were getting the therapy he deserves, I'm sure he would've taken my little mistaken tap in stride."

The server returns with some ice in a baggie, which Jenna places onto my thigh. My physical therapist then steps between Michelle and an empty chair, positioned in front of me.

Jenna directs me to elevate my leg, which I do. She returns her attention to Michelle. "How do you know I'm working with Bennett?"

A smirk crosses Michelle's face, her glossy lips twisting. "He told me."

Jenna stands to her full height, a couple of inches shorter than Michelle. "Then let me do my job."

"Like you did with your other boyfriend?"

This ramps down from entertaining to downright nasty. "Ladies. I'll be fine in a few minutes. I was surprised, that's all." The throbbing has dropped from a twelve down to a ten. Bordering on nine.

Michelle tosses her long brunette locks and points at Jenna. "Why don't you make yourself useful and get this poor guy a drink?" Her fingers swoop in to stroke the hair on the back of my neck. I move away.

"We were finished and about to return to my clinic before you got here." Jenna stands her ground.

I can't help but notice the way she used the word "my" before clinic. My palm moves and some ice falls over the side of my thigh, causing me to hiss.

Michelle bends down to check out what's wrong, her lips inches away from my junk. Jenna places her hands on her hips. "Seriously. Are you going to massage his pulled muscle or give him a blow job?"

The last two words out of Jenna's mouth are so unexpected, my lips drop open. Michelle's not distracted by them, though. "At least he'd enjoy it."

I address the annoying Michelle. "All right, I can handle this from here. Jenna's doing the right thing by icing and elevating my leg. Why don't you go on your way?"

Michelle licks her plump, glossy lips. "You can't mean it."

The way the woman's acting is nuts. We've met a grand total of two whole times. Plus, she insulted Jenna, who's standing behind her, her eyes spitting fire. I know where my loyalties lie.

"I do, Michelle. Why don't you find some other guy who's receptive?" I'm not. And after today, I'll never be.

"Well." She huffs as she stands, towering above me in the chair. "Good luck with this . . . ice queen." She flounces away.

My gaze meets Jenna's, and—despite the pain—I laugh. "She's quite overdramatic, right ice queen?"

Jenna's hand goes in front of her mouth. "I've never seen anyone handle her quite so effectively. Even Darren was taken by her, ah, décor."

"Oh, she's hot enough. But an ugly piece of work."

Jenna moves the ice pack over my thigh. "How's this feeling?"

"It's still throbbing," I confess.

"Maybe Michelle was right about one thing. I'll order us another round of drinks while the muscle calms down."

"Thanks."

She leaves to get our beverages while I rub my angry groin muscle. This sucks. I thought I was making much better progress. Although, our lunch provided much more insights into my physical therapist. Ones I really want to explore, despite all the reasons why we shouldn't.

Jenna returns with two glasses of water. "I wasn't sure if you wanted alcohol."

"Water's fine."

She takes a sip from her glass, then removes the ice pack from my thigh. Her fingers trace the muscle, causing me to inhale through my nose. Her gaze bounces up to me and returns to my leg. "It's tight."

No shit. "I know."

She continues to massage the muscle. She does a funky maneuver and the contraction subsides. My eyebrows fly to my hairline. "What did you do there?"

She half-smiles. "Therapist trick."

"I'll say." My fists unclench. "My pain level dropped to a six." My whole body relaxes and my eyes drift shut. A vision of my therapist floats before me.

When my eyelids open again, Jenna replaces the ice pack and retakes her seat across from me. "I'm glad I could help."

"You're a miracle worker, Miss Westfield."

She giggles before her lips close around the straw. Damn. Even her giggle is sexy. "I wish. But my degree did give me some insider knowledge that helps from time to time."

I drain the rest of my water as the pain continues to subside. "I think I'm going to stick with miracle worker." I can think of a few other descriptions I'd like to add. "Are you ready to go back to work?"

The moment hangs, filled with possibilities, which end when she says, "Let me help you walk to the entrance, and I'll bring the car to the front." She pushes away from the table.

"I'm sure I won't need help to the front door. It hurts but it's manageable. I need to learn how to handle this pain in the future, just in case." Tossing the baggie of ice onto the table, I get to my feet. The first few steps are pretty horrible, but then I get my "sea legs" and walk, albeit a bit unsteadily, to the front door. I don't fight with her when she leaves to get her car, though.

To distract me from my wayward thoughts, on the ride to the clinic, I ask, "So tell me more. How many therapists work for you?"

"All told, ten. I'll add another five when I get the third building." She makes a left turn. "I loathe the hiring process, but it's a necessary evil."

"I hear you. I'm involved in hiring roadies and techs for our tours more often than I care to be. The other guys in the band don't like to be bothered, so I get to represent UC in the interviews. At least the candidates are screened before I'm part of the process."

"Lucky you."

Something in the tone of her voice speaks to me, perhaps determination or hope? "You said you want ten clinics?"

"Yes, ten is my goal." She turns her head toward me, her ponytail swinging. "I want At Your Service PT to become a household name around here. Not because I'm looking to increase the bottom line, but rather to help people after surgery or who get injured, like you."

Her generosity of spirit shines. "A worthy goal."

She pulls into an empty parking spot. "Are you sure you want to do more therapy now? You could wait and come back tonight. Or, after the incident at lunch, perhaps even tomorrow?"

"With only a few more days, I think I need all the pointers I can get. I'll take this session slower, if you don't mind." I join her in front of her car, my pain level settled around a five.

We wait for the elevator. Emptying my thoughts of everything—and everyone, living and dead—except for the beautiful woman next to me, I turn toward her and cup her smooth cheek. "I'm so impressed with you, Jenna. I have faith you'll reach, and even surpass, your dreams."

Her head tilts upward.

Filled with unavoidable desire, I'm drawn to this intriguing woman.

My mouth descends toward hers.

We share a breath.

The elevator pings its arrival and she rushes into it.

Chapter Thirteen

My heart races as the elevator doors close and Jenna disappears. She didn't look up at me at all. What the fuck just happened?

I can't go up and do PT with her as if a massive bomb didn't explode between us. My fingers rake through my hair, and I turn away from the elevator. Outside, I consider my options—do therapy now, call a car service, or walk back to my rental. Waves crashing in the near distance make my decision for me. I start in the direction of the ocean.

My pace is hindered by the lingering pain. Thanks to Michelle. The odd sniping between her and Jenna during today's lunch confirms I'm on Team Jenna for sure. *As if there was any doubt.* I rub my fingers over my lips, still warm from our shared breath.

What the fuck am I doing? She's Darren's girl.

He's gone whispers through my mind.

Yet she remains his. *Do Not Fuck* list is forever.

The wind whips around me. At least this cold air is clearing my thoughts, until a new one appears. Of a more practical nature—I need a winter coat. I've mainly been inside, but this sweatshirt won't cut it.

A couple of clothing stores beckon, so I enter the first one. A helpful woman in her mid-sixties approaches, asking what she can do for me. From another salesclerk half her age, I'd assume this line was a come-on. From her, though, I understand she's being friendly.

"I need a winter coat," I admit.

She smiles. "We have the perfect choices for you. You wear a long, right?"

Gotta hand it to her, she knows her stuff. "You got it." She leads me to a rack with several choices, and I pick a navy blue long wool coat with a funnel neck, for which she praises my style. *Something to brag about to Nese Dalton, UC's new stylist.* She holds up a nice scarf and matching gloves, to which I nod. Go big or go home, right?

Once outside again, I button the coat's four buttons and ensure the new scarf covers my neck. Much better. I continue walking to the boardwalk and face the angry ocean, the frigid breeze causing me to add my new gloves to my winter ensemble.

The waves mirror what's going on inside my mind. Why did I almost kiss Jenna? What must she think of me? Will she continue doing my PT?

"Bennett," someone shouts my name.

Wonderful. Now I have to deal with the public. I turn in the direction of the voice and King waves at me. At least he's not a foe.

"Hey, I thought that was you," he says as he approaches. Today, he's wearing a black peacoat to guard against the weather.

"Hi. What brings you out to the ocean on such a gorgeous day?"

We both chuckle at my joke. "Yeah. It's days like these that I miss California." He blows on his bare hands. "But it doesn't matter, I always love communing with the waves. What drew you out here, Bennett?"

"I'm from Jersey and the ocean's in my blood too." A biting wind rolls in from the ocean. "Although it's fucking freezing out here."

"Yeah. Want to grab a cup of coffee with me?"

Why not? A little extra time between Jenna and me is for the best. "Make mine a tea, and I'm there."

Within minutes, we enter a coffeeshop. After placing our orders, we sit at a table by the windows. "How's PT coming along?"

"It's coming," I reply. "Had a bit of a setback today, though."

"What happened?"

King's nice, however he's not made it to acquaintance level yet with me. To be fair, I only have gradations of acquaintances, but I'm still not about to pour my woes out to an almost complete stranger. I opt for the lesser of all evils. "You remember Michelle, right? The woman I met with you on my first night in town."

"Big lips, tight clothes."

"The one and only."

King's name rings out over the sound system, and he excuses himself to get our drinks. I appreciate his thoughtfulness. He comes back and hands me my hot water and teabag, this time an herbal. Seemed appropriate, given I need to calm the fuck down.

He sips his steaming hot coffee. "What did Michelle do now?"

"I was out to lunch and she bumped into me. More like hip-checked me right at my muscle pull. Hurt like a bitch."

King pulls a face. "Oh man," he offers in sympathy.

I dunk my teabag into the cup. "To say I saw stars is an understatement. Felt like all my therapy went out the window."

"I watched you walking here from outside. You were doing alright." He sips his coffee. "I mean, I could tell you were going slower and were favoring one side, but you didn't appear to be injured."

"Because I got help right away. The server brought a makeshift ice pack and I elevated my leg." And Jenna did a massage trick on it.

He taps his coffee cup against the table. "Makes sense. At least there was no lasting damage."

To my groin pull. Another couple strolls in and says hello to King. He leans toward me. "They bought a house down the street from here with a sick view of the ocean."

The way his face lights up reminds me of how Jenna describes her budding PT empire. "You must love being a real estate agent."

"Yeah, I do. Never thought this is where I'd end up, but I'm happy. Helping people buy and sell rocks."

"Almost as much as your father's concerts." I pause. "Your brother's too."

He chuckles. "Let's say real estate turns me on like performing does for them." His amber eyes bore into mine. "And for you."

I chuckle. "I get it." With a squeeze, I place the teabag onto a small plate and take a sip. Warmth slides down my throat, leaving a soothing wake. "It's great to get on stage with a bunch of guys and share our music."

"You sound just like Dad." He grins over the rim of his coffee mug. "As for me, I get that rush with real estate. Although, when the TV show hired me to play opposite Angie, I had no idea what I was getting into. She's taught me a whole lot more than real estate." His eyebrows wiggle.

"Two kids later, I'd say she sure did."

He takes another swallow of his java. "To be honest, we both taught each other. I was a reckless playboy back then, spending all Dad's money. I had no purpose in life. Angie made me take the real estate exam where I found my passion."

"I can't imagine doing anything other than making music, which I discovered when I was seventeen, so I get it. Wandering aimlessly through life can't be too gratifying."

"Have to say, I enjoyed myself back then. However, it's way more meaningful now."

I sip my tea. "Glad Angie set you on the straight and narrow."

"You have no idea. When you meet someone who clicks with you, grab on to her. She can change your whole world, which can be scary. Although, I can't imagine spending my life with anyone else. Hell, before her, I couldn't imagine spending more than a night with any woman."

Sounds like my life. "What you and Angie have is special."

"It is man, it is." He finishes his coffee and offers to drive me to my rental. Since I don't want to face Jenna yet, I take him up on his offer.

Inside the rental, I wander through the kitchen to the living room. I even open the patio doors for a minute before the cold drives me back inside. I'm too restless to take a nap and too wired to watch a movie.

I put my new coat on again, and walk down the street to the arcade. A game of Asteroids Deluxe should help clear my brain. A couple of empty machines await, and I choose the one I played on my last trip. Might as well try to beat my score on this machine.

After a few rounds, I wipe the sweat off my brow. My alias of Benjamin Howell now shows I'm number eight on the leaderboard. I glance around and realize the arcade has filled. Guess school let out. I relinquish my machine to a kid who appears eager to play.

It's time for me to face the music, or rather my physical therapist. *Who I nearly kissed.* But I didn't.

I slip into my new warm winter coat and hike the blocks to the clinic. If the adrenaline from playing the arcade game revved me up, the cold wind keeps me in check. I arrive at the back door, unnoticed by the citizens of Aroostook. Being off-season has its perks.

I stand outside the building, trying to get the courage to go up. All I need to do is take the elevator to the second floor, go in the back room, and start doing my exercises. Jenna will see me and come out to supervise. That's it. Easy peasy.

Then why is it as though I'm getting ready for my own execution? It was no biggie. It was so nothing she's probably already forgotten about it.

My last thought spurs me to test the door, which is unlocked. I refuse to dwell on what this fact could mean as the elevator takes me to the second floor.

Too soon, I slip into the back exercise room and hang up my coat, then deposit my sweats next to it. On bare feet, I look for the towel I use when doing the slide-and-squat exercise, but don't see it.

My chest expands. Time to face the music.

I approach her office door. Since I've never knocked before, I guess I shouldn't start now. I fling her office door open only to see Jenna tossing some paperwork into a messenger bag.

She flinches. "Bennett. I wasn't expecting you."

Chapter Fourteen

"I'm here to do my second round of therapy." I enter her office.

She drops some papers onto her desk. "Right."

"If I didn't know better, I'd think you were sneaking out of here." We were getting along great. Until—*let it go, Bennett*.

Jenna's hand rubs up and down her arm. "I wasn't sneaking. You weren't here, so I wanted to go home and change."

"Why? Have a hot date?" With Austin the Asshole?

She moves her shoulders. "Sure do."

All my bravado slides to the floor. Why wouldn't someone as smart, kind, and gorgeous as her have a date? My gaze bounces from her messenger bag to the floor. "Oh." I suppress a sigh. "Do you have another therapist I could work with tonight?"

"No."

My shoulders straighten. "Message received. Loud and clear." I turn toward her office door.

"Wait," she commands. "What I meant was I can work with you. I do have a date tonight, but not until a bit later." She closes her eyes. "It's my birthday and I'm going out with my mother to celebrate, like we do every year."

"Oh, Happy birthday." Heat flares up my neck. Now I feel like a schmuck. "I don't want to keep you from your family gig." This will be the second time this week she's eating dinner with her mother. Such an occurrence is so far outside my own experience it's as if she's speaking Japanese.

"No worries." She places her half-full messenger bag onto her desk. "Seriously. I'm not picking Ma up until eight."

Keeping my gaze glued to the floor, I reply, "Then I better do my PT in record time."

"Get started and I'll be there in a few."

"You got it."

I return to the exercise room and start my normal exercises. *Act normal, Bennett. Forget earlier's non-event.* Jenna enters and oversees my exercises, making adjustments as needed. Her hands don't linger on my thigh, yet they don't bounce away from it either.

We get to the towel on the floor and squat one, which I do with care. After the hip check from Michelle, I don't want to aggravate it.

"I think you can add some weight to the squat," Jenna pronounces.

My forehead wrinkles. "Weight?"

She hands me a twelve-kilo kettlebell and tells me to take it slow. "You seriously want me to do a squat with this? It's twenty-six pounds!" My voice lifts at the end.

"I'm sure you lift much heavier."

"Yeah, when I didn't have this groin pull," I grumble and switch the kettlebell between my hands.

"It's only one kettlebell between your two hands. If you want to get better, you'll need to add weight to this exercise. You need to be using weights on a barbell before you're out of here."

"You're a sadist." Now my mind conjures Jenna wearing skin-tight black leather and in all sorts of kinky positions. Fuck.

"I'm not, Bennett. You were the one who's been harping on getting better for the tour, which starts in what? Less than a week now."

"Yeah."

"To do that, you have to keep pushing yourself. There's another set of exercises I want you to try, but you need to master this one first." Her chin lifts.

I pass the kettlebell between my hands again. "Another?"

"At least one."

Knowing I need to do this for the sake of my career, I get into position. "Fine. I'm going to take this slow."

She nods. "You can do it."

Her confidence in me spurs me to try. My foot slides out and I bend down into the squat. The kettlebell takes me off balance, which forces my inner thigh muscles to work. And by work, I mean throb. I bite my lip to keep from crying out in pain as I stand.

"One. Awesome job," Jenna encourages.

I repeat the exercise, willing myself not to cry.

"Two."

With deliberate breaths, I force myself to do more reps. When I get to ten, Jenna takes the kettlebell from me. *Thank God.* I focus on breathing.

"Great job, Bennett. I know it was difficult, but you're in great shape, so I knew you could handle it."

She offers me a towel, which I use to wipe my face. Sweat drips down my neck and beneath my clothes. Out of frustration, I peel my T-shirt over my head and toss it toward the rest of my clothes. I dry my torso.

In a hushed tone, she says, "Oh."

I glance over at Jenna, and her hand's in front of her mouth. Her eyes are wide open and she's staring at my chest. I look down and pluck at the necklace she gave all the members of UC that Christmas so long ago. "We all still wear ours, Jenna. Even gave one to Tris."

She whispers, "You do? You did?"

"Yes." I fiddle with the UC pendant. "You may not know this, but these necklaces mean a lot to the band. I wear it as a reminder of the thing that took me away from a bad situation and gave me purpose." Like real estate for King. "We always wear them."

Darren was wearing his when he died.

"I have Darren's," she admits.

Her confession is so low I almost don't catch it. "Really?"

She nods. "His mother gave it to me before the funeral. It's in my jewelry box."

I don't know how to respond. Over the years, the band and I have often wondered what happened to his necklace, assuming he was buried with it. I'll have to share this detail with them when I return for the tour.

"I thought you only wore it when you were performing. Like a prop with all your rings and bracelets."

It doesn't go unnoticed she admitted to knowing what I wear onstage. "The necklace means much more than that." Case in point, my fingers and wrists are now jewelry-free. Following an awkward silence, I continue, "Well, I guess it's ice time?"

Bit by bit, she brings herself to her full height. "Yes. You did great this afternoon. You're making good progress." She walks over to the freezer as I lie down on the table, my hand covering the UC pendant.

When she doesn't place the ice pack on my leg, I peer over at her. She's studying my body, and I resist the urge to flex. "I'm ready when you are."

"Right." She shakes her head, causing her ponytail to swing. Her steps bring her next to me and she places the ice onto my thigh.

"Tsss," I groan. "I'll never get used to how cold this is."

Jenna sets the timer. "Don't be a baby—it's good for you."

"I'm not being a baby. This shit's fucking cold." *Maybe I did sound a little whiny?*

"I'll be back soon. Should I turn on a lullaby for you?"

"No," I retort. "Some Hunte would rock it."

"I'll see what I can do." She changes the channel on Spotify. "Backdoor Clouds will have to do."

Alone in the room, I listen to "Broken." This song is sick, especially during the drum solo. Darren used to love this group, even getting tickets for him and Jenna at their New Year's Eve concert in Colorado. I'm sure Jenna never knew about his obsession since the concert happened after he had passed.

Grabbing the UC pendant, I tuck my thoughts about Darren into it. This pendant holds all my secrets. About Mom. Dad. Lissa. Curtiss. I give it one more—while she's off-limits, Jenna's intriguing me. The song changes to one by Cole Manchester, and I get lost in "Taboo."

Soon, Jenna returns and retrieves the ice pack. Should I bring up the elephant in the room? Her grey eyes focus on putting it away, on stopping the music, on adjusting her scrubs. Anywhere but on me.

I sit up and fix the bottom of my shorts.

Here goes. "Jenna, about what happened earlier—"

"It was nothing. No big deal."

She sounds so convincing I decide not to touch this subject again. "So you and your mother are going out tonight to celebrate your birthday, huh?"

"We are." She pulls out her phone and checks the time.

"You know, I don't have any dinner plans tonight. Or any night, really, while I'm here." I force my eyes to look like a basset hound's. Those dogs have the saddest eyes I know.

"You don't? I'm sure you could make friends with anyone."

How wrong she is. I don't do friends. "People who don't know me would only see the rock star. I don't want to be him." I pause. "Tonight."

"The Huntes set you up in a wicked rental. I bet it has a kitchen."

I lift my shoulder. "It does, smarty pants. I don't want to eat alone, though." I double down on my puppy dog eyes.

"Well, maybe I can ask my mother if she wouldn't mind a rock star barging into our girl time."

"Don't put it that way. I may be a rock star when I'm on stage, but right now I'm just an injured guy. Interested in not eating alone." Perhaps getting to know his physical therapist a bit better. *Perhaps?*

"Fine. I'll ask if I can bring a stray patient with us."

"I suppose that sounds better."

She picks up her phone and walks into her office. Jenna Westfield is unlike anyone I've ever met before. She's amazing as a physical therapist, yes, but it's more than that. Something in her wounded soul calls out to me. Makes me feel seen. Adrenaline rushes through my bloodstream as if I were about to take the stage. As a distraction, I toss my T-shirt and sweatshirt over my head and pull the sweatpants over my shorts.

"So, it seems Ma has a soft spot." Jenna walks into the room. "You've wrangled yourself an invitation to join us for my birthday celebration."

I clap. "Can't wait."

"Hmmm," she adjusts the strap of the messenger bag over her shoulder. "I'll drop you off to change before heading home to do the same. I'll pick Ma up and be back to your rental in an hour."

I close her car door in front of my rental and wave as she drives away. Then it hits me. I'm going out for her birthday dinner—with her mother. I'm not prepared for this. What background do I have dealing with mothers? Mine certainly is not the standard bearer.

Ignoring the voice in my head mocking my intrusion into her celebration, I let myself into the rental and change. A nice pair of pants and a button-down shirt should look good no matter what type of restaurant. Which I presume is a nice one, since they're celebrating her birthday.

The clock above the stove reads seven-thirty. With thirty minutes to spare, I lock the rental and walk as fast as I can, which isn't too fast, thanks to my injury, and enter a neighborhood stationery store. I choose a birthday card that's not sappy, featuring flowers on the front. I check out the novelty items for sale, hoping to find a nice gift. Nothing snags my attention, so I simply pay for the card.

On the sidewalk, I check my cellphone and realize I still have fifteen minutes. There has to be another store around here. Of course, everything's closed. All except for the arcade. She did say she used to hang out here as a kid. Maybe this would be the perfect gift?

By eight, I stand outside my rental, rubbing my gloved hands together. Headlights turn down my street and pull over in front of me. Bending down, I wave at the two women inside, then take my time climbing into the backseat. "Hi, Jenna, Mrs. Westfield."

"Please call me Faith," her mother replies.

"Faith," I repeat. A reminder to have faith she won't be anything like my own mother.

Jenna waves at me, her blonde hair loose for a change. Looks fan-freaking-tastic. "The restaurant is about fifteen minutes away, so get comfy."

Her mother turns on the radio to an oldies station. The two talk in quiet tones.

What have I gotten myself into?

Chapter Fifteen

The hostess takes one look at me and ignores the rest of the customers, including Jenna and her mother. She scribbles something onto a notepad and rips it off, passing it to me. Without checking it's her phone number—because all these notes are the same—I stuff it into my pocket.

"For later, okay?"

I'm used to this type of behavior, yet I know it's not welcomed by Jenna or her mother. I lean toward the young lady. "We're here celebrating her birthday." I tip my head toward Jenna. "Can you please check your reservation book?"

"What?" Glazed blue eyes meet mine.

"Our reservation," I persist.

"Oh." Her pen slides down the book. "For Westfield, right?"

At least she remembered this part of her job. "Yes."

Fake eyelashes bat at me. She picks up three menus and instructs us to follow her. If her hips swayed any faster, she could get a job as a metronome. She escorts us to our table and makes a show of giving us our menus. When she gets to me, last, she bends over and whispers in my ear, "I get off at eleven. I can make your evening better than your sister and mother ever could dare imagine."

I shake my head and tilt my head back to her ear. "She's not my sister." Her cheeks hollow and she scurries away.

Laughing, I take the napkin off the plate and flick it before putting it on my lap. When I look at the table, both my dinner companions are staring at me with identical expressions. I keep my mouth closed.

Mrs. Westfield—Faith—is the first to break. "I have to know. What did you say to that trollop?"

I like this woman. "Only the truth."

She starts to open her mouth, but Jenna barges into the breach. "Believe me, you don't want to know. Don't forget, Bennett here is the reckless one."

I scowl at my physical therapist. Her mother pats her daughter's hand. "Oh yeah. I remember now." They both turn toward me.

"I'm not reckless. I may have done some stupid sh— stuff, but I'm not irresponsible. I'm the one who handles all the band business, after all." That's the truth.

"Fine," Jenna acknowledges. "You're sort of the ringleader. The guys all follow your lead."

Somehow, I'm not sure she means this as a compliment. I don't get to question her because she receives a text. "It's from Kara," she tells her mother. "She wishes me a happy birthday."

Her mother's smile could be seen all the way to Manhattan. "Did you tell her you're out to dinner with me?" Grey eyes, so like her daughter's, swing toward me. "And Bennett?"

"I said we were out celebrating. I didn't mention anything about Bennett."

"The man is right here, Jenna. Tell your sister," her mother tusks.

Jenna blows her hair out of her eyes. "How about I take a photo? Speaks a thousand words."

Faith replies, "Good thought."

The server arrives and Faith asks him to take a photo of all three of us, which he obliges. Drink and meal orders given, he disappears. Jenna taps on her phone, then places it on top of the table. "Sent."

I remember Jenna telling me she and her sister aren't close on account of the fact she's ten years older, married, and lives in the City with her two kids. I address Faith. "What does Kara do?"

"She's an anesthesiologist in Manhattan. Her husband's a cosmetic surgeon."

My eyebrows raise. "Health care is in your family's blood."

Faith preens. "Sure is." She taps Jenna. "My little Jenna already has two physical therapy clinics and is working on another. I'm so proud of her."

Faith's obvious pride in her daughter's accomplishments is in stark contrast to how my own mother is with me. For a moment, I long for such a loving relationship. In my next breath, I shut it down. It is what it is—no use in wanting something I'll never have.

After the server delivers our drinks and leaves a bread basket, Faith asks, "So tell me, Bennett. How did you come to be part of Untamed Coaster?"

Her question makes the tips of my ears heat. Do I tell her the version we share with the media or give her more of the real scoop? I don't know what Jenna's told her, so I start with the sanitized version.

"It all started when we worked together at an amusement park ages ago. We met because we were assigned to a rollercoaster ride called Untamed Coaster. Formed a lifelong bond and here we are today."

Like magic. No problems. No difficulties to overcome. Except she knows we lost Darren.

Jenna doesn't let my story stand. "Now, Bennett, that's not the full extent of it. I remember Darren telling me he had to practically beg you to drop out of high school and join the band."

Yup. Like that, I slink lower on Faith's ranking scale. Her daughter's an anesthesiologist, her son-in-law's a cosmetic surgeon, her other daughter owns two—soon-to-be three—physical therapy clinics. Me? I'm the deadbeat dropout rock star at the table. Wonderful.

"Seems to me you made a good decision," her mother says. Her eyes are clear and steady. She's not lying.

"I'd like to think so." I fiddle with the fork at my place setting. "I got my GED, though. The band all got into prepping me."

Jenna tucks her hair behind her ear. "I can only imagine how Darren helped. What was his specialty? Annoying teachers? Music theory?" She pauses. "How about creative writing." The gleam in her eyes extinguishes as she travels down this dark path.

I decide to lighten them up again. "No, he was a hardass over history."

Jenna sits back. "History?"

"Yup. He used to hold up the GED study guide and quiz me on dates. He did this for hours. He didn't know a single one of them himself, but he made sure I knew them. I remember he used to make up songs for the major battles of the Revolutionary and Civil Wars." I chuckle, still able to hear echoes of his crazy lyrics.

Faith joins me with a light laugh. "I can only imagine. Did he have one for the Gettysburg Address?"

I tilt my head. "All I remember is 'Four score and seven years, oh what the heck time is that? Who talks like that anyway? Guess it doesn't matter cause Abe boy said it. Oh-ah.'"

All three of us are laughing when our server delivers our meals. Before we dig in, Faith wipes a tear from her eye. "'Abe boy'?"

I shrug. "Darren liked to personalize historic figures. George Washington was Georgie. Martin Luther King, Jr. was Marty." More laughter, even from Jenna. It feels good to talk about Darren without having such a dark cloud associated with his name.

Faith regains her composure. "So Darren convinced you to drop out of high school to join the band. What did your parents think?"

My good humor is short-lived. I pick up my fork. "My dad had passed away a few weeks before. My mom and I aren't too close, so she didn't mind."

Faith's smile falls off her face. "Oh, I'm so sorry. I'm sure it was a difficult time for all of you."

I need to right this ship. Without looking at Jenna, I say, "Well, over a decade has passed. I've always taken care of my mother, so I think she forgives me." For cutting out of town, sure. Not for the other. Never for that. I lean on my forearms. "The guys and I get together and play music. We've added Tristan on keys, but otherwise, we're still the same group who got together and played since high school. Except now we have fans."

Nice whitewash. No mention of the groupies. Or boasting about our platinum records and awards. We all dig into our meals. The flavors are delicious.

Jenna swallows. "Darren used to say UC was a cohesive unit. Don't you all still hang out even when you're not performing? He said you were the quintessential band of brothers who also rocked the house."

"Maybe in Darren's eyes, that's how UC was. He was best friends with 007"—I look at Faith and amend—"Our bassist, Pierce DeLuca. They were almost inseparable." I leave out the part about them sharing *everything*, until Jenna came along. "They were the ideal you're talking about."

"Darren talked about hanging out with you guys on the bus, going from concert to concert. He had lots of great things to say about you and the rest of the band." Jenna addresses her mother. "He didn't lie to me about that, I'm sure."

"I'm sure he didn't," Faith responds. "Maybe Bennett here has a different outlook?"

I don't want their pity. I don't want to speak ill of the dead. I don't want to be thought of as antisocial. I'm not. Simply like to keep things close to my vest, as the saying goes. "Listen, Darren's version of UC is a nice ideal. Something we should all strive to achieve."

My response satisfies Faith, who puts her glass down on the table. "Seems to me the band is a great group of friends who are enjoying the high life. Nothing wrong with that."

A flicker passes between the two women. Something unspoken. Jenna changes the subject to our lunch today. "Then Michelle came out of nowhere and hip-checked poor Bennett, hitting his injury point-blank."

"Oh no," Faith's grey eyes sear me. "Are you alright? Jenna's told me all about your progress."

I rub my thigh. "I'm good now. Rest and icing it helps. Of course, so long as your demon daughter isn't making me stand on one leg and do tree pose."

"I do no such thing!" Jenna roars, her fork landing on her nearly empty plate.

I wink at her and direct my attention to her mother. "Did you know your daughter has no sense of compassion? I begged her not to make me hold the yoga pose for longer than thirty seconds, but she wouldn't hear of it."

"Jenna!" Faith accuses my physical therapist. "Tell me you do no such thing. Bennett needs to heal, not be sent to the hospital."

I place my hand over my heart. "I swear."

Jenna gets a wicked glint in her eyes. "I only told him to do the pose because he said my exercises were too easy for him, considering what good shape he's in. I didn't want to disappoint."

Gauntlet thrown. "I never made such a statement. You were the one who told me to take off my shirt so you could massage my thigh better." Take that.

"Oh yeah?" Jenna counters. "I've seen better six-packs in liquor stores."

Faith intervenes. "So he has a six pack?"

Busted. I lean back and watch Jenna try to squirm off this hook. One of her own making.

"It's not too defined," she starts. "I mean, if you squint real hard, you might see a few dips and divots."

I cross my arms. This is getting interesting.

She glances at her mother. "Besides, he was sweating after doing squats. I only suggested he take off his shirt—" She stops talking.

"So you could ogle my goods?" I supply. *Love that I got her to lie and say she told me to take off my shirt.*

"No, you pervert." She tosses her crumpled cocktail napkin toward me. "For you to rest comfortably."

"I think that clears everything up," her mother quips. Returning to her daughter, she asks, "I do need you to back up a little. Did you say Michelle was the person who bumped into him during lunch?"

Jenna sighs. "Yes. She showed up at the restaurant."

"From out of nowhere," I supply.

Faith nods. "I can only imagine. That girl's been a thorn in your side since forever."

I wait for further explanation, but none comes. So I ask the obvious question. "Why?"

The two ladies look at each other. Standing, Jenna excuses herself to go to the bathroom and her mother dives in. "Jenna and Michelle went to school together—from elementary through high school. She always was jealous of my Jenna. When they were seniors, Jenna had this boyfriend. Thad? Theo? Tim? Something like that." She shakes her head.

When she doesn't continue, I prompt her. "So Jenna was dating this guy?"

"Oh right. Yes. They were dating a few months when all of a sudden Michelle got a makeover. Highlighted her hair, fake lashes. Changed up her makeup and started wearing tight, tight clothes."

"Still does."

Faith continues as if I hadn't spoken. "Before the senior prom, Jenna was convinced Thaine... That's it! Rhymes with rain." She taps her brow as if to congratulate herself. "Anyway, she was positive Thaine would invite her to be his date. Only the invite never came because Michelle went over to his house and asked him first."

I can only imagine what her invitation consisted of—probably at least a hand job. No horny seventeen-year-old would turn that down. Hell, I wouldn't at that age. The thought of Lissa giving me one would've sent me over the moon.

"My Jenna was devastated. Especially when the photos came out and the couple was all over each other."

"So Michelle stole Jenna's boyfriend. Seems like Jenna was the one who would have the axe to grind."

Faith takes a final sip from her drink. "I don't know all the details, but I think Jenna might have done something, because one day, Michelle showed up with a brand new, short haircut."

I rear back and laugh. Only Jenna. "Oh my. Remind me never to get on your daughter's bad side."

"Anyway," her mother elongates the first syllable. "Soon they both went away for college. Michelle got an art scholarship, but it apparently didn't go anywhere since she now works as a receptionist for a local doctor. She does do everything in her power, however, not to refer patients to Jenna's clinics."

All her trash talk about Jenna makes sense. "Guess she never got over the school rivalry."

Jenna slips into her seat. "Everything alright here?"

"Of course, Sweet Pea." Faith turns toward me, the last bite of her entrée on her fork. "Please finish your story, Bennett. Where is your mother now?"

I won't give up too much information, even to such a nice lady. One who calls her daughter Sweet Pea. "She lives in New Jersey." I stop, then add "Where I'm from."

"I'm sure she has a great support system around her. Like I do here in Aroostook."

"The people around here seem nice," I deflect. Faith is so different from any of the other mothers I've known. To be fair, I don't have much of a relationship with the band's mothers, except Mother Hilliard—who's faded into the background since Darren passed. "Present company included."

"Why, thank you." Her stomach gurgles, causing her hand to land on top of it. "Oh my. Please excuse me, I think it's my turn to use the ladies.'" She gets to her feet and leaves.

"I like your mom," I admit.

"She's pretty awesome. I've been through so much with her. She always gives me the best advice." Jenna tucks her blonde hair behind her ear. "Ma's had it rough, though. My father split when I was only five."

Words fail me. I reach out and clasp her hand.

She stares at our joined hands. "Thanks. I was young and don't remember much. Kara resented me for the longest time about it, saying I broke up her family. Since she's gotten married, I think she has a different perspective on things." Her hand moves from mine to the salt and pepper shakers on the table.

"You didn't do anything wrong," I feel compelled to tell her.

"I know. Babies don't solve problems underlying a marriage."

Wow. That's some deep shit. "Shrink?"

"Years," she admits. She moves the remnants of her food around her plate. "Ma's an amazing woman. I hope to be worthy of being her daughter someday."

"You already have two physical therapy clinics under your belt. The way she talks and looks at you, I'd say you are more than worthy."

"Thanks."

The woman of the hour returns. "Guys, I think I'm going to head out. I ate something that didn't quite agree with me."

Jenna pushes away from the table. "I'll get the car brought to the front." She opens her purse to look for the valet ticket.

I'm about to stand when her mother says, "No. Stay. We haven't had dessert yet, and you and I both know that's the best part of the meal."

"Ma, I don't want you to go home by yourself."

"Nonsense, I do it all the time. Can you please order me a car service?"

Sensing Jenna's dilemma, I whip out my cell and call one up. Selfishly, I want to spend alone time with my physical therapist. "All ordered."

"Aren't you sweet? Thanks." Her mother bends down and whispers something in her daughter's ear, to which Jenna seems to disagree. I'm sure it's about her ducking out early. In any event, the pair end their standoff when I say the car's out front.

With a hug for her daughter and a small wave to me, Faith exits the restaurant.

"Everything okay?" I finish my drink.

"Yes." Jenna plays with her hair. "I don't like Ma leaving early."

"I'm sure she'll feel better soon and you two can go on a makeup date." Something in her demeanor tells me she's not sharing the whole truth. "Sweet Pea."

Jenna's scowling at me when the server comes and clears the plates. She drops a dessert menu for us to share, so I slide into Faith's abandoned chair. Not without aggravating my pulled fucking muscle, though.

Ignoring the throbbing, I ask, "See anything you like?"

I sure do.

Chapter Sixteen

Jenna steals the last bite of tiramisu. "That was delicious." She wipes her lips.

I'll never finish a meal again without thinking of the glorious noises coming out of her mouth. "I can tell you enjoyed it."

A blush stains her cheeks. "I didn't want you to have any doubts."

She's sweet. All of a sudden, I remember the birthday card and gift I have for her. I signal for the server, ask for the dessert plates to be taken away, and a couple of glasses of champagne brought over.

"Why on earth did you order that?"

"Because it's your birthday. You need to celebrate."

She motions toward the table. "Isn't that what we were doing? Dinner with Ma. The tiramisu?"

"They were merely a precursor." I reach into my pocket and hand her my card. "Happy birthday, beautiful."

"Shhh, keep your voice down. Don't want to tip off the other diners."

The idea of serenading her holds a lot of appeal. "I wish I could, but I'm trying to keep a low profile out here. Besides, I don't do *a capella.*" The one and only time I did was when I was five and rehearsing a song for Father's Day. Mom put her hand over my mouth, saying my voice could make my sister roll over in her grave. Over the years, I've gotten over her criticism, although I refuse to sing without instrumental backup.

"Oh, right."

She looks at the envelope in her hand, which I urge her to open. She takes her time reading the thoughtful message written by the card company. Wish I could do it half as well as them. Next, she opens the gift card to the arcade and starts laughing. "No way!"

"Cut me a break. I was limited in time and location." I pull out my phone and tap a few things. "There. Now your birthday is programmed into my calendar forever. I'll never miss another one of your birthdays."

She shakes her head. "You're crazy."

"Seems like you're going to have a blast at the arcade with a crazy person then." I'm proud of my gift to her. I rented out the entire arcade for a few hours on a date of her choosing, figuring we can use it in between my therapy sessions.

"Bennett, I haven't been in there for years."

I rub my hands together. "Then you better be ready for me to whoop your ass!"

Her eyes turn to slits. "Don't be so sure of yourself." Her palm brushes over her shoulder. "I have skills."

I laugh. "Oh, it's on!"

I motion for the server to bring the bill and pass her my credit card without looking at it. Jenna huffs, "You didn't have to do that. I invited you to join us."

"For your birthday," I supply. "Not letting the birthday girl pay for her own celebration. What kind of guy do you think I am?"

Her hand rubs her throat. "I'm not sure."

I don't respond to her quiet words, which provide me with a ray of hope. Standing, we walk over to the coat check, and I help her pull hers up her shoulders. My hands rest on them for a moment before taking my new winter coat and sliding it up my own arms.

She turns and places my scarf around my neck, tugging on the ends. I have the sudden urge to taste her lips, which I bet are better than any of the amazing food we enjoyed here.

I reach out to caress her cheek.

A teenage boy wearing a jacket proclaiming him to be the valet approaches. "Can I get your ticket?"

Her lips purse, as if she's holding herself back from something we both want. She turns from me, her hand slipping into her purse and retrieving a small piece of paper. "Here you go. I'll wait for my car. Take your time."

Before I can object, she's out the door. Perhaps running from the feelings swirling between us?

I huff a breath and ready myself for the ride home. I know Darren placed her on the *Do Not Fuck* list, but does it really still apply now? I mean, it's not like I'm stealing her away from him. When we arrive at my rental, maybe I can invite her in for a nightcap?

Smirking, I open the restaurant's door to a feeding frenzy. Paparazzi swarm Jenna at the valet stand, screaming at her.

"Are you out with Bennett Hardy?"

"How do you know the rock star?"

"Where did you meet him?"

I step forward and the vultures latch on, screaming my name. Asking more questions about what I'm doing in Aroostook and who the blonde with me is. At least they haven't figured out Jenna's identity. The need to protect her swells within me.

Raising my hand, I address the crowd. "I'm in the Hamptons for some R&R before Untamed Coaster goes out on our new tour."

My words don't seem to satisfy them, though, as they continue pummeling me with more questions. At least I drew their attention away from Jenna. How did they know she was with me, anyway?

The attendant drives her car up the drive, inching forward so as to avoid the media gaggle. Personally, I wouldn't mind seeing a few of them run down. Or at least jumping out of the way.

Finally, the harried valet leaps out of the car. I glance at Jenna, who's surrounded by reporters, like I am. Unlike me, all the color's drained from her face and her eyes have glazed over. Despite knowing how much this will suck, I brush past them and walk—faking a normal gait through clenched teeth—toward the driver's seat. She's in no condition to drive up the street, let alone all the way to my rental.

Ignoring the paps, I approach the valet and pass him a good tip. "Help her into the car."

"Yes, sir." The kid glances at the money I handed him. "Will do, right away sir."

At least one problem solved. With a final wave to the media, I slip into the driver's seat, blocking the stabbing pain emanating from my muscle pull. Seated, I close the door, push my seat backward, and click my seat belt while the noise raises by decibels when the passenger side door opens.

Paps continue to throw questions at Jenna, who remains immobile. I need to get her out of here, so I honk the horn four long times. My distraction works because she hops into the car and slams her door shut, despite reporters' hands trying to keep it open. I push the button and lock them all out.

"Ready?"

My question isn't met with any answer—snarky or otherwise.

This is bad. I put the car into drive and move forward at an even pace. Several of the reporters jump out of my way, which gives me a small bit of satisfaction.

When we turn onto the main street, I let out my breath and place a hand on my thigh, where I massage the throbbing pull. The adrenaline from dealing with the paps is replaced with the agony I'm putting my groin pull through. Driving requires me to use my right leg, and my thigh protests.

The need to protect this fierce, formidable, *fragile* woman outpaces my own injury. "How are you doing, Jenna?" I dare not switch my eyes from the road since I haven't driven in . . . months. This task, combined with my spasming leg, requires all of my attention.

We drive for a couple of blocks before I realize I have no idea where I'm going. "Jenna?"

Her head swivels toward me, which I count as a win. However, her distant expression warns of her mental state. "Can you please set up the GPS?" While I don't want to waste a moment of driving any place we don't have to be, now's not the time to admit this fact.

When she doesn't speak, I shut off the headlights, turn down what's marked as a "Dead End," and stop on the side. I want to pull her into my arms and tell her this will pass. Hell, I simply want to hold her. But my leg hurts too fucking much for me to do anything other than focus on getting us home. Satisfaction rumbles through me when a passel of reporters drive by on the main road.

"Jenna, listen to me. I'm a big story in this small, sleepy town during winter. If I were here in the summer, I'm sure I wouldn't be a blip on their radar."

Her grey eyes blink. "I froze out there." She licks her lips. "I was surprised."

Over my complaining leg, I reach over and brush her hair off her cheek. "Anyone would be shocked when a pack of wolves descends without warning, Sweetheart." *Sweetheart?* I'll unpack this term later.

"Yeah."

"Please know this will blow over. I'll speak with Luke about the best way to make them go away."

She opens her mouth and a stream of air comes out. Shaky hands corral her hair into a ponytail, which doesn't stay put. I place my finger on her bottom lip over the protests of my thigh. "They'll go away. I promise."

"Thank you. I trust you."

I puff up at her words. When has any woman ever trusted me

other than to give her an orgasm? "I won't let you down." I glance at the screen on the console. "Now, can you set up the GPS so we can get out of here?"

"I can do that." She gathers herself and hits various buttons on the dash.

I return to sit properly, massaging my thigh. My head follows my progress rather than hers.

"There. All set."

The disembodied GPS voice instructs me to return to the main road, so I make a U-turn and off we go. We make small talk on the way back to town, going through windy roads that challenge both my driving and physical abilities. When a deer leaps across the road, I come to a fast halt, which brings about another bout of pain that I hide from my physical therapist. She doesn't need to deal with my issues after the ambush at the restaurant.

At long last, we stop in front of a traditional two-story house. In the summer, I bet it has a nice lawn and flowers. "Uhm, Jenna. I know the GPS says we have arrived, but this isn't my rental."

Her hand flies to her mouth. "Oh no. This is *my* house."

Chapter Seventeen

S ilence stretches between us.

I want nothing more than to spend the evening with her. Hold her. Make her feel safe after the paps ruined her birthday. "Jenna," I begin. "Do you want me to stay?"

She doesn't answer for a long time. My stomach churns to the beat of my throbbing thigh. At least not driving has alleviated some of its anger.

Her finger points toward the garage. "You can park in the driveway."

"You got it." I put the car into drive and complete the task with only minor additional pain. Must be the buzz running through my body. I refuse to jump to conclusions about what staying at her home means, but I seem to be making progress on something I only recently realized I wanted.

When I shut off the car, she opens her door and springs out. I open my door but my exit is neither fast nor graceful. When I'm upright, little pants escape.

"Oh no." She shakes her head. "Are you all right? No, of course you're not. You shouldn't have been driving. It taxes your groin muscle too much. What was I thinking?"

She continues rambling until I raise my hand. "Stop. We made it here without being followed. That's a win." Cutting into the dead end was a gifted choice. I take one step away from the car and wince.

Her hand comes around my waist. "It's my fault you're hurting. Come on, let's get you into the house."

The time from her driveway to her front door takes at least ten hours—really minutes, but who's counting?—since I need to stop several times. When we're finally inside, she shuts the door, turns on the lights, and hangs up her coat, all before I can do anything more than lean against the wall and catch my breath.

Jenna places her hands on my arms. "Bennett."

I force my gaze to hers.

"It's my turn to take care of you. Think you can walk to the kitchen?" She points to a room about a million miles away.

My head shakes. "No, I—"

"I get it. How about you sit down right here?" She indicates the chair in the foyer. Only a couple of steps away.

"Better," I rasp.

She assists me down to the chair. It's wooden, but it gets my weight off my thigh, which is all that matters.

"I'll be right back." She disappears into the kitchen, presumably to get another ice pack. I don't think I'll ever order another drink on the rocks for as long as I live.

Sure enough, she emerges with another one in her hands. She hesitates before handing it to me.

"You need to take off your coat."

My fingers reach the buttons, but it seems like my fine motor skills were left in the car. I drop my hands. She takes over, making quick work of opening it and helps me slide it down my arms. She stares at my pants, then glances deeper into her house.

"I hate to say this, but you'd be more comfortable with your leg elevated. Do you think you could make it to the living room? I promise you'll appreciate it."

I'm so tired. I want this pain to stop. If she thinks this is a better idea, though, I suppose I can manage it. "My last move."

Smiling, she replies, "You got it."

Jenna helps me get to my feet. I leave my coat on the chair, and with unsteady strides, we walk into the living room. She has an upholstered sectional against a window facing a large-screen television. The walls are painted grey with orange and yellow pillows. "I like it in here."

"Thanks. I do too." Before I collapse, she instructs, "Take off your pants."

I smirk. "While I'd love to, I have it on good authority I'm not allowed to have sex until I'm healed. With the way I'm feeling—"

"What's your pain level now?"

"About a nine."

"Meaning a twelve." She bites the inside of her cheek. "We have to get these pants off you so the ice will be directly on your thigh." Her fingers open my buckle.

While I want to tease her, I don't have the energy. Dealing with the fucking paps and driving zapped all of my reserves. I help her roll my pants down my legs, then lower my boxer-brief-covered ass onto the sofa. With efficiency, she removes my shoes and socks as well as my pants from around my ankles. An instant later, the ice pack lands on my thigh. Followed by a throw blanket, I presume for my modesty.

Coldness seeps into my bones. "Fuck!"

"Ice is good for you." She pauses. "Unlike me. I'm sorry, again, for how I froze back there. And for making you drive me home." She hangs her head.

With my leg outstretched, and the bloody ice pack on it, I feel better already. If we were close enough, I'd tilt her chin up toward me. *Maybe more.* "Just a temporary setback."

"If I were a responsible therapist, you wouldn't have had *any* setbacks." She takes a seat across the room. Too far.

I pat the cushion next to me. "I'd feel better if I didn't have to raise my voice to speak with you." She slumps, then stands and crosses the great expanse—truly, mere feet. She sits beside me, though not close enough. "Better."

Jenna plucks at her pants. "I had a wonderful birthday, Bennett, the ending notwithstanding."

"I'm glad. I did too. Your mother is very nice."

Her expression lightens. "She's my best friend. We've been through so much together."

Because I need to touch her, I reach over and slip my hand over hers, entwining our fingers. "I'm happy you have someone so close to you."

"You have that too, with the band."

I don't contradict her. Why bother? While I'm suffering actual pain, she's the one who dealt with an undeserved onslaught this evening, one for which she had no preparation. "At least your mother didn't witness it back there."

She nods. "You're right. I don't think she would've handled it as well as I did."

I can't stop myself. "Like the professional therapist you are?" I squeeze her hand, letting her know I'm teasing.

Her head tilts toward mine. "Not everyone is used to people chronicling their every movement, from where they buy coffee to when they go to the gym."

I hate to bring this up, but it's the truth. "They used to follow Darren."

"Well, true. But they weren't as rabid over him as they are over you. We did get questions lobbed at us in the airport once, but generally, he wasn't their focus."

Her explanation rings true. For whatever reason, I'm usually the lightning rod the media pursues. "I hear you. But all the guys get their time in the burning sun."

She doesn't continue this conversation. "How's the pain level now?"

"It's dropped down to maybe a high six."

She chuckles. "Your descriptions are hysterical. Most people would call it a seven." She comes to a temporary halt. "Or a nine."

I lift our joined hands to my mouth. "I'm not like most people."

Beneath mine, her fingers open and she slips from my hand. Rubbing her newly freed palms against her uninjured thighs, she stands. "Yeah, well, what are we going to do with you tonight? My guest room is upstairs."

I glance at the staircase and resist the urge to cry like a baby. "I can stay right here. Do you have an extra pillow or something?"

"I do." She rushes up the stairs like a gazelle and returns with linens and a pillow. "Here you go."

"Wow. All I need is a blanket."

"Use them all." She removes the ice pack and checks my thigh. "I think it's calming down. Leave it on for another ten minutes then toss it here." She points to an empty plate on the coffee table, which she moves closer to me.

"Thanks."

"No problem. I'll see you in the morning." She races away from me.

Or from what she's feeling for me?

Alone, I finish with the ice pack and drop it where she indicated. Because nature calls, I force myself to wander down a hallway where I find a half bath. It's cheery, like her, with a unique, contemporary light fixture. When I return to the living room, I unbutton my shirt and toss it onto my other clothes laying across a chair, taking my cellphone back to my makeshift bed.

I set up the pillow and comforter and snuggle under them. Be nicer if I were snuggling with the home's owner.

My fingers play with the UC pendant around my neck, which has gained even more significance after tonight. In addition to being sexy and smart and thoughtful, Jenna is an accomplished therapist, and she's caring. She almost made me believe better things can happen. Unlike the awful end to her birthday.

Stop it right there. Do Not Fuck list, remember?

I check the time. Since it's only eleven, I know Luke will still be up, and he needs to hear about what happened for a variety of reasons. I pull his contact information and press send.

"Hey there, B. How's physical therapy coming along?"

"I was making progress until tonight. Jenna, her mother, and I went out to dinner to celebrate Jenna's birthday. When we left, a pack of paps got to us."

"Oh, shit."

"Yeah."

I can picture him pacing around a hotel room, processing what I told him. "How many are we talking?"

"I'd say there were at least fifteen or twenty." I wait a beat. "All of them are stationed here in the Hamptons. My guess is they were looking for a new story to tide them over until summer."

"My thoughts exactly. I'll get our PR team on it. You'll have a plan in your inbox by morning. I wonder how they found out you were out there?"

"I don't know. I've been keeping a low profile, basically only going to PT. I did go out to dinner with King and Angie, and I found an arcade that helps me while away the hours." Michelle pops into my mind and I stare at my phone for a moment. "I did meet a woman—"

"Of course you did." Luke's chuckle floats through the air.

"Ha, ha. No, this one tried to get me to take her home, but I passed for various reasons. If I had to guess, I'd say she was the one who tipped off the press."

"It doesn't matter who did it, you know. Fact is, your whereabouts are now out to the public. Do you want me to send Elias?"

Security. I sigh. "No. I enjoy being able to move around without having someone tagging along two feet behind me. I don't want to have to deal with that here."

"All right. But if there are any more issues, we'll revisit."

"Sounds good." An inexplicable need to spill the beans about how I'm feeling about Jenna rises, which I squash. Luke's become my "good acquaintance," but he's not my friend. Ever since Curtiss fucked me over with Lissa in high school, no "friends" are needed in my world.

Luke intrudes on my thoughts. "While I have you on the phone, I do have some band business we need to discuss."

"Sure. Shoot." Perhaps this will take my mind off the woman upstairs.

"You know Chico, our guitar tech?"

"Of course I do. He's fucking brilliant."

"And leaving." Luke lets this sink in for a moment. "He just gave his two weeks' notice."

We've always treated him well—what on earth made him want to leave? "I can't believe it. Did he say why?"

"His girlfriend's pregnant."

Good Lord. "Better him than me." Truer words were never spoken. "Do you think he can transition the position to a new tech before he leaves?"

"Yeah, that's the upside. If I arrange for some interviews, do you think you could do them with me when you get back? I'll be sure to let the candidates know this position starts immediately."

My mind replays Jenna complaining about hiring new physical therapists. How she hates the process. Once again, I'm grateful I don't have to deal with any preliminary shit. "Sounds good to me."

"Will you be ready to perform for the tour? When are you planning on getting here?"

I run my fingers through my hair. "If I had to go onstage tonight, I'd fall flat on my face. It was a long, fucking day, thanks to the press. However, before tonight, I would have said I was making progress. I'm starting to be able to move laterally." I smirk, remembering how Jenna described the exercises.

"That's something. I guess we can be happy this isn't a boy band of the nineties with choreography. You only have to stand and walk across the stage." He chuckles. "I'm sure your fans wouldn't mind keeping you in one place for a bit."

"I hope you're right. I still have a limp sometimes, but I'm sure I can play it off. It's the sudden moves that get me."

"Well, you still have a few days left to rehab. Use the time wisely."

So long as I'm ready to hit the stage on day one. "I will."

"Hey," he interrupts me as I'm about to end the call. "Know I'm on your side, B. If I could change the dates, I would. We can make sure you ice it—or whatever you do—all the time except for when you have to be onstage. The rest of the guys are ready to help, too. We got your back."

His words sink into my heart for a moment, then bounce off when my mother asserts herself, mocking me for getting injured in the first place. I'm nothing more than a meal ticket to Luke, who doesn't want his cash cow to give him curdled milk.

"I hear you. Have a good one." I kill the call.

I collapse onto the pillow and close my eyes. In the morning, I'll get the PR team's plan for how to address the media and will discuss it with Jenna.

My *physical therapist*.

I only wish I still considered her Darren's ex. No, Jenna's so much more—kind, caring, capable, insightful, sweet. She understands me like no one else *ever* has. She encourages me to try to dip my big toe in the friendship pool. She makes me want to be a better man.

I huff a sigh. Things are about to get messy.

Chapter Eighteen

Sunlight streams through the window. Where are the blackout shades? I must've forgotten to pull them in place last night.

The smell of coffee reaches my nose. I *know* I didn't set up the coffeemaker last night. My right eye pops open and I'm greeted with orange and yellow, two colors not in my rental's palette.

I sit up, the blanket falling to my waist, exposing the necklace on my naked torso. I didn't fuck Michelle last night, did I?

Realization sets in with a vengeance, reminding me of everything that occurred—resulting in my spending the night in Jenna's house. How her mother left us before dessert. How Jenna moaned over the tiramisu. How the paparazzi attacked her when she was getting the car.

I fumble for my phone and pull up the expected email from our PR team. Shit. This has to be over two pages long. I skim the bolded headlines: Say you're out in the Hamptons for some R&R. Do not mention your injury unless you want the press to be all over your rehab. Tell them how excited you are for the movie and tour.

It's the final one that captures my attention: How do I want them to handle Jenna?

Handle Jenna?

The team gives me different options, if-then scenarios. If you want to distance yourself and the band from her, then we suggest going to a different clinic. If you want to protect her out of loyalty to Darren, then we understand and suggest you make a statement to the effect you're spending time with her out of pity.

Pity?

I continue reading to the end, which causes me more concern than the tone of the entire thing. The PR team concludes by saying Jenna causes negative reactions among UC's fans, so they prefer option one. If I'm in agreement, they give three alternate places to try. Other rehab clinics are listed, with their contact information.

My eyebrows shoot together. Jenna's not something to "manage." She's a real human being who's been through so much—if not *more*—than the band. I'm certain she hasn't confided in me a fraction of all she dealt with following Darren's death. I'm not going to cause her more pain.

I reread the PR email's last section, and anger boils up from within. I'm not leaving the poor woman to fend for herself like we did following Darren's death. Back then, the band was in freefall. Now, it's only me falling apart. I tap my thigh, which doesn't hurt this morning. Yet. Give it time. Especially with the exercises Jenna has planned.

I write a terse email to the PR team, saying I'm not turning my back on Jenna. I'm also not here out of pity. Pity! For fuck's sake.

Ditching their "professional" suggestions, I begin to brainstorm my own. Remembering Mom's diatribe, I don't want to tell the world how stupid I was to pull my groin. Lying low in the Hamptons seems plausible, but for the weather. Maybe I can say I wanted to enjoy the beach in winter? But my family's from the Jersey shore. What if I reached out to Jeremy Davis? He took a positive spin in his article in the *Record News* about UC.

"Hey there," Jenna intrudes on my musing. "Brought you some tea. I remember you prefer it to coffee." She hands me a mug with the tag for white tea hanging over the side and sits on the other end of the sofa, tugging on her robe to keep it closed.

My thoughts scatter. "Thanks." I blow into the steaming hot mug.

"I hope I didn't interrupt anything. You looked deep in thought."

Do I share what the PR team said? Maybe some of it, considering she's implicated. "I was trying to work out a strategy to get the media off my back out here."

She takes a sip of her coffee. "Oh. They were, uh, intense last night." She pulls out her phone. "Did they post any articles today?"

Shit. I didn't have time to check what they wrote. "I didn't look. They probably didn't disclose much more than my general location." Why didn't I look at this before my emails? I can only imagine what they had to say—Jenna's carrying my baby or we went off and got married. I rush to *The Gossip*, a well-known sleazy tabloid. I'm not quick enough.

"Oh." Jenna's palm covers her face. "At least they spelled 'Black Widow' right."

"What?"

She hands me her phone and my stomach plummets. This is much worse than I imagined. The headline screams, "Black Widow Picks Her Next Victim." Beneath it, the article states I was out to dinner with Jenna Westfield, formerly Darren Hilliard's girlfriend, who died a couple of years ago in an overdose. The implicit gist is Jenna's killing members of UC, with me next on her target list.

"Jenna, oh my God. I'm going to kill those fuckers." I drop her phone onto the coffee table.

She doesn't shed a tear, merely rubs her thumb and pinky together. "Those reporters have no idea how their words hurt. They're only trying to sell magazines. Or get clicks."

I can't let her handle this all by herself. I toss the blanket onto the floor and pull her body into mine. "Jenna, I'll fix this." I rub my hand up and down her back, her head cradled against my naked torso. "They're going to be sorry they messed with me."

Her breathing comes in short pants, but she doesn't make any other sounds. I continue comforting her, even in this small way. "I need to come up with a story about why I'm out here. Something better than I came out to the Hamptons for some rest and relaxation." But what?

"King and Angie."

I look down at her, trying to make out what she's suggesting. It's difficult when she's so close. I inhale her unique vanilla-floral scent. "Maybe the Huntes invited me out to Aroostook, is that what your suggesting?"

She doesn't respond with words, but her blonde head bounces on my pecs.

I work through her suggestion. "Because they're raising their profile out here?" Sounds lame.

Jenna pulls away—my necklace peeling away from her cheek—grey glossy eyes boring into me. "Maybe they were trying to get you to buy something out here, and are wining and dining you?"

A slow smile crosses my face. "Since they know I'm going out on tour soon and won't have time to check out properties when I'm away."

"You can be a hard guy to pin down." The mere fact she can tease me at this moment speaks volumes for her character. "I've heard you don't own any houses?"

Her question makes me sound like a vagabond. "I bought a place for my mother." Which she left last year for a place that suited her better.

"Oh. Very nice of you."

A vision of Dad lying on the floor flashes. I didn't do it to be nice. "I like your idea. If this PT thing doesn't work out, I can get you a job in PR."

She stares at my abs, but not out of desire. "I hate to be the subject of the press again. I thought I had left this all behind."

I continue to stroke her back. "They were looking for an angle about why I'd be here with you. On the bright side, at least it means they don't know I'm seeing you for physical therapy."

Her chin lands on my pec and she taps my chest, over my heart. "There is that."

Her sweet, simple gesture makes my breath catch. "Yeah."

My gaze eats up her gorgeous face, attached to my torso.

She doesn't move.

I take a breath. One. Two.

I lower my head, and our lips meet. Like a forgotten chorus, I slant my mouth over hers in an intimate introduction. My breathing increases, and my palms cup her cheeks.

She's been a forbidden fruit for so long, but now my hunger is unleashed. I trace her closed lips with my tongue, and they part beneath it. Not needing a second invitation, I swoop in and move my hands to her back, pressing her closer against me.

Her mouth tastes of coffee and simply Jenna, a potent combination. One I could savor for the next few hours.

Or days.

Or years.

Beneath me, Jenna's hands slide up and play with the hair at the nape of my neck. Her fingernails dig into my hairline, causing a slight prick of pain, which she smooths over with her talented fingers.

I groan, pulling her body closer to my hardening one. Until an off movement reasserts the muscle pull, and my thigh starts throbbing.

I spring back from her. "Aww, fuck." My hands land on my thigh.

Her expressive eyes sweep over my body and widen as she realizes what happened. She also knows how much I wanted her, as my underwear does nothing to hide my rock-hard erection.

"Let me get an ice pack."

Before she can move, I grab her wrist. "No. I need you here next to me more."

Her body stiffens, and I know our moment is lost, yet I'm not sorry it happened. I wasn't thinking of Darren when I was kissing

Jenna, and I certainly didn't kiss her out of pity. She's a captivating, intriguing, brilliant woman. Unlike any I've ever known.

However, the way she's worrying her bottom lip—the one I was caressing a second ago—screams the opposite about me. Us. Even though she doesn't push away from me, I know she wouldn't welcome my touch now. I drop my arm and she flees.

My leg extends, ready for the dreaded ice pack. While I wait, several texts ping. Before I can read them, Jenna reappears with it in her hand and I prepare for the cold.

Instead of doing the expected and passing me the ice pack, she lowers to her knees and tenderly places it over my muscle. "How's that?"

My cock didn't get the message she's off limits. Jenna clearly knows how she affects me as it's basically staring her in the face.

"It's," I begin. "Challenging." The left side of my mouth crooks upward.

"I can see that." Her eyes close for a moment. When she opens them again, shiny grey irises appear. "I'm not sorry." She kisses me again, far too fast, then sits in the chair across from me. She picks up her coffee cup.

We return to sipping our hot drinks as if we hadn't just kissed like horny teens, the quiet between us a sharp contrast to the prickly ice on my thigh. My mind reels from our kisses, and my body wants more. Well, except for the part wrapped in ice at the moment. To distract myself, I scroll on my phone.

"Got some texts?"

"Yeah." I glance up at her, "The other band members are checking in with me. Guess they read the same article."

"Nice of your friends." She replaces the mug onto its saucer.

My stomach clenches. *More like keeping tabs on their frontman.*

"While you're replying to them, I think I'll go change." She stands. "Maybe you can also reach out to King and Angie?"

Just like that, she's back to the business at hand. Given she's being raked over the coals, I can understand her thought process. "I'm not sure." I lift the ice pack and return it to my thigh. "Think they'd be upset if I don't buy?"

A devious smile crosses her face. "You never know. You could fall in love out here."

Love? Is she joking?

What if she's *not?* I wait for my body to revolt but it never does.

What if I already have?

Chapter Nineteen

While Jenna's getting dressed upstairs, I draft an email to the PR team outlining her idea. It might work. Looking for real estate is always a good way to sideline the press. Who knows? Perhaps it's time for me to put down roots?

Roots?

Aroostook does have its charms, considering King and Angie are a cool couple. Not to mention whatever is going on between Jenna and me. And her mother's sweet. The more I think about the idea, the better it feels. I prefer this coast to LA, although my rental out there was lit. I bet the Hamptons could offer something just as nice. If not better.

Before Jenna returns, I've tossed the ice pack onto the plate and managed to get into my clothes from last night. Looks like I'm the one doing the walk of shame today.

If only. Doctor's orders be damned.

Dressed for the day, Jenna bounds down the stairs. Smiling at her from across the room, I say, "Let me check outside to see what we're dealing with."

"What do you mean? You don't think the reporters figured out where I live, do you? I've moved since—"

"I'm not sure." I turn to her. "You didn't move because of Darren, did you?"

Her lips purse. "Not entirely. The reporters left after a few weeks, so it wasn't them. I thought I needed a do-over."

I open my arms wide. "Come here."

She hesitates for a minute, then walks over to me. My arms close around her. For once, I don't want to ravish her, but make her feel protected. Well, a little ravishing wouldn't hurt either. But I mainly want to give her comfort for my recent failure.

I step back. "Let me take a look." Walking-slash-quasi-limping to the front door, I peer through the sidelights. Sure enough, at least ten cars are parked outside. Shit. My shoulders slump.

From across the room, she asks, "How bad is it?"

I have to tell her the truth. She deserves this much from me. Besides, it'll be impossible to hide when we get outside. "Only a few intrepid reporters." My mind whirls with how we're going to get into her car. Plus the fact I have to appear one hundred percent healthy doing it.

"Not awful."

Ten could turn into fifty in the blink of an eye. "Change in plans." I hope she's okay with this. "How about I call King and Angie now and let them know about our little scheme. Which may not be so far-fetched after all."

Her eyebrows raise. "No?"

"Turns out Aroostook has its appeal."

She beams at me, making me think I made the right decision. I know better than to get my hopes up, though. Lissa taught me that lesson back in high school, which only reinforced Mom's refrain. Still, I deserve a quick shot at fleeting happiness.

I dial Russo Real Estate. Angie soon is on the line, joined by King at my request. I outline our idea and ask them to find me a house in the ten-million-dollar range. They agree and promise to be at Jenna's house within the hour, not without receiving a warning from me about the media swarm awaiting them here.

We sit, and Jenna forces my right leg up onto the sofa. "At the very least," she says, "you'll get to see more of my beautiful town. Even if you don't buy anything, you'll enjoy what the Huntes have to show you."

"Us," I correct her.

Her head tilts.

"If you think I'm going to buy a house without a second opinion, you're crazy. After all, it was your idea I do this in the first place."

"Only as a way to throw off reporters." She wags her finger at me. "It was all you who decided to make this real. Besides, I need to get to the office."

"You're the boss. You deserve the morning off."

"Oh no," she protests. "I have a meeting."

"When?"

"At two o'clock."

I toss my head backward. "We'll be done well before then."

I can tell I've won the argument, but she doesn't back down easily. "You'll have to do your two sessions of physical therapy back-to-back."

"Small price to pay." Spending all day with this woman is not a hardship. Learning more about King and Angie and the town is a bonus.

A honk outside announces their arrival. Ignoring the paparazzi, they pull into the driveway, next to Jenna's car. King opens the driver's side and rushes to open the passenger door, where Angie steps out. To the screams of the paps, they approach the front door.

"I think you should stay hidden," she says.

Jenna's thoughtful comment warms my soul. "I think you should too. Just open the door and step back."

The swing of her ponytail signals her assent, and soon the couple sweeps into the small foyer, the front door slamming shut behind them. Angie's brown eyes sweep over Jenna before landing on me. "Are you two all right?"

I raise my hands. "Been better, been worse."

King chuckles. "One way to look at it. When you warned us about some reporters here, I thought you were exaggerating. Felt like my dad was in town."

At least he has some familiarity with their tactics.

"We rushed out here and didn't check the internet," Angie explains. "What's going on?"

I fill them in on the press reports about Jenna, who disappears into the kitchen to bring refreshments. "So, I need to rehabilitate her reputation while not giving away my true reason for being here. We thought checking out properties would be a good cover. Although"—I notice their hunched postures—"The more I consider this idea, the more I like it. If you show me a property that wows me, you might have a sale."

Angie's the first to recover from my two truths. She stands taller and rubs her hands together. "In that case, we're going to give you a choice you can't refuse."

Jenna enters the room. "Is that a bad *Godfather* reference I hear?"

"Seems like it," I quip.

Jenna slants me a quick glance as she puts a tray of coffee mugs onto the table. In a flash, I'm back to our initial meeting at the club, debating the merits of the first versus the second film in the iconic series. How our normal conversation made me feel *seen* for the first time in ages. How the real woman in front of me stirred something long forgotten deep within me.

How is she doing it again?

King lifts a brown bag I hadn't noticed. "Picked up some bagels that will go great with your coffee." He looks at his wife. "Angie's taught me never to go to someone's house without some food."

"Awesome!" Jenna reaches over and takes the bag. "Let me get a platter and some plates, and I'll be right back." She disappears into the kitchen again.

"Let's have a seat and talk about the properties," Angie suggests. "And discuss how to handle the media." Her eyes dart toward the window.

Once we're seated with drinks—Jenna brought me another tea—and bagels, we strategize about how the morning's going to go. Angie shows me listings for a few different properties, and I pick two to visit, mindful of Jenna's time. We also decide to go in two different cars as a diversion and because Jenna needs to be at the clinic for her meeting.

I test my leg, which feels relatively normal. For recent days. "I'll drive."

Jenna crosses her arms. "I was in no state to drive last night, but I'm capable today. I don't want you to put more strain on your leg than absolutely necessary."

I counter, "How will it look to the reporters if I let you drive?"

We're at a standoff.

King suggests, "How about this? Bennett, why don't you come with us? It'll look like we came here to pick you up to scout houses. Jenna can meet up with us. Might even throw the vultures off."

I consider his idea, but don't like how it leaves Jenna vulnerable. I've been dealing with paps for years. She hasn't. "No. I don't want to leave Jenna to the wolves."

"What if we switch up the order?" Angie queries. She addresses me. "You can go with King, and I'll ride with Jenna. You two can even speak with the press while we leave first. I bet none of the reporters will follow us when the story's talking with them."

Her idea makes sense. We can be the decoy, so to speak. I'll put out the story that I'm checking out properties. "I think it may work."

We sit and make small talk, getting to know each other better over our makeshift breakfast. My mind, however, runs amuck with a potential fly in the ointment—how do I account for being with Jenna? No way am I telling the reporters I'm here for physical therapy after my stupid jump onstage. Nor am I discussing Darren. Perhaps he can provide cover, though?

When the ladies take the dirty dishes into the kitchen, I turn to King. "Hey, the paps will want to know why I'm here with Jenna. Since I need to keep my physical therapy off their radar, do you think they'd buy I'm catching up with Darren's ex-girlfriend?"

He winces. "I'm not sure about that one. The best decoy tactics are closest to the truth, at least that's what Dad always says." He goes silent while his biceps flex. "How about saying you came here because of our television show and ran into her in town? Then you went out to dinner to catch up?"

"You know, that might work. It'll loop you guys into the press, since it'll appear I came here to seek you out. Will that be a problem?"

He grins. "Nah. Call me a media whore." We're chuckling when the ladies return into the living room.

Angie takes one look at her husband and says to Jenna, "Don't ask."

King and I laugh even harder. This relative normalcy is unusual. I like it.

All too soon, Jenna and Angie prepare to go to Jenna's car. "Wait," I stop them. "How about we all go out together and I divert their attention with our cover story. In the meantime, King can help both of you into Jenna's car and then you drive off? We should be only five or ten minutes behind you."

We can see them off, then monopolize the press. As we put on our coats, I ask King, "How are your evasive driving tactics?"

He wraps a scarf around his neck. "I don't get to brush them off too much anymore, but I'm sure it's like riding a bike." He puts a hand on my shoulder. "I'm ready for them, don't worry."

About as prepared as we can be, I open the door and walk out of the house. Taking my time—both to allow King to help the women into their car as well as not to let on about my injury—I draw the reporters' attention. The screaming begins, questions being hurled at me from all sides.

"Does the rest of UC know you're out here?"

"Does Jenna have anything to do with your appearance?"

"Are you dating the Black Widow?"

No one takes notice when Jenna's car starts. After the ladies pull back from the driveway, King joins me.

"I didn't think my appearance in Aroostook would cause this much of a ruckus," I say. "Must be a slow news time for you all, being winter and all."

"What drew you to the Hamptons?"

My gaze takes in the clear blue sky. "I came out here to check out real estate." I turn to face King. "This guy has a show on television, if you didn't already know, and it makes all the homes out here seem like the place to be. So, I took this little break before Untamed Coaster's tour starts next week to visit for myself. I heard you all don't bother celebrities much in Aroostook." I give them a pointed glare.

"We are excited to show some properties to Mr. Hardy," King picks up the mantle, allowing me time to verify all the reporters are still here with us and not following Jenna's taillights. At least this part of our plan worked. I tune back in to hear King explain, "We're off to look at houses. Because these are private properties, I don't expect to have you travel with us. That is, unless you're ready to shell out some of your money to buy a house yourself. In which case, give my office a call." He chuckles.

Gotta hand it to King. He knows how to handle these vultures. We turn toward his SUV when the same pap as before screams, "What about the Black Widow?"

I stop and turn toward the firing squad. "Her name is Jenna Westfield. She was my bandmate's girlfriend, which means she's part of the UC family. I didn't know she lived here until I ran into her in town, and we decided to go out to dinner last night to catch up. Nothing more."

I leave the gaggle and concentrate on taking normal steps toward King's Audi. My entire body's strung so tight, all I want to do is ram my fist into the reporter's face. But I know the deal. If I show his questions annoy me, the rest of them will jump on the bandwagon.

Not for the first time, I'm grateful Faith had to duck out of dinner early. She doesn't need any of this hell raining down on her.

As soon as my ass slides onto the black leather seat, I slam the door shut. King turns on the SUV, locking the doors. I push the seat back as far as it will go in order to stretch out my right leg. We reverse out of the driveway at a snail's pace. I force a smile and wave at the reporters as we finally get onto the street and pull away. When we're out of their line of vision, my head slumps against the headrest.

"Thanks, man. You did great out there."

King replies, "Sort of like I've done this before, huh?"

I check the sideview mirror. "How many are following us, do you think?"

"I'd say more than half. Ready?"

My hand grips the grab bar, my knuckles turning white. King floors it and we race down the residential side street with an angry group of reporters on our ass. I don't bother to turn around. In fact, I keep my eyes shut as he races over the roads like the pro he is.

When we stop at a red light, I turn my face toward him. "You've had more than your share of opportunities to evade them." Not a question.

"I didn't lie. I know my way around their antics. Plus, after a couple of years as a real estate agent in this town, I know these streets like the back of my hand." He makes a quick turn. "Jenna's lived here her whole life. I'm sure she took evasive maneuvers although none of the paps were following her and my wife."

"Thank God. I can handle them on my tail, not theirs."

"I hear ya, bro." We ride in silence for a while. "Jenna seems nice."

I appreciate King's not-so-subtle question. "We're not together. She was dating the keyboardist for my band until he died a couple of years ago." I swallow the lump in my throat. "I like her."

Why did I confess this to a near stranger? Braxton Hunte's son or not, I don't know him. Hell, I don't know his father too well either. Or his brother Trent, for that matter.

"Hey, no worries with me. I get it. Before I met Angie, there was no way I was going to settle down." He makes a quick right, then a left. "When you know, you know. Until then, enjoy the groupies."

I grin at his remark. With a father as infamous as his, I'm sure he's seen more than his fair share of my lifestyle. Women throw themselves at me on the regular. It just happens none of them compare with Jenna.

King turns into a long driveway and pulls behind an oversized house, where Jenna's Lexus is parked. Both she and Angie are outside, chatting as if they were old friends even though they've only met at professional functions until now.

I gather my strength and open the door, meeting King near the headlights. "Fancy meeting you here," he quips, then kisses his wife on the cheek.

I appreciate the security. "This house allows me to hide from the paparazzi, so that's a plus already."

We walk through a fence and tour the backyard first. Angie begins her description of the property, pointing out the view of the water from here. It's quiet. A far cry from LA or New York City, appealing to me in a way I never expected.

Angie addresses me, "Want to go inside?"

I check with Jenna, who admires the park-like backyard, with its dock. We have some time to kill. "Why not?"

Chapter Twenty

Unfortunately, the inside of the house did not live up to its grounds. We stand in the dated kitchen, and I admit as much to the real estate agents. For her part, Jenna doesn't say anything but her facial expressions say she agrees with me. Besides, for five million, I don't want to buy a fixer-upper.

Angie takes it all in stride and passes me another piece of paper. "I think you'll like this one. It's double the price but is done from top to bottom."

"Sounds better." Hell, if I am going to buy a new home, I don't want to have to dick around with making improvements to bring it up to this century.

Car keys twirl around King's fingers. "Think it's safe to go in our own cars?"

I bet he said this for me, thinking I have a thing for Jenna. Well, if I'm being honest with myself, he's not wrong. I'm being sucked into her aura of authenticity, and I like it. What does she want with me, though? I'm merely a patient in her eyes. Our few kisses can be chalked up to misguided judgment. Or maybe she has a thing for rock stars? However, she did agree to tour houses with me. This has to mean something. Doesn't it?

Jenna surprises me by responding, "I think the coast is clear. I haven't seen a reporter since we got here, and I've been checking all the windows."

"Then it's settled. King and I will see you at this next house in fifteen minutes." We walk out with Angie and King, who lock up behind us.

"I can drive," I offer. Inside, I think: Please don't make me, though. If the paparazzi find us, I don't want a repeat of last night.

"It seems quiet now, Bennett. I'll drive." She presses her key fob and the doors unlock.

I'm still a gentleman. I walk to her door and open it, bowing low. "After you, Candy Kong."

Her giggle is my reward for remembering the girlfriend of her favorite arcade game, Donkey Kong. This is Jenna's first sign of humor since we checked the tabloids this morning. The sound makes my stomach flip, and not in a bad way. Once she's seated, I close her door and walk to the passenger side.

"My leg doesn't hurt today," I note.

"Great. I was hoping you'd say that. You've been rehabbing hard. So long as you keep to linear movements, I think you'll be fine."

I click my seatbelt. "Do you agree with me about this house? The interior didn't live up to the exterior?"

She starts the car and plugs in the address to the next property into her GPS. "Yeah. Too bad, though. It's on a gorgeous lot."

She enters an empty street, and I release my pent-up worry. We're alone on the road. "I appreciate you taking time away from your work to help me escape the press."

"It was actually a little fun," Jenna replies. "Sort of cloak and dagger. I appreciate how you deflected them."

"They have no right to call you nasty names. They're idiots."

"Not sure about their IQs, but I'll give it to you, they're a nasty group of people. Seems like all they want to do is sell photos and lies."

The tight skin around her eyes gives away how much their nick-name hurt her. "Hey. We know the truth about what happened. You had nothing to do with Darren's death. Nothing at all. Hell, you probably kept him from overdosing several times before."

Her fingers around the steering wheel tighten but she doesn't say anything. Which leads me to believe she did stop him before that night.

"You did, didn't you?"

The GPS now has her full attention. I don't push, I don't have to. I replay her reaction when I had to tell her of his passing. She was out of her mind with grief, sure, but there was a discordant note I never quite placed. Like she thought his death was inevitable. A burden she carried for too long.

This line of thought brings me to 007, and the fact he was in Darren's room that terrible morning. Like he routinely checked on his best friend. As if he knew something bad could've happened during the night.

I shelve my thoughts about 007 and focus on the woman here with me. "Jenna. I'm sorry." What else can I say?

"It wasn't my fault, I know that. He was my boyfriend, not my responsibility. It sucks how he died, and I wasn't able to stop it." She pulls up to the security guardhouse for the community and gives him King's name. Sporting a new temporary pass, we push forward.

In the driver's seat, she appears tiny and fragile. But I know this woman is anything but—she's running two, soon to be three, physical therapy clinics. There's true grit in her. No wonder Darren fell head over heels for her.

"You're right. His death is on him. If he was aware he wasn't keeping track of when he took meds, he should've written the doses down."

"I told him to do that." She continues to stare at the road.

I turn in my seat, with care. My thigh doesn't protest. I reach out and stroke her arm. "He was a great guy, and he treated you like the princess you are."

She bounces backward. "I'm hardly a princess."

"Well, I think so for the both of us. Don't beat yourself up anymore, okay?"

She inhales. "I think we're here." She turns off the road and drives up a long driveway, parking next to King and Angie, who open our doors for us.

"Welcome to Secluded Rest," King announces.

I like the name already. The thought of having some secluded rest, away from prying eyes of all types, has appeal.

He runs down the exterior description, including the mile-long circular driveway and old-growth trees. We walk up the stairs—I slow us down, but no one seems to care—and go through a double-door entryway that opens into an oversized foyer, featuring two coat closets and a two-sided curved staircase up to the second level.

"Wow." Jenna's assessment isn't wrong.

"Yeah, wow."

King and Angie show us the public spaces, including a massive family room complete with a fireplace. The kitchen is Gordon Ramsey-worthy. Several other rooms complete the first floor, including a guest bedroom with an *en suite*.

"This room, tucked into the back of the house, could be converted into a music room without too much effort." King leads us to a large room in the center of the house, without any windows. "My father said he prefers to practice without access to the outside to distract him. I thought you might like the same."

I walk around the room, picturing the band in here with their instruments. Me? As the lead singer, I only need a music stand. If I were to host UC, which I've never done, this room would be perfect. I give King a nod and we move outside.

"Out here," King continues, "there's a pool, outdoor kitchen, fire pit and, of course, the ocean."

"Of course," Jenna murmurs.

"This is great," I admit. "Does the boat come with the property?"

"It doesn't mention it on the listing, but I can check for you," Angie replies. As if this is a done deal.

Jenna makes a beeline toward the gardens, bending down to examine the plants. "She's something special," Angie notes, her gaze following Jenna throughout the yard. "I can see her blossoming, with the right partner."

"I can too," King adds.

Too bad that partner won't be me. Not because my emotions aren't involved, though. I simply can't imagine she'd be interested in another UC band member.

"I'm not him." I walk and, unseeing, end up in the outdoor kitchen. My rental in LA has one of these, but this one is even more tricked out. A wine fridge, built into rocks, pushes it over the edge.

Angie gathers us together and takes the tour upstairs—I manage them, although slowly—pointing out the five bedrooms, each with their own full *en suites*. All of the rooms are painted different yet coordinating colors, evoking a spa-like environment.

We walk down a long hallway. Before we come up to the primary suite, King stops, grins, and points.

"Holy moly! Is that an elevator?" Jenna's exclamation is adorable.

I've been to many a house with an elevator, and this one here does increase the appeal of this mansion, despite it being way too big a house for only me.

King answers, "Sure is. For times when the stairs are simply too much. Or," he focuses on my thigh, "if you have an injury."

"Seems like the owners thought of everything," I remark.

"Sure did." Angie leads us farther down the hall and opens the doors to the primary suite. The view is stunning. It overlooks the backyard and the ocean beyond.

"This is amazing," I say. My feet take me to the French doors, which lead to a sizeable balcony.

"Told you Aroostook would grow on you, dude," King says.

A crash comes from the bathroom, which causes me to spin in

that direction. Which, of course, causes my muscle to spasm. My head flies up to the sky. "Fuck!"

Jenna rushes to my side. "Oh no. I'm so sorry. I was checking out the shower and dropped the standing towel rack."

I take in her explanation, but it doesn't soothe my fucking thigh.

"I'll go get an ice pack." Jenna's out of the room in a flash.

Angie takes over. "Let's get you into this chair."

King helps me limp to a club chair beside the bed. I sit and raise the leg rest, which relieves some of the pressure.

Two alarms go off. Both King and Angie check their phones, dismissing the notifications. Because I want attention off my injury, I rasp, "What's up?"

Angie replies, "We have a meeting in our office with the studio in a half-hour."

"We can skip it," King interjects.

My head shakes before my mouth catches up. "No. I don't want to be the reason you skip a meeting." I place my hands on the armrest and begin to right the chair.

Jenna runs into the room. "I found this towel. Not my ideal ice pack, but it'll do."

Angie asks, "How long should he have it on?"

"Thirty minutes," my physical therapist replies in time with my mental answer.

The couple exchange a glance. King says, "Jenna, if we show you how to lock up, would you mind taking care of that for us? We need to get back to the office before then and we don't want to interfere with Bennett's recovery."

I hate feeling like a baby.

"Are you sure that would be all right?" Jenna doesn't direct her question to me, rather seeks confirmation from Angie.

"Yes, it's perfectly fine—the homeowners aren't in town anyway." Angie points. "We weren't able to show you the basement, which has a bowling alley, massive bar, state-of-the-art workout room, some arcade games, and another full bath."

"I'll take your word that it's gorgeous." In the chair, I ensure my leg is stretched and my thigh covered with the ice. King and Angie nod at me, then they leave. Jenna follows them.

A few minutes later, Jenna approaches me again. "What's your pain level?"

"Right now, I'd give it about an eight." Nearing ten, but I keep this to myself. She already feels bad enough.

"I'm so sorry about the noise."

"You didn't mean it."

She goes to lift the ice pack again, and I catch her wrist. "Let it be."

I pull her downward until she's sitting on the arm of the chair. I slide my butt to the side and she slips into the main chair with me. I cup her cheek. "Distract me."

She sucks in air. Her eyes roam over my face, her pink tongue peeping out of her mouth. I want to kiss her silly, but I don't know if that's what she wants. Or needs.

Since when do I wonder what a woman needs?

"I've watched your performances on YouTube with the new guy."

"Tris," I supply. "He's great on keys in a different way than Darren was."

"Yeah. I hear you." She twists her hips so her left one rests on the main cushion. Her arm snakes toward the ice pack, then detours to my forearm. "You guys are great."

"Thanks." For some reason, I want to confess a truth to her. Something that's been eating at me since dinner. "We're not really friends, you know."

She tilts her head.

"UC. Granted, we've known each other for ages—well, except Tris—but I don't think of the guys as my friends. Don't get me wrong. We laugh a lot and perform together onstage. But I don't consider them to be my friends."

Jenna continues stroking my forearm. "None of them?"

"Not really." No one knows about my mother. Or cares to delve too deep into any of my lyrics. "When we're not on tour, we don't hang out together."

"But Darren used to get together with Pierce all the time."

"Well, true. Those two were rather inseparable."

"What about River and Cooper? They always were hanging around with Darren. I remember him telling me about their exploits."

I swallow. "Yeah, well, they did graduate high school together. They formed Untamed Coaster before I joined it."

Her hand stills. "Aren't you lonely?"

Ever since Dad died, I've been on my own. *No need to get into the lying POS, Curtiss.* "My best friend growing up was my father. He died when I was seventeen." She has to understand this. She was raised by a single parent.

"But your mother—"

"She's still alive. We've never been close."

She squeezes my arm. "I can be your person."

I want to shake my head to confirm I heard her quiet offer right. Instead, I place my hand over hers. "Are you offering to be my—?" I can't voice the word.

Grey eyes, opened wide, lift to mine. "I'd like to be your friend."

I squeeze her hand. "I'm not sure I would know what to do with one of those, Jenna." I do know what I want to do with the woman almost in my arms, though. "Come here."

Something breaks inside me. I drag her to my body and kiss her as if this was my last opportunity ever. She's stirred up all sorts of odd feelings in me, ones I haven't felt since my high school girlfriend. I pour my heart out to her with my touch. She fuels my hunger, kissing me back as if I mean something to her.

I leave her mouth and trail tiny kisses down her neck, around her chin, and end at her ear. After nibbling on her lobe, I blow into it, which causes her body to roll into mine.

The ice pack falls off my thigh and onto the floor.

She giggles. "I think your thirty minutes is done. Let's get you downstairs and into the car." Rosy-cheeked, Jenna scrambles off the chair and removes the ice pack. "Put the chair into its normal position and I'll help you up."

It's bad enough she has to give me physical therapy. She doesn't have to help me stand, too. "I can do it. My pain level has dropped."

"To what? A level seven?"

I query my body. "Yeah."

She grins. "Get the footrest down." After I do this, she continues, "Place your hands on the arms and stand."

Using all my upper-body strength, I get to my feet without her help. "See. Told you I could do it."

"Impressive. Now let's try to take a few steps."

I do, the pain from my pulled muscle manageable. Especially when I limp. However, I do admit defeat and take the elevator to the first floor. In the foyer, I catch my breath while she returns the makeshift ice pack to the kitchen.

My mind spins with our interlude upstairs. She wanted my kiss. I sure as hell wanted hers. Can we really be starting something new and different? Can we do this without Darren in bed with us?

Her slender arm goes around my waist. "Ready to do this?"

"I am. Thank you, Jenna. For everything."

"You're more than welcome." She rests her head on my shoulder for a moment. "Let's go."

We make it all the way to the car where I lean against the door while she locks up. She presses some buttons on her phone. "There. Texted Angie that we're leaving. Now's the big question, where do you want to go? To your rental to change? Or directly to the clinic?"

I dip my head. "I've been in these clothes since last night, and they're not the right ones for therapy. Do you mind taking me to my rental? I'll be quick so you can make your meeting."

She adjusts her ponytail. "Sure thing."

We get into the car, which takes me longer more because I antici-pate pain rather than feel it. "What did you think of the property?"

I consider her question. "I like it. The views are amazing, and I love the backyard. There seem to be a few too many rooms, though. What do I need with so many bedrooms?"

"What if the band wanted to crash at your place?"

"Didn't you hear what I told you? We don't hang out when we're not performing."

"I heard you. I just think it's sad. You're missing out on so much. I remember Darren telling me about backyard BBQs and going to visit sites in various places when you guys were touring."

"Yeah, well. Those were his experiences."

She stops at a light and turns her head toward me. "What did you do when they were out?"

I shrug. "Dunno. Probably hung out at a local bar or club."

"Sounds lonely."

My lip quirks. "I can assure you, I wasn't alone."

"Hooking up with random women is different from spending quality time with friends." She presses on the gas when the light changes.

Friends. There's that word again. I'm not ready to confess my utter lack of them—correction, my lack of need for such frivolity. "I'm a loner. I prefer it that way."

Her finger taps against the steering wheel. "You do you." Her lips purse.

Why does it feel as if I sabotaged anything between Jenna and me before it even began?

Chapter Twenty-One

We continue in silence for a few minutes until she pulls up in front of my rental. "We're here." Her door handle clicks.

"Great." I open my car door and stand, taking long, yet careful, strides toward my front door. Seems like the paps haven't figured out where I'm staying since they're not camped out on the sidewalk. I enter the code and let her enter before me.

"Make yourself comfortable. I'll only be a minute."

My body takes me down the hallway to my bedroom, where the door closes with a snick and I lean against it. My phone rings to the beat of Eminem's "Cleanin' Out My Closet." It's Mom. *Hell no.*

I toss my cell onto the bed and cross the room to get my physical therapy workout clothes. After all, that's the only reason why Jenna's in my house, to take me to her clinic. I strip and take a shower, remembering everything that's happened over the past twenty-four hours. My physical therapy. Dinner with Jenna and her mother to celebrate her birthday. Being chased by the press. At least King and Angie helped save the morning.

Those kisses.

Soapy water runs down my body and onto the shower floor. My head lowers, watching it circle the drain. Metaphor for my life.

I wrap a towel around my waist and toss one over my head, drying my hair. My stubble needs a trim, but I'm not taking the time to do it now. I walk into the bedroom and pick up a pair of underwear. Dressed in another pair of grey sweats, I suck in troubled air stirred up by the paparazzi. I pause for a minute to remind myself that despite the current difficulties, I am Bennett Hardy, lead singer of Untamed Coaster. I can take whatever the universe dishes out today and make it my bitch. *Jenna's help doesn't hurt.*

Returning to the living room, Jenna's on her phone. She holds up a finger, indicating I should wait so I go to the fridge and take out some orange juice. It's impossible not to eavesdrop. "I know, Ma, I'll be careful. It's not me they're after."

Guilt pings through my armor. I've been so selfish, shoring up my story about why I'm in town. I glance over at her and notice her wiping her eyes. No matter what, she doesn't deserve this. When she catches my interest in her, she turns her back and lowers her voice. She even walks over to the sliding glass doors and slips outside.

I've been an ass. I tried to distract the press away from her, yet they still shouted questions at me about the "Black Widow." She didn't kill Darren. Truth be told, she tried to save him. How can I lure them away from her? I send a text to UC's PR team, asking for more ideas. Ones that will help *her* situation over mine.

The woman taking up more real estate in my mind than the properties we toured reenters the rental. With an overly perky tone, she asks, "Are you ready to go to the clinic?"

"Sure." I drain my cup.

On the ride there, the question flows out of my mouth before I can censor it. "How's your mother doing? I'm sure she's worried sick about how you're being portrayed in the media."

Her shoulders rise then fall. "She remembers how it was for me when I was together with Darren. She knows the deal."

"You didn't sign up for this when you agreed to take me on as a patient. The press shouldn't treat you this way."

"I'm sure you explaining things to them this morning will make them back off."

If only her optimism coincided with my experience. "I hope you're right. Hate to say it, but they don't go away fast. Especially when they're in a news slump."

Her chin lifts. "Then we'll simply ignore them."

She turns toward her clinic, where news vans are lined up on the sidewalk. Immediately, I drop the seat so it's flat and turn my head to avoid being identified. "Drive to the back of the building. They won't be able to take photos back there."

As she passes them, she provides a running commentary about all of the telephoto lenses point at her car. "So much for them going away," I remark.

Jenna parks and I right the seat. She yanks on her ponytail. "Reporters aren't back here and we need to get into the building. Are you ready? We'll take it slow."

Her face shows nothing but determination. I scan the rooftops, confirming we're free of photographers. The buildings behind us are all private property, so the vultures can't lawfully trespass there, either. Good for us. "Will your other patients have a difficult time getting into the clinic? Think we should go elsewhere?"

"I refuse to be run off my own property by a bunch of reporters. Let's go." Without waiting, she opens her car door.

Once inside, she presses the call button for the elevator. If I were worthy of her, I'd drag her into my arms and comfort her. But she deserves someone who values friendships and has a caring family. Neither of which are me.

Her chest rises and falls several times as her breathing comes in staccato, quiet pants. The media must have freaked out this brave woman. We enter the cab where she presses the button for our floor.

The doors close.

The air twists.

The pit of my stomach churns.

I brought this pain to her doorstep. I want to do whatever I can to ease it. "Jenna."

She doesn't say anything, merely flings her body against mine. My arms close around her trembling body and I realize how much this is taking out of her. My nose lands in her hair, inhaling her perfume, filled with floral notes of rose and jasmine, finishing with a bright citrus and vanilla. Whatever it is, I like it.

I like her.

Too. Damn. Much.

"I reached out to UC's PR team about this mess. I should hear back from them with a new strategy after my exercises."

Her words are muffled as they're said against my chest. "Appreciate it, Bennett."

The elevator pings and I kiss the top of her head. "Are you ready?"

She steps back and my body weeps, uncaring how undeserving I am of this intriguing woman.

"I think so." She squares her shoulders and walks out of the car.

When we enter her office, the Asshole lies in wait. "Miss Westfield. Oh my God. What is going on outside the office? Are you alright? Why are they here? Why are they calling you the Black Widow?" He pulls her into a hug.

Seriously, dude? Standing right here.

She resists his embrace, which is all the sign I need to rush forward. "I'm the draw for them. Because I'm a rock star, the press loses their minds when I do something as mundane as stepping foot into the real world." *And you, Asshole, with your geeky glasses and scrawny body certainly do not cause any type of pandemonium. Or even mini ripples.*

Jenna breaks away from him. Placing her hand on my arm, she says, "Yes, they're here because you are, Bennett. I'm something old they like to resuscitate when they don't have anything else to discuss."

She's not wrong. Except for the fact they wouldn't be bothering her if I wasn't here.

My guilt can't take hold because the Asshole steps between us. "This just sucks. For you and all the patients. Do you think you should be here?" He touches Jenna's shoulder and my heart rate spikes. Oblivious, he continues, "Maybe if you lay low for a few days, they'll move on?"

This is the first suggestion Mr. Touchy-Feely's made that makes sense. Since the paps haven't figured out where I'm renting, perhaps Jenna could stay in my rental with me and do private PT? Although, security is zero there.

With steel in her spine, she replies, "I can handle them." Jenna turns to me, eliminating his contact. Smooth. "Why don't you get started in the other room, Bennett?"

I war with myself. Should I stay or leave? I don't want the Asshole to have any more one-on-one time with my girl.

My girl?

With a curt nod, I enter the exercise room. I need to keep her safe at work. She shouldn't be alone in her house, either. It's not protected.

Determined to figure this out—and to block Austin the Asshole's moving in on Jenna—I hit the first exercises. As I'm finishing up the first round, a ping from my cell announces a new email. I make quick work of the remaining reps and grab my phone. Sure enough, the PR team sent me an email. I skim the contents, for once gratified with their hard work.

Jenna breezes into the room carrying a heavier kettlebell. "This is for your lateral exercises," she explains.

Not even her adding weight to this difficult exercise ruins my upbeat mood from the email. However, one rep in and I'm singing a new tune.

"If I didn't think you could do it, I wouldn't have added the extra weight."

"Tell that to my leg," I breathe through gritted teeth.

"You're doing great. You really are in good shape."

Her compliment goes a long way toward helping me complete these exercises. When I finish, I drop the kettlebell to the floor with a loud thud.

No sooner does it land, but she points to a barbell. "We'll try using this next time. Until then, how about we do something new with bands?"

She leads me through another set of grueling exercises which tax my groin muscle, but not beyond my limit.

When we break for the session and I lie down on the table to get another round of ice, I ask, "Where's Austin?" Kudos for not referring to him as the Asshole.

"I sent him over to the other clinic. The receptionist was diverting patients over there anyway, since the media isn't over there."

"I feel terrible for how I've disrupted your life. But I might have a solution for you."

"I'm all ears."

As she massages my thigh, I share the email. "Hayden Vaughn on UC's PR team suggested I take you to a safe house, as it were, while they get restraining orders against the media to keep them away from you. I'm fair game, being a public figure, but you're a private citizen."

She stops, pressing her fingers on my upper thigh. My cock twitches.

"A safe house?"

"Nothing FBI-like. I'm thinking a couple days rental of the gated house King and Angie showed us today with the long private drive-way, Secluded Rest. Your house is too open, and my rental too easily accessible. Once the wolves figure out where I'm staying, I won't be able to keep them away."

"I like my house."

I shake my head. "You don't have to move away. I'm thinking you stay away from it for a couple of nights, until the restraining order is in place. By then, I'll almost be on tour anyway." I swallow over the boulder in my throat. I don't want to leave her.

Like Lissa abandoned me for my ex-best friend Curtiss. Like my father did when he died. Like Mom wrongly insists I did with my sister.

"Do you think a restraining order will work?"

I blink. "I'd usually say no, but in your case, I'm more optimistic. You're not a public figure nor are you dating one." A pang of longing washes over me. "They'll have little option but to let you be."

"I hope you're right. Otherwise, my best hope is for some other celebrity to draw them away from me."

The only other celebrities in the Hamptons at this time of year that I can think of are King and Angie. "Should we ask the Huntes to help us out? They can raise their profile by faking a fight or something."

Her nose scrunches up. "No way. I'm not going to drag someone else into this mess on purpose."

The mess I set in motion by pulling my groin muscle and hiding it from the public. But if I hadn't, I wouldn't have reconnected with Jenna. Who, now, I can't imagine not speaking with on the daily. She challenges me to see things differently and try new things, something I didn't realize I need in my life. I want to get to know her more. Much more.

"Yeah. I agree." I toss the ice pack to the side and sit up. "I'll fill King in on our plan and make it happen."

"Who knows?" Jenna says. "You might decide to keep the mansion and even expand your circle of friends so they can visit."

Not going to happen.

She tidies up the exercise room.

Even though she might be a good reason to amend my long-held beliefs.

Chapter Twenty-Two

"Are you ready to go to my rental?" I ask Jenna. "It won't take me long to pack."

She sighs. "I wish it didn't have to be like this. Do you think they'll bother Ma?"

I can only hope they don't dig into Jenna's life. "I want to tell you they won't, but it's a distinct possibility. If you think it would help, want me to put security on her house?"

Her thumb and pinky rub together. "I hate they can do this. Reporters shouldn't be allowed to be so disruptive. We're only trying to live our lives."

My arm goes around her shoulders. "I know. I'm sorry." Despite going against every molecule in my body, I add, "If you'd prefer, I can make a big deal out of leaving Aroostook. Reporters will follow me to wherever, and you'll get your lives back."

Please say no.

The wait for her to respond is agonizing.

"I don't want you to leave when your injury is still unhealed. You'll have to start over with a different physical therapist, which isn't fair, either."

Is this a win? She said she wants me to stay, so I'll take it as one.

"It's settled then." I want to hug her but manage to keep my arms at my sides. "Let's hit up my rental first, since I hope the paps don't know where I'm staying. I'll pack and we'll go back to your house for you to get a bag. I've called and we can meet King and Angie at Secluded Rest."

Her eyes smile. "Sounds like a plan."

She gathers her paperwork and meets with the clinic's receptionist, explaining she's going lie low for a few days until the media attention wanes. The fact we're going to be together for the next few days doesn't escape me.

We take the back elevator down to the ground floor and make our way to her car. "I can drive," I offer.

"No way," she huffs. "I'm not going to ruin all your progress by making you get behind the wheel. Get in, Mr. Lead Singer."

She's never treated me like a famous musician, and her nickname doesn't sit well with me. I open her door. "I'm just a guy, Jenna. I do a job, but that's not who I am."

She tosses her purse in the seat behind her and slides into the driver's side with ease. Her head tilts up. "You don't seem to have much of a life outside of the stage."

Unsure what to do with her observation, I slam her door shut and make my way to the passenger door. Once I'm inside, I say, "I'm always busy, either with UC-related stuff or representing the band at clubs or parties. I think that's a full life."

"It is." She turns on the car. "I apologize. I was out of line." She doesn't sound apologetic, rather resigned.

Despite wanting to challenge her further on this, I let it go. After all, why bother to fight when I'm leaving soon?

Story of my life.

As she drives to the front of the building, I drop the front seat down again. "The media are surrounding the car," she narrates. With the windows closed, I can't make out whatever they're screaming, but I can only guess.

After she turns right out of the parking lot, I sit upright and watch the reporters as they begin their pursuit. When we approach a stop sign, I instruct, "Don't stop, Jenna. Keep on going."

Looking determined, her right foot presses on the gas. We make several quick turns and lose most of the reporters. A few of the more intrepid ones follow. "So much for being under the radar," I note as we pull up at my rental.

We fight our way inside and slam the door shut. "Jenna, if it's like this here, your place is going to be much worse." We walk into the kitchen. "Impassable."

She protests, "But my clothes, my things."

"We can buy new stuff for you." Her expression falls. "I don't think we should go back there now. It'll be a madhouse."

I can hear Mom from here. *This is what you do, mess up everyone's lives.*

"I needed to get a few new pieces of clothing anyway," she rallies. "It's fine. I can handle this for a couple of days. Then everything'll return to normal."

I complete her thoughts: When I'm gone.

"Make yourself at home while I pack my stuff. I won't be long." I leave her with the fridge open and enter my bedroom. At least I've packed and unpacked my suitcase a million times while on tour, so this chore is completed in under ten minutes.

I wheel both pieces of luggage out to the living room. "Ready."

She shakes her head. "I don't know how you can live out of a suitcase. I used to say the same thing to Darren. He always replied it was part of the gig, and touring was something to be enjoyed."

"He was right." I join her at the kitchen island. "Listen, the press is a pain in the ass, for sure, but they don't know what's inside here." I tap my chest over my heart. "They make up crazy stories, but I know the truth. UC's PR team usually comes through with debunking the most outlandish stuff they dream up. Try not to let them get into your head. They don't deserve it."

She plucks at the label on the water bottle. "I'm trying. I'm not cut out for this life." Her lips rise in a half-smile.

"I don't know. From where I sit, you're not letting them calling you a Black Widow get to you. Don't. Keep up your barriers."

"I'm trying, but it's hard. I don't like having a barrier."

My hand covers the top of hers. "You keep the people you love inside with you. All the rest of the world can believe what they want. That's all I'm saying." Guess that's why it's so easy for me. I don't have people inside the barrier.

My cell breaks the extended silence. Despite knowing exactly who it is, I pull it out of my back pocket and stare at Mom's name. I close my eyes.

I'm about to decline the call, when Jenna says, "It's your mother. She must be worried sick about you." Her chin tilts. "Take it."

I don't want to answer the phone with Mom on a good day. Today certainly does *not* qualify as one. "How about this? I'll call her when we've settled into Secluded Rest." The phone rings again.

"Promise?"

"Yes." On an exhale, I send Mom's call to voicemail. "Let's get ourselves to the mansion."

Big, grey eyes meet mine. "Can we at least drive by my house to see how bad it is? Maybe I can squeak in?"

How can I deny her this simple request—one I brought to fruition. "Sure. But if it's nuts, we're not going near it, you hear me?"

"Thank you!" She wraps her arms around me for a fierce hug. "I'm sure they won't be camped out at my place."

Wrong. I keep my opinion to myself. Together, we each take a piece of my wheeled luggage, and I put the backpack on my shoulders. "Are you ready to face the music?"

Her head shakes. "Always with the band references, huh?"

I shrug. "It's what I do."

"Well, true." Her shoulders plop downward. "I'm ready."

I open the door and go out first to try to deflect the reporters. She clicks to unlock her trunk, and I stow both pieces of luggage and my backpack in it while she rushes to the driver's seat. I stand and close the trunk, then turn to face the vultures.

"Don't you guys have something better to do than interrupt my vacation?" I whine. "I'm out here for some R&R. Can you please give it to me?"

"Is it true you're buying property in Aroostook?"

"Why are you spending more time with the Black Widow?"

"Are you moving in on Darren's girl?"

This last one hits a nerve. I stop in my purposeful walk to the passenger door. "I can safely say Jenna Westfield is her own woman and doesn't belong to anyone. I would hope you would understand that."

I open the door when another pap's question sails through, "Are you excited for your tour?"

This one I can answer. I push away from the car. "I am very excited to go out on tour with Untamed Coaster. Following the amazing movie that chronicled our struggles over the past years, we're ready to get back to performing."

"Bennett, how is Tristan integrating into the band?"

"Bennett, who is writing the songs for the next album?"

"Bennett, will Jenna be joining you on tour?"

It's like I unleashed the furies on UC. I raise my hand and they quiet somewhat. "I would appreciate your giving me some space before I get on the road."

It's as if I didn't say anything, as the screamed questions continue. With a wave, I slink into the car and lock my door. "Still think they won't be camped outside your door?"

"I hope not. But you really handled them well."

She starts the SUV, and we pull away. I turn around to check on their status but my pulled muscle protests. My hiss of pain causes Jenna's head to spin toward me. "You need to massage it, so the knot loosens."

I try, but without too much success as we weave through the town. To distract myself, I say, "I'll be happy when we're in Secluded

Rest. Doing my PT there for a few days, without running into reporters, will be like heaven."

"Pain scale?"

"Not too bad. Maybe a seven."

"Which means a high eight."

I don't correct her, simply watch the houses pass until we turn onto her street. Reporters dot the landscape, but it seems passable. Somewhat. "Do you think you can handle this, Jenna? If not, we certainly can order whatever you need."

Stubborn jaw set, she replies, "I'm going in." She maneuvers her car passed the few paps into the driveway. "I never use the garage because it's filled with stuff."

Still rubbing my thigh, I reply, "Understood. Keep your head down and walk straight to your front door. Don't answer any questions."

"What about you? How are you going to walk without a limp?"

"It's not like I have much of a choice. I'll get out and walk in front of the car, then you join me, and we'll go in together." Come to think of it, if we wanted to divert the reporters, we should've gone straight to the mansion. "Wait. I think we shouldn't go in, especially since you'll be bringing luggage when we come out."

I can see a war brewing in her eyes. "I only need a few things. How about I use what could be considered a large purse?"

"Better." I inhale. Since she's not backing down, I ask, "Ready?"

At her nod, I get out of the car and ignore both the screaming from reporters and my thigh. My only goal is to get her inside the house so I can collapse. This was a bad idea. Yet . . . I couldn't deny her some small comforts considering I'm the guy who's preventing her from staying here.

When I round the front of the car, her door opens and she pops out. The reporters scream more questions at her, but we ignore them and soon are inside the house. She urges me to the same sofa I slept on last night. "Stay right here. I'll get you an ice pack before I get my things."

Because I'm tired, I don't protest. Soon she deposits the ice onto my thigh. "Now call your mother."

If I refuse, I look like an asshole. "Fine," I grumble and pull out my cell. With any luck, she won't pick up.

"Bennett?"

No such luck. "Hi, Mom. I saw you called but was in the middle of something. Is everything all right?"

Jenna gives me a sunny smile and heads upstairs. If only she knew.

"I saw you're in the headlines again, this time for stepping out with your dead bandmate's girlfriend."

"It's not like that. I told you I pulled my muscle and needed physical therapy. Miss Westfield is a damned good therapist. Nothing more." I adjust the pack on my thigh.

"The news is reporting it like you and she are shacking up."

"How many times do I have to tell you not to believe anything you read or hear? You know how it is. Reporters are always looking for a story. Or making one up." I hit my good thigh. Gullible people like her believe their lies.

"I do know stories are usually based on truth."

"I don't want the press to know about my injury. Nothing's going to stop this tour, and I don't want their speculation." I stare at my cell. "You haven't told anyone, have you?"

She cackles. "Who would I tell? Ramona? She doesn't care anything about your type of music."

At least that's something. "I've told you a million times to stop reading the tabloids and seeking out shit online."

"Don't do this, don't do that. You're not the boss of me. If you'd let your sister live, I'm sure she wouldn't treat me like the dog you do."

And here we go. If I'd had any say in the matter, my twin would be here right now. I close my eyes and take a deep breath. Do not engage. "You know I'm only telling you this for your own good."

"What you think is my own good," she sniffs.

Time to change the subject. "What did you do today?"

"Ramona took me on a walk inside the mall."

"Sounds nice." Better than railing against me. "Did you buy anything?" Like Jenna's going to have to, because of me.

"No! I wanted to get a blouse, but she said it was too big for me. I know my size. I know it would've fit me perfectly. That Ramona thinks she knows everything. Like you do, Bennett. Neither of you know anything!"

Round Two. I need to end this. "I'm sure she meant well."

"Just like the Black Widow you're hooking up with now. I'm sure she meant well when she killed Darren. Maybe she'll do us all a favor and take you out too."

My blood pressure spikes. "Perhaps if you were a sane human being, you wouldn't have run Dad into an early grave."

The line disconnects.

Jenna steps into the room. "Guess the call didn't go well?"

Chapter Twenty-Three

Fuck. How much did Jenna overhear?

I take my time removing the ice pack and placing it on top of the platter on the coffee table. "My thigh feels a little better."

She comes over and picks up the ice, then disappears into the kitchen. I take this moment to get to my feet, spying her oversized purse on the floor. Looks like a laptop case. Smart.

Jenna crosses the threshold. "No matter how much she tries your patience, you can't replace your mother."

She doesn't know what that woman has put me through my entire life. "Your mother is great, Jenna. Mine is not."

She crosses her arms across her chest. "Every mother deserves respect, Bennett."

"Growing up, Dad used to say something like that to me."

"Would he be proud of your last conversation with her?"

I drop my head. No, he wouldn't. My hand goes behind my neck. "Probably not," I mumble. Jenna remains silent. "I suppose I could send her a little gift to smooth things over."

"Smart man." She picks up my cell, where I had dropped it after Mom disconnected our call. "Start now."

"Bossy."

She shakes my phone at me.

"Fine," I grumble and take my cell from her. Dad used to give her chocolates on the regular when I was growing up, which seemed to mellow her out. She could use some mellowing now. I search for the best chocolates in the world and place my order. "There. Done."

"Good job."

Somehow, I know the kudos from Jenna will far exceed any thanks I get from the woman who birthed me.

"I want to call King and Angie to confirm everything's a go for us to hit up Secluded Rest." At her nod, I hit send on my phone and am connected with King.

"Hey, King. Jenna and I are ready to go to the mansion, if you got the permission?"

"Sure did. I figured you didn't care about the price."

My eyebrows raise. "Of course not." I don't even ask how much, as it doesn't matter. All that's important is getting us away from the reporters. He says he'll meet us there to get us situated.

"King will meet us there to let us in. Are you all set?"

She nods and picks up her "purse," adjusting the strap over her shoulder. "Yup."

"No. Wait. I should carry that for you. The press will have a field day if I don't."

She tugs on the straps. "No, it's not necessary. If you carry it, they'll think it's luggage. This way, I can keep up the ruse it's my purse."

Damn. She's brilliant. "You know, you're right." I motion for her to proceed me. "Lead the way."

She giggles and my cock takes notice. *Down boy.* My eyes fasten on her ass as she opens the front door and we face the media gauntlet again, which has grown since we've been inside. She tosses her "purse" into the backseat and once again takes the driver's side. After closing her door, I make my way over to the passenger side and get in, extending my leg to its full length.

Jenna backs up and the reporters rush to their cars. Her palm contacts the steering wheel. "Why can't they give us a break?"

I repeat what the PR team says all the time. "It's their job."

"Their job sucks."

"Yeah. Wouldn't want to be them." I chuckle. "You don't have to drive like a bat out of hell this time. The mansion is in a gated community, remember? They won't be able to get past the front gate."

She relaxes in the seat. "You're right." A slow grin takes shape across her face. At the top of her lungs, she screams, "Follow me, boys!"

My head bounces on the headrest as we drive at a normal pace, stopping at stop signs and obeying traffic laws. She turns into the community and we approach the gate.

"Hi. We're going to Secluded Rest."

The guard behind the desk asks, "Name?"

Jenna glances at me, to which I tip my chin. I'm sure King gave them her name. "Jenna Westfield."

A beat passes before the guard scribbles something down and hands Jenna a piece of paper. "Keep this on your front dash. From now on, all you'll have to do is show this and you'll be let in." It's an extended stay pass.

Jenna puts it down in front of her. "Great. Oh, and see all those cars behind me?" She waves behind us.

The guard peers out. "Hard to miss."

"Don't let any of them in. They're reporters."

"You got it. Have a good day."

With that, we enter the community and drive toward the mansion overlooking the water. "You have a devious streak in you, don't you Miss Westfield?"

Her teeth worry her bottom lip. "Only when it's called for."

"Remind me not to earn it."

"Keep up with your exercises and treat your momma with respect, and we'll be good." She turns into the long driveway.

One out of two will have to do.

King opens my car door. "Glad to see you made it." He gives me a light punch on my shoulder.

"Yeah, well, looks like a nice neighborhood . . ." We chuckle.

Jenna joins us with her oversized purse over her shoulder. "I popped the trunk with your luggage, Bennett."

"Thanks." I turn toward the back of her car, King in tow, and grab my backpack. "Would you mind grabbing those for me? I hate this." I point to my leg.

"Understood." He lifts my luggage out of the car and looks around. "Where's the rest of Jenna's stuff?"

"Because the paparazzi were all over us, we decided she couldn't take anything bigger than what she has. Otherwise, the rumor mill would get worse." I slam the trunk closed.

"Oh, man. That sucks." We roll my bags to the front.

King addresses Jenna. "I'm sure Angie could help you get anything you might have forgotten."

Grey eyes dart between us. "I was thinking I could go home and get a change of clothes tomorrow. Maybe even stay there."

"No way." I stop. "You saw the press staked out at your house. I won't let you go back there while I'm here. It's not safe."

Jenna's left arm covers the other. She rubs up and down the strap. "It's not me they're after."

"You heard them. They're just as rabid for intel about you as they are for me."

King stays silent, observing.

I continue, "At least I gave them a plausible story about looking for properties. What's your angle?"

She straightens her shoulders, her lips in a thin line.

"That's what I thought." I turn my head toward King. "Let's go in."

The three of us go to the front door, where King produces a key from the lockbox and hands it to me. "I'm removing this while you're here. You can drop the key off to the agency before you leave, or give it to Jenna to do so after you've left."

His words pinball through my body. I don't want to leave her here. All alone to handle the press. *Who am I trying to kid? Even though I'll be the one leaving, it still feels like she's the one abandoning me. Like everyone else in my life.*

King ushers us through the front door. I'm once again hit with the massive foyer, high ceilings, and open concept. Not to mention the view of the ocean through the wall-to-wall windows in the family room. It's breathtaking.

And big. I don't need such a huge place.

Jenna points to one side of the staircase. "I'm going to put my things in a bedroom." Without waiting for a response, she runs up the stairs.

King says, "Let's take the elevator."

"I hate this fucking muscle pull," I grumble as we wheel my luggage down the hallway. Pressing the button, the door opens and we get into the cab with my luggage—with room to spare. "Shit. This thing is big."

King smirks. "I hear that a lot."

I like this guy. "Yeah, me too." Although not from the one woman who I'd like to hear it from. I bet Jenna . . . *A needle scratches across the record.*

King asks, "What was that out there?"

"Huh? What do you mean?"

The doors open and we walk toward the primary suite. In a higher voice than his usual baritone, King imitates me from outside the car. "'I won't let you go back there while I'm here. It's not safe.'"

I flinch. "Jenna's my responsibility. She wouldn't be in this predicament but for my stupid injury." I pound on my right thigh.

"Uh huh."

We wheel my luggage into a huge walk-in closet.

"Between you and me, that's not the only reason." I shrug off my backpack and place it on top of the quartz-covered closet island. Why am I confessing all this to King, whom I barely know? Perhaps that's why?

"We thought we saw sparks between you two."

"It's complicated. She used to date one of my bandmates."

We enter the main bedroom. "The one who overdosed?"

I nod. "Darren. He was a good guy. His overdose was a mistake, not intentional."

"I hear you. Happened to my father's original drummer back in the eighties. None of Hunte touches the stuff anymore." He turns his head. "Me neither."

There's more to this story, but I remind myself we're not friends. No one is. I'm not in a position to dig deeper into his story. Instead, I say, "Darren's the reason I didn't take the doctor up on prescription pain killers."

"How's your leg, anyway?"

I take his off-ramp. "Rehab is going well, but sometimes it hurts like a motherfucker." I pause. "Don't tell Jenna that, though."

He laughs. "You're secret's safe with me." King holds up the lock-box. "Well, I think you have everything you need in here. Let me know if I can help you out in any other way." He walks toward the doors. "And good luck with your girl."

I open my mouth to argue that she's not my girl, but he's already gone. *Just who am I trying to kid?*

Chapter Twenty-Four

I sit on the bed. What am I going to do with my girl, as King called Jenna? My cell pings with an incoming text, which I gratefully pick up.

LUKE

How's it going, B? Think you'll be ready to perform in front of thousands in 4 days?

Four days until I take the stage. How did the time disappear so fast? My hand rubs my thigh, and I look down. His implied ending echoes in my mind—please don't make me reschedule at this late date. There's really no choice.

It's going great! I'll be ready.

.   .   .

Three dots pulse while he types a response. I'm too impatient to wait, so I click the telephone icon.

"I was typing my response."

"You know me, Luke. You take too long to type."

He chuckles. "Damn autocorrect is not my friend. So, rehab is going well, I take it?"

"Yeah. It's hard, but I'm getting through. Already up to the intermediate exercises."

"Sounds good. Don't push yourself too hard, though. The band wants to start the tour as planned, but only if you're ready."

"I'll be ready. Flare-ups still happen, but usually because I'm not being careful. So long as I don't do something stupid again, I'll be fine." I hope.

"I've seen some footage online of you in the Hamptons," Luke continues. "Has the PR team been good at handling everything?"

"For the most part, they've been on point. We did have to leave our respective houses, though."

"What? Where are you guys now?"

"We're in this huge mansion on the ocean that King and Angie Hunte showed us when we were trying to fool the reporters into believing I was looking for properties out here. Turns out the owners aren't in town and said we could lay low here. It's in a gated community with a long-ass driveway. No reporters allowed."

"Sounds perfect." He takes a breath. "So, you're there with Jenna?"

"Yeah. You know what they were calling her. Her house was mobbed by reporters. She can't go back there until I'm gone." Even afterwards, I'm debating how safe she'll be there. Maybe I should buy her this mansion, and she can move Faith in with her?

"Be careful, B."

His warning is something I've told myself countless times. Still.

"We're ducking the reporters like usual. The UC PR team is even getting a restraining order for her."

"What's going on between you two?"

That's the million-dollar question. The way we kiss sets my blood on fire, but I'm not sharing this with Luke—we're not "friends." I play it off. "What on earth are you talking about?"

"When you answer my question with a question, I know the cocky lead singer of Untamed Coaster is getting in deep."

How do I counter this? "She's Darren's girlfriend. She's on the *Do Not Fuck* list."

"Was," he clarifies. "And Darren's request died with him."

I stare at the tray ceiling. "None of us would dare touch her." Although I already have. My cock twitches wanting to again.

"I think Jenna's a great woman. Smart. Talented at her job. Hell, she got Darren fixed up in no time. She's working wonders with your injury too."

"She is." She's remarkable. Funny. Smart.

"Do you like her?"

There it is. The question of the year. "Of course I like her," I explode. "I shouldn't. Can't. Do." *Oh shit, did I just admit this out loud?*

He sucks in his breath. "All right. This changes everything."

"No," I backtrack. "You got it wrong. She's my physical therapist. Nothing more."

He rattles, "I'll need to prepare the guys. 007, especially, will have a hard time with this."

The extent of my idiotic attraction to Jenna hits me between my eyes. "I won't pursue her. It's not fair to the band. Besides, I'm outta here in four days." *Still have ninety-six hours.*

"It's fine if you're with her."

"I'm not."

"Just give me the word. I'll need a heads-up to prepare the band."

"Again. Not needed."

"Didn't have this on my bingo card."

"Luke, listen to me! We're not together." Why does saying this make my stomach punch in on itself?

"I got you, B. Listen, I should get going. Lots of details to tie up for the tour. Good luck with your physical therapy." He pauses. "And your therapist."

The line goes dead before I can refute his innuendo. Fuck. I toss my cell onto the bed as Jenna enters the suite.

"Hey there." She's back in her scrubs, with her hair in a ponytail, a chipper smile gracing her face. Too chipper.

If she knew what I was discussing with Luke, I'm sure she wouldn't be so happy. Not going to ruin her mood, though. "Hi." I stand. "Let me put on my shorts and I'll be ready to start."

"Perfect. I'll set up in here while you change."

I retreat into the huge closet, and slip my workout shorts up my hips. My shirt is tossed onto the carpet. "Okay, I'm ready."

Jenna pauses in setting up the mat on the hardwood for me to do the towel exercises. She swallows before donning another sunny smile. *Yes! She's not immune.* "Great."

She adds more weight to my first round of exercises in order to increase the level of difficulty. It hits me like the heavy kettlebell. "Where did you get these weights and the mat?"

"Austin brought them over."

The Asshole is here? No sooner than the thought enters my mind, than he saunters into the bedroom. *My* bedroom.

"Hi there, Bennett. Jenna asked me to bring over all the equipment you need for your rehab." He drops a barbell onto the floor. It thuds.

"Great," I reply, focusing on my exercises rather than Jenna's work colleague.

I don't pay attention when he walks over to her side and looks over her shoulder at her paperwork.

Refuse to raise an eyebrow when he makes her laugh at some stupid comment.

Will myself not to rip his arm off his body when he touches her forearm.

It's when he corrects me, I lose it. "Jenna's my therapist. What she says goes," I snarl.

Jenna leaves whatever she was doing and comes over to us. "What's going on here?" She seems befuddled.

What's going on is the Asshole is sniffing around you and you're mine. Do Not Fuck list be damned.

"I was giving him some pointers on the exercise," the Asshole whines.

"I was doing it the way you taught me," I counter.

"Oh. Bennett, would you mind doing another rep for me?"

I do the most perfect rep in the history or reps. No one could do it better.

The Asshole leans closer to her. My grip on the kettlebell tightens. He says, "I told him he should flex his foot for a better result."

Jenna turns her body to face his. *I'm right here!* She reaches back and fiddles with her ponytail holder. "Austin, Bennett has a groin pull. To rehab this muscle"—she points to my upper thigh—"we want to elongate it. Which means what?"

His head drops. "You point the toes."

"Correct. Now I do understand why you were thinking he should flex his foot for mobility, but that's not our priority at the moment with him."

"Ah, I understand now."

Wow. She's both teaching him and not putting his initial thoughts down. What a concept. No wonder the Asshole is like a little dog, lapping her up. Hell, I don't know much about physical therapy, but I'm getting a bit of a woody from how she handled him.

Jenna touches my leg. "Good job, Bennett."

I resist the urge to smirk at him. Barely. "Thanks."

"Now, I want to try a new exercise with you." She shows me a balance training exercise, which I mimic. After a couple of minor adjustments, I'm good to go. She continues to explain the exercise to the Asshole.

She should be working with patients. She's amazing at it. Or she could be a professor, given how she's teaching him shit in a dignified manner. Not an administrator. I need to get to the bottom of the mystery of why she left something she was born to do.

I move on to the towel squats, adding the barbell this time. I concentrate on the movements, taking them one step at a time. While I may not be fast—yet—I've got this. Once all my exercises are complete, I lie on the bed for the ice pack cooldown; I smile to myself. Ice Cooldown. Maybe this could be a new song title?

From the doorway, Jenna bids the Asshole a good evening. Because I want to be sure he leaves the mansion and doesn't hide somewhere to kill me in my sleep—or seduce her in hers—I suggest, "Why don't you show him out, Jenna? This place is huge, and we don't want Austin to get lost in here."

"Good idea," she replies. "Let's walk you to the front door."

"See you soon, Bennett," the Asshole says.

Not if I can help it. I raise my hand. "Bye." Look how nice I can be.

When I no longer hear their low voices, I concentrate on the ice pack on my thigh. I loathe being incapacitated in any way, and this is wearing on me. I want to climb a rock wall with the band in New York City. Take the stage without worry my groin pull will flare. Feeling helpless does not sit well with me.

Jenna returns to my room. Alone. She sits on the edge of the bed, too far away from me. "Tell me about your upcoming concert."

"It's going to start our comeback tour. The movie actually launched us back into the public eye, so we're going to capitalize on the hype. We'll be on the road for more or less of the next year."

"Wow. I didn't realize the tour was going to be so long."

"Platinum Records, our label, wants us to go all over the world to remind our fans who we are."

"As if they could forget you guys." She removes the ice pack. "How's it feel?"

"Cold."

"Then it was doing its job. Want to explore the basement level? We never did get down there before."

"Sounds like fun."

She assists me off the bed. Even though I don't need the help, I'm too much of a bastard to turn her down. She challenges me. Doesn't let me get away with anything. Treats me like a regular human being. I don't want to resist her any longer. The kisses we've shared haven't been enough.

We walk to the elevator and take it all the way down and enter the enormous basement. The exercise room is the first thing we see. "Shit. This place is dope."

"It is," she agrees. Her fingers brush over the exercise bike and free weights. "Maybe we can move your rehab down here tomorrow?"

"Don't see why not. I own this place, at least for the next four days."

"I feel like a kid in the candy store. Let's go see what else is down here." She trots ahead of me, oohing and aahhing over the bowling alley. "Oh my goodness!"

Her exclamation brings me to her side. My eyes widen. "Arcade games."

Without another word, Jenna runs to the Donkey Kong machine while I start the Asteroids Deluxe. We spend the next half-hour grunting and yelling and wailing and cheering.

She's the first one to step back. Adjusting her ponytail, she says, "That was fun. I even made it to the bottom of the leaderboard." She points to her name at the twentieth position.

I run my fingers through my hair. "My time at the arcade has paid off. I'm number seven."

She giggles. "Impressive. The twelve-year-old inside you must be jumping for joy."

This. This right here is why Jenna's so special. She can see the little boy I was—rather imagine me as an idealized version of him. I'm not merely the lead singer of Untamed Coaster, the unofficial leader of the band, or a rock star with all that entails. To her, I'm a regular guy. Another human being with a profession—not defined by it.

Do I think of myself outside of it?

When I'm performing, I'm in my element. I get a rush from taking the stage and singing UC's songs, many of which have hit the top of the charts. Tons of perks follow this job, like money and chicks, tempered with the annoying media attention. But Jenna's the first person to want to know who I am beneath all those trappings.

The walls surrounding my entire persona start to tumble. For the first time in a long while—since my high school girlfriend's betrayal with my ex-best friend, since Dad died—I'm willing to allow her to see who that man is. If there's anything to see.

I walk over to her and run the back of my hand down her cheek. "Tween Bennett wouldn't understand how insightful you are."

Her hand covers mine. She swallows but remains silent.

I continue, "How do you do it? You see beneath the hood, beyond the rock star standing in front of you."

Her arm falls, and mine follows. "You're part of a band, a group of guys who play music together. That's what you do, not who you are."

My lids close at her profound statement. One I couldn't have accepted a couple of years ago. When UC was at the top and Darren was still our keyboardist. After everything that's gone down, now I think I'm able to believe her. But what happens if all that's underneath is a black hole?

I open my eyes and stare into her grey ones. "What if there's nothing there?"

My whispered words cause her to flinch. "There is. I've seen it with how you interact with the band. With Luke. With King and Angie." She steps forward and taps my chest over my heart. "Beneath all the cocky attitude is a heart filled with so much love, ready to come out."

This woman. I don't know if she's right, but I want to prove she's not wrong. I want to be worthy of such a description. "Jenna." I scan her face, from her blonde hair pulled into a ponytail to her unique scent of roses and vanilla to her features, unembellished by plastic surgeons or a ton of make-up. She possesses a rare, true beauty. It steals my breath away.

I stare at her capable fingers. "I hope you're right."

"Believe me, I am."

She says this with so much conviction, I can almost believe her.

Time stands still.

I breathe her in.

Her phone blares. She checks her cell and murmurs, "I have to take this."

Chapter Twenty-Five

Phone to her ear, Jenna walks deeper into the basement while our conversation swirls through my mind. I want to be worthy of her belief in me. Could she make me a better man? Disbelief roars through my body. Do I want her to?

After a few minutes, she reappears. "Ma wants to know if we'd like to go to her house for dinner?"

Sadness washes over me. Unlike mine, I know how much her mother means to her. However, with the reporters all around, I don't think it's a good idea.

I'm about to tell her no when she shakes her head. "We'd love to, but I need to get Bennett stage-ready, so we need to do more physical therapy. We've hit crunch time."

Nothing about the paps. Makes sense for her to protect her mother. Besides, my option for security still is on the table.

She walks around the exercise room and arcade, not stopping in one spot for too long, chatting with her mother. Her voice is pitched low, but I'm not tempted to intrude on their conversation any more than I already have. Instead, her belief in me—I'm more than a rock star—plays on repeat.

Stopping next to me, she says, "All right, Ma. I'll keep you posted." She disconnects the call. "It's better she thinks I'm working than running from the media. She's still not over everything that went down with Darren."

We need to talk about her ex-boyfriend, the guy who saved me from spending my senior year of high school at my mother's house. Hell, we need to discuss whatever's going on between us. So many heavy thoughts swirl.

Her stomach growls.

Food takes priority. "How about we go upstairs, light the fire, and order takeout?"

She rubs her stomach. "Yeah, it's been a while since we both ate. Let's go." She heads toward the stairs. From the third one, she raises her eyebrow. "Coming?"

Not yet. "Think I should take the elevator?"

"No. You don't have any luggage with you and the exercise will do you good. Take your time."

Bolstered by her approval, I walk over to the staircase and take the steps up at a snail's pace, hanging on to the handrail. My groin muscle protests a little but it's nothing I can't handle. Once we get to the kitchen, I plant my ass on a stool in front of the huge island. Resting my elbows on the quartz, I huff, "I made it." Wish I wasn't so winded.

"Good job." She looks around the kitchen before pulling out a box labelled "Local Restaurants."

Impressive. I'd never seen such a box. My phone and Google usually do the trick.

She remarks, "At least they're organized. I have one of these at home. Makes life so much easier." She flips through various menus and holds one up. "Italian?"

Whereas she's controlled and systematic, I'm more of a fly-by-the-seat-of-your-pants type of guy. We couldn't be more different, yet why does something in her call out to my soul? "Sounds good to me. I'll have chicken parmesan." It's my go-to Italian meal.

"I'll order the same. Plus a bottle of red."

"Now you're talking my language." I'd prefer a Manhattan, but wine with Italian food is always a good choice. "Make it a Barolo."

Her eyebrows lift, but she places our orders, which will be here in forty minutes. I like how capable she is. Most of the women I hook up with either don't eat or leave all the decisions to me. It's nice to be pampered by a woman who knows her own mind. Another first.

I tug on the end of her ponytail. "You're unique."

"Wouldn't want to be considered boring," she quips. She opens various cabinets. "Aha! Snacks before dinner."

She pulls out chips. Then she checks the fridge, holding up some cheeses and even a salsa. "I'm too hungry to wait."

She doesn't pour the chips into a bowl, but rather opens the bag and dips one into the salsa jar. She turns the opened bag toward me. "Have some before I eat them all."

"Then you won't be able to eat your dinner." I grab a few chips. Once I've finished crunching, I add, "Can't have that, can we?"

She examines a block of cheese. Satisfied it's still good, she cuts a few pieces and puts them onto a plate. "I didn't realize how ravenous I was. I suppose we should replace whatever we eat."

I shrug. "I doubt the owners will even miss it. This seems to be one of several houses they own, given the furnishings and their being away. I don't think they keep tabs on their chips."

She pauses. "Probably not. But I would feel guilty."

I can't imagine any of the women who I've spent time with ever caring about a couple of chips they've eaten. Or even bottles of vodka and gin they've consumed. The way she cares about others is novel. Refreshing.

"Jenna, I appreciate how honest you are."

"Only trying to treat others the way I want to be treated, the way Ma raised me. That's why I could never understand the paparazzi. They're rude and pushy."

"And they make shit up when they don't have a story, or there isn't one to tell." Snagging a piece of cheese, I stuff it into my mouth.

"I guess it's their job. If no one wanted their photos or fake articles, then their profession would disappear."

"I don't see that happening anytime soon."

"Me neither." I force myself away from the island and head toward the fireplace in the next room. "If we want to be able to eat our dinners, I think we should stop with the appetizers." I flick the switch and the fire springs to life.

Jenna joins me in front of the fireplace, dusting off the remnants of our snack from her fingers. "The fire feels good."

I face her. "Jenna, I want to kiss you for being such a wonderful human being. I want to hold you to my body and absorb your goodness into my soul. What are you doing to me?"

Her hand flies behind her head and she tightens her ponytail holder.

When her arms return to her sides, I reach behind her head and pull the holder out of her hair. "I prefer your hair down."

"Oh," she squeaks. "Darren did too."

His presence can be felt in the family room as if he were here now. Am I simply a stand-in for her ex-boyfriend? "Do you miss him?"

"Every day." Pained grey eyes search my face. "As time has passed, it's gotten easier. He used to call me his Perfect Ten. Not as a reference to my body, clearly, but because I always asked him for the ten top things about whatever he was doing." Her cheeks half inflate. "Top ten things about whatever city he was in. Top ten things about touring on a bus. Top ten things about writing music."

There's so much to unpack. She's never asked me for any top ten list. I rest a beat. "Which is why you want to open ten clinics."

Her hand flies to her chest. I don't think she's going to respond, but she does. "Yeah. I want to honor him in this small way." Her shoulders rise on an inhale.

I hate seeing how broken she still is. I want to hold her and make it better. I can't resist. "Come here." I open my arms, and she walks into them, resting her head against my lower pec.

I don't want to be a substitute for Darren, though. Hell, we were in the same band. How can she see me as someone different? Unlike me, our keyboardist had a wicked sense of humor. He gave the devil a run for his money with his pranks.

I'm his opposite. I've been described as "cocky," "arrogant," and "confident." Obviously, those writers didn't know me too well. Fine, I use my rock star status to get what I want, but that makes me practical. Also, I keep to myself—which probably has been misinterpreted. I'm a loner. Jenna is not.

"Darren was a great guy," I allow. "He invited me to join UC when I was seventeen and spurred me on to get my GED. He always was the life of the party." Until he wasn't.

She nods against my chest. "He had a big personality, true. But that's not what drew me to him." She steps back. "He treasured his mother and sister and set them up financially. Darren celebrated his roots with parties and lavish gifts, probably because he didn't have much growing up. It was only after I came into the picture that he spent any money on himself."

"I remember a certain tricked-out motorcycle as his first purchase," I correct her.

"Well, true. But it was the only purchase he made for himself when you guys hit it big." She leads me to the leather sectional, where we sit next to each other. "He was so proud of the band. He used to go on and on about how exciting it was to be on a journey with his best friends."

"007 was his best friend."

"Yeah. He considered the rest of you—Coop, Río, and you—to be right up there, you know. When I came and saw you all together, I saw it too. The comradery among you five was untouchable."

Among the other four, I can see it.

She touches my hand. "You always were slightly different. You were with the band, but not. I often wondered about your distance. I even discussed it with Darren, who blew me off. Was I wrong?"

The million-dollar question. "I'm honored to be part of UC. We have a blast performing. It's different now, with Tris." My eyes flick to hers. "I enjoy being on tour."

"Never putting down roots."

How can I answer her? I do what I do best. Deflect. "I'm in this mansion right now, aren't I? Considering purchasing it."

"Seems like you are. But if it weren't for your injury, you wouldn't be, though."

My bravado flees. "You're probably right." About all of her observations. Dare I share one of my secrets? Her nose tips toward mine, her eyes searching for more. I can give her this. I *need* to. "You weren't wrong. I'm friendly with all of the guys in the band, but I wouldn't call them 'friends.'"

She bites her lower lip. "You've said this before. Why?"

I rub two fingers over my own nose. How to explain this so she understands? "From a young age, I was taught people would let me down. I had a girlfriend my junior year in high school—the only one I've ever had—who dumped me like a bad song lyric the minute a senior sniffed around her and invited her to the prom. I was devastated. Then my father died. When I was invited to join UC, it was an escape from my ugly reality." I slam my lips shut. Not going into Curtiss. Or worse, my so-called "sister."

"I'm so sorry. But"—she brushes the hair off my forehead—"Those things happened years ago."

"Years of writing songs and performing, winning awards." Hooking up. "It's been a ride."

"But not a blast?"

"I've enjoyed myself," I correct her. *Never fully let loose.* "There have been some excellent times, for sure. Lots of laughter." Which I never participated in with abandon, but I did join in the hoopla. "I know I'm blessed."

"You deserve to be there as much as the rest of them." When I rear back, she adds, "Not more than. You are all in it together. Untamed Coaster is a band. You're one of the brothers."

"UC wouldn't exist but for the team around us. Our label, manager, PR team. None of us could do it without the others."

"Exactly my point. Your group is intertwined."

I pop my chin in the air. "Good way of putting it." Intertwined, but not friends. We get along, enjoy each other's company. Nothing wrong with that. I still maintain enough distance in case it all falls apart. Like it almost did when Darren died.

"Enough about me, Jenna." I stroke her hand. I need to understand what's going on between us. "What are you doing here with me?"

Her eyes track my fingers. "Your physical therapy."

I push, "Nothing more?"

"You're my patient. There are rules."

I draw a treble clef on her hand. "In case you haven't noticed, I'm not much of a rule follower."

Her eyebrows rise then lower. "Hashtag truth."

Our contact—my finger to her hand—scorches me now. The same way it almost blew my head off during our first kiss. The all-encompassing feelings I felt during our—way too short—make out sessions. What is going on here? I kiss her hand. "Do you feel it?"

My question hangs over us.

The doorbell blares.

She announces, "Food's here."

Chapter Twenty-Six

Instead of answering "no," Jenna scurries toward the door, which serves to convince me that my feelings aren't one-sided. What to do with them? Can we get beyond the ghost playing the keys between us?

I walk to the dining room to set the table and stop. This room is too big for the intimate conversation we need to have. So, I return to the kitchen, glance toward the island and then spot a small banquette tucked into the corner. Perfect. I make quick work of setting a couple of placemats down before she returns with the bags.

Handing her a plate, I take mine and slide the chicken parm onto it. If I were alone, no way would I bother with such niceties. With Jenna, I want to be more civilized. At least for dinner.

She carries her plate over to the dinette and sits on the cushioned banquette. I join her, sliding in next to her rather than doing the more expected thing and sitting across. My body crowds hers into the cozy nook.

She picks up her fork.

I do the same.

She cuts a piece of chicken.

I mirror her action.

She brings it to her lips and bites.

My cock shifts. When she finishes chewing, I bring my forkful of chicken to her mouth.

Grey eyes blink.

She opens her lips.

I deposit the food into her mouth.

After her lips close, I pull the clean utensil toward me.

A "pop" is the only noise she makes. I adjust my erection, which is begging for the same kind of attention.

"Good?"

"Very," she replies.

I mimic her next few actions, feeding her my dinner despite wanting to taste my meal. I simply want to taste her more.

Her knife and fork clatter to her plate. "Bennett, what are you doing?"

Damned if I know. "Taking care of you."

"I'm a big girl. I can do it."

With any other woman, I wouldn't bother. With Jenna, feeding her amps an unknown protective streak in me. "Maybe I want to." I lean in, offering her another piece of chicken, to which she scrunches her eyebrows and shakes her head. Hint taken. I take my first bite of the meal and my mouth explodes with delicious flavors.

My head leans back and I emit a groan. "This is fucking good."

Next to me, Jenna giggles. "Bet you're upset by how much of yours you gave to me."

"No." I sit upright, donning a smirk. "But I do want to eat it now."

I shovel forkfuls into my mouth, enjoying the vibrant Italian meal, punctuated by her floral-vanilla scent. After a moment, she picks up her utensils and continues eating. We don't speak another word until both plates are clean.

"So good." I extend my arm on the top of the banquette behind her. "I don't only mean the food, although it was pretty fucking excellent."

"Darren always loved Italian too."

This is the opening I need. "Are you really okay about what's going on between us, considering he was my bandmate?" I replay my word salad. I'm usually much more articulate—hell, I write lyrics for a living.

She licks her lips. "Darren still means a lot to me, even though he's been gone for a couple of years. He opened up my life to experiences I never would have had. He made me laugh." A sad smile emerges. "I'm forever grateful he was in my life."

Makes two of us. Guess he sort of saved us both.

"I like you, Bennett. This version of you anyway."

My brows pull together. "What do you mean? What version do you see?"

She twists in her seat, dragging one leg under the other. In her quiet, deliberate tone, she says, "The one who needs help and guidance. Who needs the physical therapy I can provide." She takes a breath. "Not the arrogant one who performs in front of thousands of people. Who discards women and drinks like they're candy. Or the one who's hiding his injury from the world."

"That's a mouthful." I take a minute to digest what she piled on me. "There are expectations of me as the lead singer for UC. I have to always be 'on'—for the cameras, reporters, fans. You've seen, first-hand, how the paparazzi can be. I've had to build a layer of protection around me, otherwise I'd go insane. I give them what they want, they print whatever stories they see fit. The wheels go round and round."

"Wow. That's just," she tosses her napkin onto the table, "cynical. When do you have time for a private life?"

Private life? I haven't had one of those since I joined the band. Except. "I got my GED. That was something I did for me."

She nods. "True enough. How about a more recent example? Do you have any hobbies?"

A smirk crosses my face. "Arcade games. Especially Asteroids Deluxe."

"Touché. You've been playing a lot of that here in Aroostook. When was the last time you played before you got here?"

Her question brings me up short. "Honestly, I can't remember."

She goes to fiddle with her ponytail, only to realize I took it out. Her arms return to her sides. "Tell me, when was the last time you went off the grid to do something for yourself? Something *you* wanted to do, without any expectations or cameras?"

"I went on vacation to Ibiza not long ago."

"Which is a place for the rich and famous to party." She twirls a lock of hair, biting her lip. "Darren knew how to turn off the fame, and be a more subdued version of himself. It doesn't seem to me that you ever shut down your public persona." She tosses her hair behind her shoulders. "I'm your polar opposite, not your plaything."

Her words lodge in my heart. "I've been more real with you than anyone else in memory." My only girlfriend, Lissa, pops into my mind. I was an inexperienced teenager back when I was with her. After her, too. No one scaled the wall of infinity she left behind. I didn't want anyone to try. Until now. "I want to allow you beneath the surface." I blink. If there's anything to see.

Her grey eyes get wide. "You've said it yourself, Bennett, many times. You don't do friends. You like your life that way."

My heart rate speeds up. "Maybe no one's made me want to dive deeper?"

She shakes her head. "I'm a physical therapist, not a psycho-analyst."

"I don't need a shrink. Just someone who challenges me." I follow her lead and put my napkin on my plate. "You do, Jenna. You don't care I'm a rock star with legions of fans. You don't let me get away with shit. *Au contraire*, you treat me like a normal human being. Hell, any other physical therapist would've been kissing my ass and letting me skip workouts. Not you. You didn't let me get away with anything."

"For your own good."

I acknowledge her defense with a hand wave. "You also didn't drool over my body, make inappropriate comments about my injury, or try to massage my cock when you were working on the muscle pull."

Her nose wrinkles. "No self-respecting physical therapist would do any of those things."

"Believe me, they would. I was lucky you were in the audience when I got hurt. If a groupie got a whiff of my injury, she would've blown me to make it better." I don't censor myself. Jenna needs to understand my life in order to appreciate how difficult diving deeper with another human being is for me. "I'm under no illusions that another female physical therapist wouldn't try the same." I fold the napkin.

"I don't believe you about the women in my profession. Your attitude shows how jaded you are."

We're getting nowhere. "How many boyfriends have you had since Darren?"

She pulls her leg out from under her and sets it down on the floor. "What concern is that of yours?"

I have an unquenchable need to touch this woman. Feel her. Worship her. My hand contacts with her shoulder. "You must feel this thing between us. Hell, when we kissed, it was unlike anything I've ever felt."

"I fail to see what one thing has to do with the other."

"Because it's bad enough I have to compete with a dead man. Who else do I have to fend off to reach your heart?" *Heart?* WTF am I saying? In the past, if it didn't have to do with pussy, I wasn't interested. Yet, with Jenna, everything's turned on its head.

She remains silent, so I press, "Austin?"

My question gets a reaction. "Austin?" She rears back. "No. He's an employee. Nothing more."

"Not from my vantage point. But I digress. If not him, then who?"

"The cocky lead singer of Untamed Coaster doesn't 'do' girlfriends. Or care about relationship status."

"He might not, but I do. Only with you." There. I've said it. Laid my heart bare. My gaze bores into hers, trying to dip into her soul.

Her head bows. She whispers, "None."

The enormity of her answer weighs on me for a second. It doesn't matter the legion of women I've been with—so it cannot matter the small number of notches on her bedpost. "All that matters is what's between us now. It's unlike anything I've experienced before. Have *you* ever felt like this?"

She licks her lips. "It's different with you," she admits. "Maybe because you're uncontrollable."

I sit taller. "Uncontrollable?"

"Wild. Spontaneous. Daring."

A slow smile creeps across my face. "I like being all those things."

She tucks her hair behind her ear. "None of them are me. Nor do I want them to be."

"Oh, come on." I tug on her hair to dislodge it from behind her ear. "Staying here with me was spontaneous. Taking me on as your patient was daring." I lean in closer. "Kissing me was wild."

She focusses on my lips. "It was that."

I lean closer still. "Want to be wild again?"

I don't press her. I've never forced myself on a woman before and I'm not starting with this one, who means more to me than any of the others. She's real and brilliant and challenging. Three things I didn't know I needed in my life.

"I think I do."

This is all the permission I need, as my hands cup both of her cheeks and I bring my lips to hers. One touch is all it takes before the wildfire reignites in my soul. With a moan, I give all of myself to her. Well, all I can considering our confined space.

My hands skim her torso, cupping her boobs. She's natural, which is another thing I like about Jenna. Nothing on her is embellished— she's not trying to become an Instagram model or get picked off the casting couch. She eats normal-sized portions. Kisses me like I mean something to her.

I take a breather. Before I know what I'm spouting, the truth leaks out. "Jenna. I've never met anyone like you before. I like who you want me to be. I want to be him. For you."

She touches my hair, my ears, my nose. "I understand why you keep this hidden from the world." Her hand covers my upper left chest. "I only wish you'd let me or your bandmates inside your real world."

I'm not about to let anyone into my "real world," let alone this beautiful creature. "Believe me, it's much better this way." I trail kisses down the side of her neck, pausing as her pulse pounds.

She tilts her head back to give me better access. Being no fool, I take her up on her unspoken offer. Soon, though, this banquette is too constricting. I want more room to spread out and enjoy her. "Up."

"What?"

"What I want to do to you requires we have more space. A lot more space."

"Oh," she pants. "I, uhm . . ."

No time for her to worry about something stupid, like the dishes aren't put away. Or the curtains aren't drawn. Or whatever nonsense is running through her beautiful mind.

I tug her shirt up and over her head. It lands with a tiny plop on the floor. "Unless you want me to lay you out on this table. Which would mean I'll have to toss these dishes onto the floor."

That gets her attention. I suppress my chuckle when she leaps from her seat and skirts around the table, causing me to get to my feet and hiss. Stupid fucking groin pull. I remain still for a moment, until the pain dissipates, then walk to the kitchen island. Hopefully Jenna didn't notice.

"How's your leg?"

Leave it to my observant physical therapist. "It's fine. I'm more interested in how you're doing." I don a lascivious grin, one I hope hides my pain.

Her head tilts. "How about we put more ice on your thigh."

"How about we don't?"

"Which leads me to believe you need it now more than ever. Come on." She disappears, and the freezer opens. I hear her rummaging with a baggie, then the clinks of ice. Her blonde head appears next to mine. "Why don't you sit in the family room so you can stretch out?"

I need to turn this table back to the fevered kisses. "How about this? We do a little hot, then cold."

"Excuse me?"

"If I have to have another freaking ice pack, then I'll need something to warm me up. I'll sit on the sofa over there"—I quirk my head toward the family room—"and you play nurse. Then I'll play . . . My voice trails off. *Pimp. Dom. Alpha.* Jeez, all these are not what I'm looking for.

Jenna rescues me. "Randy teen?"

"That'll do."

We relocate to the family room, where she slaps the ice pack on my thigh as soon as my butt hits the leather sofa. When she's finished inspecting my muscle pull, I grab her around the waist.

"I've never seen a nurse as sexy as you, Miss Westfield. Especially one without a shirt."

Her brow arches. "A gentleman such as you, Mr. Hardy, shouldn't speak of my state of undress."

"Even if this 'gentleman' was the cause of the article of clothing being missing?" My hands reach out and weigh her boobs. Not huge, but definitely more than a mouthful. "Let me reciprocate." I toss my shirt somewhere into the room.

Her gaze lands on my necklace, then lowers to my tattoos. Her breath catches. "Oh my."

"You know what, nurse? It hurts down there too."

"Looks like it might." Her hand remains on my thigh.

I reach around and unhook her bra, with practiced ease. "I think these might be a good distraction."

My lips close in on her nipple, sucking. Her back arches, giving me better access. Without hesitation, I nibble and then lave her distended nipple. Then I move to the other boob. Have to give them equal time.

I slide my hand down to her pants and pop open the button. My fingers dip inside, reveling in her warm heat.

"I need to check the ice pack."

My fingers tap against the sofa as she stands and takes a step. I reach out and grab her around the waist. "Where do you think you're going?"

"I was giving you some room. Because of the ice, you know?"

"Good try sweetheart." *Sweetheart.* There's that word again. I tug her body and she comes closer to me. We both watch as her zipper lowers.

Her pants and panties sail to the floor.

She stands before me, naked. "You're beautiful, Jenna. Do you know that?"

A bemused smile crosses her face. "I'm nothing special."

"If you believe that, then you've been hanging out with the wrong men." I'm sure Darren wouldn't let her believe such foolishness. I shake my head to clear it. The only people in this relationship tonight are Jenna and me. All others can fuck off. "Open your legs."

"What?" I tap the insides of her thighs, and she complies. No sooner are her legs open, then I rub her clit. "Oh!"

"I like the sound of that, Jenna." My fingers do a circling motion, causing her lower torso to roll for me. The ice pack falls off my thigh and lands on the floor, but she doesn't notice. I'm too wrapped up in bringing her pleasure to care.

Her hands blindly reach out to hold onto my shoulders, causing her boobs to dance in front of me. I do the only sensible thing, and latch onto one while my fingers play her like a well-tuned guitar. I want to make her scream in pleasure. Lose herself to me. This is happening.

My mouth moves to her other nipple. I dive deeper into her wet core, and make a come-hither motion to hit her G-spot.

"Bennett." Her breathing turns erratic, her hips moving in time with my fingers.

I circle her clit, wishing it were my tongue rather than my fingers doing the work. Next time. Eyes closed, her body is mine to direct. She keeps climbing and climbing, but never lets go.

She needs to surrender.

I bite her nipple, then soothe it with my tongue. She's like a live wire, ready but unable to explode. I pull back. My fingers continue to play music only she can hear. Her breathing becomes more labored, sweat drips down her torso onto mine. I want her to be free.

Unable to do any more for her in this position, I say, "Come for me, Jenna."

No sooner is my command out of my mouth, then she blows apart. Her core clutches my fingers in a vice-like grip, even more liquid coats my fingers. She screams something undecipherable as her back arches. I've never seen anything more beautiful in my life. I'm fully hard.

She collapses and I catch her by her shoulders, directing her onto the sofa next to me. Her head connects with my chest, and her hand plays with my necklace. The one she gave me so long ago. My cock twitches, reminding me he's more than ready to play.

"Oh my God, Bennett. Oh my God."

"I'm not a deity, Jenna." I kiss the top of her head. "But I can be yours."

Her hand trails down my chest to the top of my jeans. And lower. And lower. She sits up, staring down at me. "What happened? Your ice pack is on the floor."

I shrug. "I think it fell off somewhere between your calling me a god and my fingers encircling your clit. Or was it when I was kissing your tits?"

She turns beet red. I fucking love that my words—however crude —can do this to her. Her hand snakes out and she picks up the ice and returns it to my thigh.

"Shit, that's still cold."

"You need to keep it on." She stands and walks deeper into the room. She's so gorgeous, in an unassuming way. Bending down, she picks up my discarded shirt and tosses it over her naked body.

I cross my arms and fake pout. "Not fair. You look better in my shirt than I do." Something primal in me puffs out at her wearing my clothing.

"The doctor said no sex."

If the ice pack didn't do it, her latest reminder did. My cock deflates as if it were a bad boy and needed to be punished. "Nothing wrong with getting you off, though."

Her blush returns. "Thank you."

I don't think I've ever been thanked for an orgasm before. "You're welcome?" I let my question end on an upward note.

She looks around the room. "Well, I think I should go to bed. To sleep. Tomorrow's a very big day, you know? I shouldn't stay here. With you like that. I mean, keep the ice pack on for another fifteen minutes, then you can go to bed too. In your own bed. Good night!" She runs out of the room, never even stopping to clean up the dirty dishes.

If this is how she reacts to my fingers, I can't wait to see what my cock does to her.

Chapter Twenty-Seven

I wake to birds chirping and sunlight streaming through the curtains. Blue, blue sky belies the cold temperatures. It's going to be a beautiful day. An old Bruno Mars song plays in my mind, but I'm not looking for something dumb to do. No way will I ask her to marry me, either.

Right?

Shoving the blankets down my bare torso, I lean against the padded headboard. Images of last night replay. No matter how things ended, she enjoyed herself with me—and I'm the first man who's gotten her off in two years. A satisfied smile fills my cheeks.

Which quickly disappears. What if she decided I was a mistake? One she doesn't want to repeat? My fist contacts the bedding. No. Way. I can read a woman, and she was satisfied. *Wasn't she?*

The ringing of my phone startles me, and I glance down to see Luke's name. Great. Bet he's checking up on my progress. On the third ring, I pick it up.

"Hey, Luke."

"B! How's it going?"

I've known my manager long enough to know this isn't a social call—especially since we just spoke the other day. He needs to hear his asset is recovering. Plus get the scoop on whether he has to break the bad news to the rest of the band that I'm with Jenna. I tackle the first issue. "I'm doing okay. Not back to normal yet, but I'm able to walk and even take the stairs."

"That's great. Does the pull still give you problems?"

"I have a hard time imagining when it won't flare up," I confess. "But I'm able to handle things better. Physical therapy is giving me more strength and different ways to cope than I had before."

"So, the tour starts in three days." His statement hangs out there for a few beats. "Sounds like you'll be ready for opening night?"

"Yeah, even Jenna hinted I'll be ready. I'm not going to lie; I won't be able to perform the same way. No running around the stage. Absolutely no quick turns. I'm sure if I take it slow at first, it'll be fine. Thanks for working with PR to keep this a secret. I don't need my rehab publicized by the media." Even if Jenna thinks I should come clean to the public, it's one headache I don't want.

"You've made it easy, B. Have to admit, playing like you're interested in Aroostook real estate was genius."

I glance around the enormous primary suite, then steal a look at the ocean view. This place calls to me, and not simply as a refuge from the paparazzi. "It might not be a lie."

"What? Has the rolling stone decided to gather moss somewhere?" He chuckles. "Say it isn't so."

"I didn't start out looking for a place, for sure. But this property is really nice. And it's secluded. None of the vultures can get to me here."

"Welcome to the next level, B."

"Guess it happens to the best of us, Luke."

"I can't wait to see this magical place." I hear rustling of papers. "I do want to remind you, though, about your follow-up doctor's appointment tomorrow. Should I schedule another helicopter?"

I consider the trip for a second. I'd like company on the ride. "I'm sure the doc will agree with Jenna's assessment and clear me to perform. I'd like for her to be there."

He clears his throat. "So, how are things going between you two? Should I prepare the band to see her again?"

Damn if I don't want to wrap her up and keep her in my pocket all the time. I smirk, thinking of all the rehab she could do from my pocket. My morning wood agrees.

"Jenna and I have a professional relationship." No way am I throwing her under the bus. Besides, after last night, I'm not positive where we stand. "She's damn good at what she does." In and out of PT.

Luke exhales. "Good. I couldn't imagine how that conversation would go down. Especially with 007."

Darren's best friend. Another reason not to have friends. They die. Abandon you like everyone else.

As my silence lingers, Luke repeats, "Are you sure there's nothing going on between you two?"

I don't want to lie, but the truth is I don't know what's going on with Jenna. "She's my physical therapist, nothing more."

A noise from the doorway makes me turn my head, and she stands at the threshold, holding a tray laden with breakfast. Shit. Did she hear me?

"Text me the details for tomorrow, all right?" I rush UC's manager off the phone. "That was Luke," I explain to the woman approaching the bed with goodies, grey eyes staring down at the tray. I'd offer to help her, but I'm naked under the covers. Instead, I rearrange the blanket over my lower half.

"I bet he's worried about you." With jerky movements, she lowers the tray onto the bed. Several feet away, she remains standing.

"He wants to be sure I'll be ready to perform. I told him you think I'll be ready to take the stage." I drizzle syrup on the waffles I swear Jenna made with her own two hands. "I'd like for you to come with me to the doctor's tomorrow." My breath fills my lungs and stops. Everything stops.

"Oh, I think I'd be in the way." She takes a step back. "I'm only your physical therapist, after all."

I lean forward and grab her wrist. "Jenna."

Her eyes remain trained on the hardwood floor.

Dropping her wrist, I tip her chin upward. "I hope you know you mean much more to me than only physical therapy. I was only trying to throw UC's manager off our scent."

Her eyes close. "Off *my* scent?"

I drop my arm. "He was sniffing around, trying to find out what's going on between us." I whinge. "Hell if I know."

Through pink-stained cheeks, she replies, "Last night was a mistake. There, there can be nothing—you're my patient." Her shoulders square. "I'm the administrator of two physical therapy clinics. As a matter of fact, I asked Austin to come in and help with your PT today."

Ouch. I try not to flinch. "Austin," drops out of my mouth.

"Yes. He's a good therapist."

"Why?"

She takes a step back. "I have a meeting this morning and can't oversee your exercises. He'll do a great job for you."

"What meeting? Where?"

"It's with the bank about a loan for our third location." Her chin wobbles for a moment, then solidifies. "We were supposed to meet yesterday afternoon, but I left him a message when it became clear I wouldn't make it. We rescheduled the meeting to today."

A distant memory about a meeting yesterday flits through my mind. Whatever. She's not making any sense about the need for a meeting. "I thought you were using the money from working with me to get your third location?"

"Yeah, well I already had this meeting scheduled with the bank when you sort of fell into my lap. If I get this loan, I'll apply the money I'm earning from working with you for our fourth location."

Her logic makes sense, even if it does leave me to work with

Austin. "Don't you have another therapist I could work with? One who doesn't have the hots for you?"

"No. All my other therapists are busy with clients. Because the location where Austin works has been hounded by the paparazzi, he's available." Her lips purse. "And he does not have the hots for me."

I wince at her description. "I hate my presence has disrupted your business." A second later, I add, "And yes, he does."

"Well, you're leaving in three days and then things will return to normal."

Except for the fact Jenna's changed me, I admit to myself. She doesn't treat me like a rock star or some god who can get away with everything and anything. She's seen through all the bullshit, and still likes me. I grin. She also likes how I made her come on my fingers.

I lean forward. "I wanted to throw Luke off your scent because I don't know what's between us, Jenna. I like you. A lot. The more time I spend with you, the more I want to, and that's simply not how I usually operate." I wrap a lock of blonde hair around my index finger. "What are you doing to me?"

"Back at you. You weren't in my plan. No man was." She swallows. "I don't understand what's going on between us. Darren—"

"Was an amazing man." No denying this truth.

"He was." She licks her lips. "He exposed me to a whole new world, one without rules or order."

"Let me guess. You loved him despite all that."

"I did." Her head drops. On a whisper, she replies, "I need order and control, two words definitely not in his vocabulary." She lifts her head. "Or yours."

She has me there. I don't need either because everything is taken care of by others, and I don't give a shit. So long as I'm where I need to be when the gig starts, that's all that matters to me. Not to Jenna, though. Can I see her living in my world, the way she blended into Darren's?

I do. If she'll have me—which she probably won't. No one does.

"Maybe we can meet in the middle?"

She shakes her head. "I'm leaving for the meeting now. Due to the time and, well, everything, I'll stop at a boutique and buy a new suit. I don't want to have to deal with reporters at my house on top of everything. Applying for this loan is nerve-wracking enough." She takes a couple of steps away from me.

"It's your third time. Has to get easier?"

"You would think so. It was even more challenging the second time." She backs farther away. "I don't expect it to go any easier now."

I start to get off the bed but remember I'm naked underneath. Despite everything that went on between us last night, and this morning, I don't think she'd appreciate seeing me in all my glory right now. Instead, I hold my arms wide. "Let me give you a good luck hug."

"I think it's best if we don't cross that line again. You're my patient."

"Technically, I'm Austin's patient this morning."

Her cheeks lift. "You're still under my supervision. We shouldn't have done those . . . things. We can't fool around any longer."

"Fuck that."

I don't give a crap about the fact I don't have a stitch of clothes on either. I shove the blankets off my body, stand, and cross to where she's standing—transfixed. I wrap her in a hug and kiss the top of her head.

After a long moment, her arms go around my naked hips. We stand, locked together, for an exquisite beat.

Then she steps away. Without saying another word, she escapes from the room, leaving an unfinished melody of desire and confusion in her wake.

Chapter Twenty-Eight

I lean forward, slide my right foot out on a towel, lower to a squat with the twenty-kilo barbell. Austin walks around me in the basement gym, adjusting little things with my position and barking orders. Well, he is a professional after all—I'm sure he'd say what he's doing is gentle corrections. Whatever. I want him the fuck out of my house.

Crap. I'm starting to think of Secluded Rest as my house.

"Ok, last time. Keep up the good work."

This forced cheerfulness from Austin is the only bright spot of my exercises today. When I allow my mind to wander from PT, it immediately goes to Jenna. I hope the bank doesn't turn her down because she wants another location so badly. At this rate, she'll meet her goal of ten clinics in no time. And be farther away from me. I drop the barbell.

"Great job so far. Has Jenna worked with you on skater jumps yet?"

I chug water. Anything with the word "jump" in it makes me queasy. "No."

Austin rubs his hands together. "No time like the present, considering how well you've mastered the other exercises."

In addition to pursuing Jenna, this guy's a sadist. Great. "What exactly do I have to do?"

"Let me show you." He stands with his legs hip-width apart. "We'll start out slow. Just step to the left side and bring your other leg behind you, swinging your left arm out to the side and your right in front of your torso. Then repeat on the other side. Eventually, you'll work up to leaping from side to side." He demonstrates a smooth leaping motion.

I know how to fucking jump, Asshole.

Part of me wants to dive right into the deep end and jump from foot to foot. The more pragmatic part of me screams it's going to be impossible to do without aggravating my groin pull. Or worse. Set me back to the beginning.

"I'm not sure. Jenna hasn't gone over this with me."

"All right. You don't have to try this advanced exercise yet. It's the next level you'll have to do when you're ready to progress in your therapy. Guess she doesn't think you're ready for it yet. My bad."

Oh hell no. No way am I letting some sniveling, scrawny guy who has the hots for my woman talk down to me this way. *My woman?* Hell, yes she is! I draw up to my full height. "I'm sure I can do it."

"Really?"

"Yeah. I'm sure." I stand with my legs apart.

"Remember, do not jump. You only want to step side to side. Take it slow." He demonstrates what he means.

"Slow," I repeat. Part of me wants to rip off the band aid and leap, but I clamp that part down. Doing it slowly will be better than reinjuring myself.

I step to the left and tap my right foot behind, while swinging my arms. My groin twinges in warning. I purse my lips and step out right and tap my left foot behind, which causes the familiar—all too painful—throbbing in my pulled muscle. "Fuck!" I grab my thigh.

Austin rushes to my side. "You did the steps correctly and slowly. I'm surprised it hurts this much."

"Maybe why Jenna hasn't done them with me," I grit out over my panting.

He directs me to a chair. "I'll get an ice pack." Asshole disappears to the downstairs bar area while I stretch out my leg onto the over-stuffed ottoman, massaging the knotted muscle.

By the time he reappears, my breathing is under control. My anger, however, is not.

"Put this over it, the ice will relax the muscle."

I grumble, "Like I didn't already know this after two weeks of dealing with this injury." I put the numbing baggie of ice over my thigh.

"You were making so much progress, I really thought you were ready for skater jumps." He runs his palm over his forehead. "I wanted to be able to show off your progress to Jenna."

"What progress?"

The woman of the hour saunters into the basement wearing a navy-blue suit with a white blouse my fingers itch to unbutton. Not to mention her navy fuck-me pumps have to add another four inches to her height.

"Jenna!" The Asshole joins her at her side. "How did it go with the bank?"

She looks between us—me sitting with an ice pack on my outstretched leg and him standing on her right side. A sunny smile of triumph crosses her face. She doesn't even have to say the words for me to know the outcome of her meeting.

"I got it."

The Asshole's eyes get big. "You did? That's great! Congratulations." He reaches out and hugs her.

I growl. I'm sure they didn't hear me since I'm half a room away.

He adds, "So, when do we break ground?"

She laughs. "I'm going to take over an existing building, so no breaking ground necessary, Austin. I do have to marshal the contractors to do the necessary renovations, though."

She steps away from him and approaches me. "I see you're already on the cool down part of your PT. How'd it go?"

I open my mouth, but the Asshole dives in before I can get a sound out. "He did great. He has all the stage one and two exercises down, and even did squats with the barbell."

She nods, her expression pleased.

"However," he continues, causing my eyebrows to rise. "I think I might have introduced him to skater steps before he was ready. He did one and his muscle screamed in protest." He wrings his hands.

Crap. Now I have to give the Asshole some props for coming clean to Jenna. Guess he figured better he do it than me. Nice touch with the hand wringing.

"Oh no." Jenna rushes to my side. "Bennett, how do you feel?"

I look at her with my puppy-dog eyes. See, Asshole, two can play the same game. "It's calming down."

"I wanted to start skater steps today, so I don't blame you for trying, Austin."

Well, fuck. There goes my victim positioning. Jenna's and Austin's eyes meet and communicate something. I'm not privy to their PT telepathy, but it seems like they've reached a conclusion. Not sure what it is, though.

Preferring to get the spotlight onto a happier subject—and not wanting to discuss my treatment plan in front of the Asshole any longer—I say, "Looks like you also have to scout your fourth location too."

"Four?"

Jenna adjusts the ice pack on my thigh, then stands. "Thanks to Bennett, here, I've got the financing for another clinic."

That's one thing you can't give her, Asshole, that I can. Money. Now it's time for me to get Jenna alone again—I'm sick of sharing her. My fingers itch to unbutton her shirt and strip it off her body, together with the professional blazer. On second thought, perhaps she should keep them on. I can bend her over the table in the corner and live out a boss-secretary fantasy I didn't know I had.

Blood heating, I tune back into their conversation. Jenna's saying, "so that's why I want to get the third clinic up and running first."

"Agreed," he replies, as if she needs his approval.

The way he flirts with her, and is solicitous of her every need, makes me want to puke. Could he kiss her ass any harder? Enough.

I toss the ice pack onto the side table, drawing both of their attention. I raise my hands. "It's lost its cooling power." C'mon Jenna, make him take care of it.

"Austin, would you please put the ice pack into the freezer?"

His inscrutable brown eyes dart to me. "Sure thing, boss."

I don't help him, but make him pick up the ice pack. Soon, he's out of the room. I struggle to stand, testing my groin pull. Seems like the ice did the trick. "Congrats, Jenna. Told you it would be fine."

She tucks her loose hair behind her ear. "It was hard for me to believe until I was told yes."

An unknown protective streak races up my spine. "You deserve it. I know how to celebrate too. Let's go out to dinner."

Her hand flies in front of her open mouth. "Won't there be reporters?"

Shit. "There may be, but only at the door. We can find a restaurant with a back entry."

"I don't know of any."

The Asshole strolls into the room. "Any what?"

"Restaurants around here with a back entrance," Jenna oh-so-helpfully supplies.

I don't want to be beholden to this annoying gnat. He works for Jenna, gets to see her every day. Holding up my phone, I announce, "Let me text King." If anyone in this town would know of secret entrances, it would be Braxton Hunte's son.

"Good luck," he mutters. He turns to Jenna. "This is Aroostook, not swanky Manhattan."

Please let them be wrong. I want to take her out to commemorate her third bank loan. King has to come through. Which he does. I read his text aloud, "King recommends this place called The Dancing Goats. Do you know it?"

"Who doesn't," Jenna replies. All Austin does is whistle.

"I'll take that as it's good. Let me make a reservation."

"For after your second PT session tonight," Jenna adds.

"Will it include those skater steps?" If it does, I may have to rethink dinner.

She smiles. "We'll see." Turning her body toward Austin, she says, "Thanks so much for all your help this afternoon. Running Bennett through his paces can be difficult, and I appreciate it."

"Enough to let me run your next clinic? You've said so yourself, the clients love me and flourish under my therapy."

My fingers form a fist. Seriously? Have I been wrong about him? Does he want Jenna as his girlfriend or merely for a promotion? Whatever. Neither will happen if I have anything to say about it.

"I'm not sure, Austin. I need to talk with Courtney and Felipe." Jenna glances at me and adds, "They run my first two clinics. I was thinking you'd take over the sixth location. Give you more time to make bigger inroads in the community. You know how both of them do outreach with the locals, which benefits the clinics."

Gotta hand it to him. The Asshole doesn't take "no" lying down. "I'll be here when you're ready to call me up. I promise never to let you down."

"Appreciate it."

Christ. Could this guy suck up anymore? I focus on making a reservation at The Dancing Goats. I hold up my cell. "There. The restaurant will be expecting us at seven p.m. tonight. Maybe I could interest you in an arcade game before my next session?"

A tiny smile dances around her lips, and she turns back to the Asshole. "Thanks for all your help today, Austin. I plan on being back at the clinic in a couple of days."

Dismissed.

I hide my smirk as I turn toward the games, approaching Donkey

Kong. It's a good game, just not as good as Asteroids Deluxe, but soon I'm immersed.

Two games later, Jenna finally shows up. I don't ask about the Asshole—don't care. Instead, I kill another Beespy before I'm hit with shrapnel and the game's over. I claim a spot on the leaderboard—right behind Jenna.

"Benjamin Howell?"

"Ever since I was a kid, I've always been him when I play arcade games." I shrug. "Howell for Thurston Howell, III of *Gilligan's Island* fame."

Her head bobs. "Benjamin?"

"Honestly, it was the first B-name that came to mind." I chuckle.

"You're something else," she shakes her head.

I don't know whether that's good or bad, so I keep my mouth shut on the alias front. "Want to play a game? I could switch over to Asteroids Deluxe."

"Sounds good." I switch places with her, and we play our respective games, pings and zaps and our own exclamations providing the soundtrack.

I walk away first and lean against the wall, admiring the view. Jenna's taken off the blazer and is barefoot. The image of bending her over one of these games grows stronger. Or even the pool table in the corner of the basement I didn't notice before. I circle behind her, enjoying how her ass flexes with her movements. Damn.

"Ah, rats!" She steps back. "I was robbed."

I crane my neck to see what position she landed. "Number eight isn't too shabby."

"Thanks. I'll do better next time."

I like her statement because it means she plans on being here long enough to play more games. My gaze roves deeper into this area of the basement, taking in a large TV, sofa, and a jukebox. Nice. "We have some time before we need to leave for The Dancing Goats. How about I see what's on the jukebox?"

"Can't take the music away for long?"

"No way. I live and breathe it. Let's see our selection." Together, we walk over to the back wall and check it out. "Classics. Elvis Presley, Tony Bennett, Frank Sinatra." I flip through more pages, and am rewarded with more contemporary hits. "Better. They have Cole Manchester, Hunte. The Light Rail."

Our eyes zero in on the same band. She points, "Untamed Coaster."

"Yeah, well I'm not stuck up enough to play my own music. How about we try some vintage Cole Manchester, 'No One to Hold.'"

She shrugs. "I like him."

He's a good guy. His wife's pretty awesome too. "Me too."

The opening strains begin to sound, and I enjoy his piano playing for a moment. It's a sad song, for sure, but there's hope in it too. My arms itch to pull her to my body.

I hold up my hands. "Dance with me?"

She bites her lip. "Bennett, like I said before. Not a good idea. You're my patient."

I seize this opening. "Since I'm your patient, you'll definitely be accompanying me to my doctor's visit in the City tomorrow."

"I won't be needed."

"What if I forget what exercises I do? Or can't discuss advanced ones to try? I could even give up the goods about the skater triple flips."

My deliberate misnaming of the exercise the Asshole made me do today earns a giggle. "They're called skater steps or skater jumps. I want to try them again with you in our next session."

I sigh heavily. "Then I'm not even sure I'll be able to make it to dinner." I drop all pretense. "It fucking hurt."

"We'll do them together and I'll make sure they don't give you any more pain."

"Dance with me," I repeat. I take one more step forward.

Her shoulders droop. "One song."

She steps into my embrace and my body jolts. Inhaling her floral scent topped with vanilla, my chin falls to the top of her head. We sway in time with the rhythm. I'm careful not to aggravate my injury.

Her body relaxes against mine before the second chorus. Even though we're fully dressed, this feels like the most magical moment of my life. Well, next to the times we've kissed and when I made her come.

I want her to be with me.

I want to be worthy of her.

I want to share myself with her.

Following these monumental thoughts, I pull her tighter to my body and enjoy the moment. When the song ends, we remain locked together in silence for a long while. "Come with me tomorrow morning." I sweeten the pot. "I'm taking a helicopter."

Her head falls backward. "Really?"

"Yes." I get lost in her gorgeous grey eyes.

"That's decadent."

I need to appeal to her inner control freak. "Practical," I correct her. "I can be back for an afternoon of PT."

Her smile lights up her whole face. "On second thought, I guess it does make sense.

"Then you'll join me?"

She blinks. "All right."

Dare I kiss her to seal the deal? Her protests about professional requirements aside, I want to feel her lips on mine again. A moment from Quinn's movie comes into focus, where she made it clear Darren's physical therapy had been completed before they got together so as to avoid any ethical issues. This only cements her need to follow every rule to the letter. Which is *not* in my DNA.

Time to break her out of the confines. I lean forward and kiss her, savoring every second of her response. Despite not wanting to, I keep my lips closed. I'm rewarded when the tip of her tongue reaches out.

I moan and crush her to my body, my tongue exploring her mouth like a madman. Her boobs flatten against my chest. Breaking apart, I trail kisses down her throat, then fuse our mouths again. My fingers hold her head to mine.

The feel of her lips on mine is more passionate than anything I've ever felt before—except for the last time we kissed. I want to make her come again. I want more. I want it all.

A ring bounces off the walls of the basement. It's not mine. Jenna disengages from me. Eyes downcast but cheeks pink, she says, "My phone."

I kiss her again. "Don't answer it."

Her hair brushes against her shoulders. "I have to. It's my mother."

My body seizes, then relaxes. It's *her* mother, not mine. Still, I don't like sharing. I step forward again, running my finger down her pert nose. She swallows. The phone rings again. "I gotta take this." She scampers away from me.

I let her have the conversation. After all, tonight she's all mine.

Chapter Twenty-Nine

I take another spoonful of the white chocolate raspberry bread pudding. "You were right. This place is fantastic."

"I'm going to gain a hundred pounds with you, but this dessert is worth it." Jenna grins around her own spoon, filled with some sort of peanut butter chocolate concoction. For no reason at all, my cock leaps in my pants.

Shifting my weight between my hips, I admit, "I'm so glad I made it through the skater steps this afternoon, so we can enjoy this meal together." I also plan on enjoying much more with her when we get back to Secluded Rest. Where no *resting* will be done, doctor's orders be damned.

Her spoon clatters into the empty bowl. "You're getting the hang of them. Keep taking them slow, like you did today."

"Thanks to your guidance. You need to tell Austin to take a chill pill before having another patient do them."

She wipes her mouth. "I have to tell you, I was surprised when you told me he didn't take it easier on you. He's usually much more cautious."

"Yeah, well"—I place my spoon onto the saucer—"guess I'm

special." I don't share my personal opinion that he's jealous of me and the time I'm spending with Jenna. She doesn't see his shady motivations, and we're having too good of a dinner to poke this particular bear.

"I will definitely have a conversation with him."

The fact I'm leaving for UC's tour in three days, nearly two, torments me. My fingers tighten around the wine glass. I don't want to let her leave now that I've found her. I need to set up a way to keep in touch. Fly her out to concerts? Visit with her on breaks? Buy Secluded Rest so we can be together during my downtime?

Will that be enough?

"I've been thinking a lot about the tour. I don't want to leave you, Jenna."

She tucks her hair behind her ear, which she left loose for tonight's meal. "You've been doing great with your therapy. Continue doing your exercises during the tour and you'll be fine."

"I need your oversight. What if I mess something up? Like those stupid skater jumps?"

"You'll be fine. Listen to your body."

My body cries out for *her*. I lean my forearms on the table. "Jenna—"

"Yes! I knew I'd find you! It's been so long. Way too long!"

At the fan's exclamations, I pull away from Jenna and turn to the woman standing at my side. She's about the same height as Jenna, but that's where the similarities end. This chick has long, bleached blonde hair, probably due to extensions, and a rack that's definitely been surgically enhanced. It's her light blue eyes that crawl inside me, though.

No. Way.

The woman takes a step closer to me and runs her hand through my hair. I trap her wrists and shove them away from my body.

"I love your cut," she purrs. "Your hair is still one of the most sexy things about you."

My eyes bounce between my future and ugly past, now disguised as a plastic surgeon's wet dream. Who tore my heart out by dumping me for Curtiss, my former best friend. The two who cemented my desire to be a lone wolf, never to let anyone else get close to me again. I lean forward and snarl, "Lissa—"

Across the table, Jenna leaps to her feet. "I'm, uh, going to use the restroom."

I want to grab Jenna's hand to keep her with me, but it's more important for me to get rid of *Lissa Baker* so she's gone when Jenna returns. And she never comes back. While Jenna weaves away, I scan Lissa's too-thin body, noting each change with disgust. "Time's a bitch, huh?"

"You can't mean that, Bennett." She squats next to me, placing her hand on my right thigh. She giggles and, instead of warming to how adorable she is, I recoil in my seat. "I knew I was living rent free in your sexy head all these years. All of your band's songs have been about me. I hear the pain in your voice, especially when you sing 'Crushing Blow.'"

I'm so mad I cannot form a coherent thought. Between gritted teeth, I reply, "That's Darren's song."

Her fingers play with my limp ones. "I'm the woman who you told you loved. You've obviously never loved anyone since, given you've not been with anyone for longer than a night or two ever since."

For a moment, I stare at her hand entwined with mine. Her blood-red nails spur me to shake free of her grasp and rise to my feet. Looking down on her gives me a sense of dominance in this fucked-up scenario. "You're messed up, Lissa, in more ways than one. 'Crushing Blow' is all Darren."

Once again on her feet, she shrugs. "You still sang it. To me."

"You're wrong." I stare into familiar eyes, the only thing recognizable about her. "I haven't seen you in over a decade. Why are you here now?"

"I know we still have what we had back in high school. I made a huge mistake back then, and you disappeared after your dad died.

You left our hometown to be a big rock star with Untamed Coaster." Her gaze runs up my torso until they snag my eyes. "I've kept tabs on you via the media ever since. I'm an influencer now. I'm perfect for your image."

I shake my head, unable to process what this woman from my past is spewing. "What?"

Her hand snakes out and runs up my arm, squeezing my bicep. "We look amazing together. I'll never forget how you confessed your love to me. You can't simply throw away a love as pure as ours."

Love? Pure? "That's not how I remember it, Lissa." I still can't believe her name is falling from my mouth. "I remember telling you, your not saying it back, and then you dropping me like the proverbial hot potato when Curtiss asked you to the senior prom."

She flips her long hair. "Water under the bridge. I'm here now." A disgusting smile crosses her face. "I saw you were looking for properties in this town and knew I had to come here. You're difficult to catch in one place."

"Have you tried?"

She cackles. "Only like a gazillion times. I got to Ibiza the day after you left. Same with Rome, Monaco, Las Vegas." She pauses. "I'm not upset, though. Your shows have been fantastic."

Lissa wants some of my reflected fame, like a million other women. Except Jenna. Always except Jenna. Lissa's wants don't matter to me, as proven by my physical revulsion to her. I take a step away. "Listen, I'm not sure what you've read online or in magazines, but I haven't been pining for you all these years. None of UC's songs are about you."

She opens her mouth, obviously to protest, when Jenna returns to the table. She looks between the two of us. I take a deep breath. "This is Lissa Baker. We went to high school together."

Lissa juts out her ample chest. "I was his high school girlfriend."

I cross my arms. "Until she dumped me for my ex-best friend to go to the Senior Prom with him."

Undeterred, Lissa continues, "Bennett here told me he loved me."

"I was a teenager." Seriously. My gaze bounces from my high school flame to my physical therapist, and there's no comparison. My heart swells. *Oh shit.* I truly am in love with Jenna.

While I'm focused on my current feelings, Lissa doesn't wait. Giving Jenna a look that would cause another person to shrivel on the spot, she says, "He hasn't had a girlfriend since me."

Jenna's shoulders lower. "I think I should let you two get reacquainted."

No. Fucking. Way. "I don't need to get to know Lissa now—her true colors shone brightly in high school."

"Oh, come on, Bennett. You have to give a stupid high schooler a break. I've learned a lot since then." She leans forward. "I've missed you."

"I haven't missed you, Lissa. Not one bit." After her debacle, I made the decision to never remember who I've slept with. Until Jenna. Images of our first meeting back when she was dating Darren, challenging me about *The Godfather*, resurface. When she was the first one to examine my groin pull. Our time with physical therapy exercises. I walk over to Jenna.

Big, grey eyes snag mine. "Lissa looks like all the women in your life."

Without her saying, I can hear her finish her sentence and she couldn't be more wrong. Instead of trying to reason with her, I lean to her ear. "She's not you."

Lissa reasserts herself between Jenna and me, hand on my chest. "We have so much to catch up on."

I grab her wrist. The PR team has taught me never to piss off a fan, but at this moment, I don't give a shit. "No, we don't. You and I happened in the past, which is where we belong. I haven't been pining for you for a decade. Go back home, wherever that is."

Lissa's mouth drops open. "You can't mean that, Bennett. You told me you loved me." She wraps her arms around my neck. "Me."

Not only is Jenna staring at me, but we've drawn the attention of all the patrons in the restaurant. I place my hands on Lissa's arms and draw her away from me. Raising my voice so it carries, I say, "Lissa, we went to high school together. Those years are long gone. Please return to your life and I'll do the same."

Our server appears behind Lissa. "May I be of any assistance, sir?"

Thank fuck. "Could you please escort this woman away from me?"

The server touches her arm. "Miss, please let me take you to a table and let's leave this couple alone."

I dart a glance toward Jenna, who's gnawing on her bottom lip. While Lissa's being led off—screaming how we belong together—I place my hand on Jenna's lower back and direct her to the chair.

What should I do? I've never been confronted by an old lover when I'm with a woman I hope will be much more. "Jenna, I'm sorry."

She holds up her hand. "Not your fault."

"True, but I want to apologize for the way Lissa treated you." I pause when the server brings us the bill and takes my credit card. "She was wrong."

Her chest expands on an inhale. "I want to go home."

The server returns. In silence, I sign the paper, leaving him an excellent tip. He did rescue me from Lissa, after all.

"Let's go to the car."

We stand and retrieve our coats from the coat check. Of course, things couldn't remain so easy. Lissa pops up in front of me. "I know you didn't mean what you said back there. I just surprised you, that's all. How about we go back to your house and reminisce? I'm sure your mother will be so happy—she always liked me."

I snort. "Then go spend your time with her." I pull Jenna to my side. "We are leaving." I drag Jenna toward the front door.

Shit. I should've taken the back exit. Thanks to Lissa's sudden appearance, I forgot. A swarm of reporters crowd the street outside

The Dancing Goats, screaming questions about my "reunion" with my high school sweetheart. About taking her with me on the road. About whether she's the one I never got over. As a bonus, Michelle walks to the front door, through all the screaming paps.

Needing to get out of here—now—I choose the only sane option and usher Jenna back inside and steer us toward the restaurant's backdoor. Once inside the car, Jenna puts it into gear. Our ride out of town is quiet. After we turn into the gated community and Jenna shows her temporary pass, I say my first important words since addressing the media.

"I meant it. Lissa *was* my girlfriend. Ages ago. I haven't seen her in a decade."

"She did a number on you."

I tap on my leg. "She and Curtiss fucked with my head. But that's all in the past."

"If you believe that, I have a bridge in Brooklyn to sell you." Jenna turns into the long driveway to my rented mansion, her stiff body warning me more loudly than words to stay far away.

"Jenna, it's not what you think."

"Really, Bennett, then how is it? This Lissa person—who you told you loved years ago—clearly still has feelings for you. Your relationship may have ended years ago, but she and Curtiss are still playing with your mind. You've never worked through what they did to you."

"You're wrong. They mean nothing to me. Do you hear me? Nothing. You're all that matters." I clamp my mouth shut.

I need to give her time to sort through what happened, hoping she doesn't decide I'm not worth it. Because if tonight taught me one thing, it's that she means more to me than anything else in my life.

We enter the mansion and she takes off, running up the stairs. I call to her back, "Don't forget you're coming with me to the doctor tomorrow morning!"

She doesn't stop.

I only hope we can get past this. After all my jaded years, I can't believe Lissa is able to throw my life into a spiral once again.

Chapter Thirty

After a restless night, I take a quick shower and put shorts underneath my sweats. No need to get dressed nicely for the doctor, as he'll probably want to examine me. I toss a new shirt over my head and walk out of the primary suite.

I stop in front of the room Jenna's using, but can't hear any noises from inside. Is she awake? Still coming with me? Dare I knock and ask?

During what passed as sleep—more like tossing and turning and punching the pillow—I decided I need to let Jenna make her own decision about me. I don't want to strong-arm her into coming to NYC. No matter how bad it will suck if she doesn't take the flight, I can't force her to do something she doesn't want to do.

Even if I believe enough for the both of us.

I force my feet to approach the stairs, longing for the time when I could bounce down them at a fast clip. Now, I take each step one at a time hanging onto the banister, careful not to fall or make a sudden movement. When I finally reach the landing, I enter the kitchen and set up the coffee maker. For some reason, I have a hankering for the brew this morning. I make enough for both of us, even if I'm the only one drinking it.

Too restless to do anything except walk in circles throughout the first floor, I count the number of steps it takes to complete one entire lap. One-thousand, five-hundred, thirty-seven. I bet if my gait were normal, it would be much less.

If my gait were normal, I wouldn't have met Jenna again. Let her into my life. Seen what Darren saw in her—and then some.

Darren was head over heels for her, given how he showed her off at every possible moment. Whether the other ladies wanted to hear his gushing or not. If she were mine, I'd be the same. Yet, unlike when she was with Darren, we're still in the middle of my PT and we've already kissed. Done much more. What does this mean? A new thought rears its ugly head—does she only want me because I'm in the same band as he was? This can't be true.

Our conversations replay. I allow myself to believe her when she says I'm not a stand-in for Darren. My stomach knots. How can I make her believe I love her? Especially when we're not talking?

The intercom linked with the gatehouse blares and the guard informs me my car service is on its way. My heart pounds louder than when Río starts the opening for "Refocused Destiny." Is she joining me, like she promised? Should I tell her the car's on its way?

Upstairs, a door opens, causing my entire body to sag. We can work things out so long as we're communicating. As fast as currently possible, I race to the kitchen and prepare two to-go coffee cups. We meet at the front door.

I blurt out the first thing that comes to mind. "You came."

"I did." She eyes the mugs in my hand.

I pass one to her. "You've made me happy."

"Thanks. Although, are you sure you still want me to come with you?"

I don't let any space exist between her question and my affirmative answer. "Definitely."

She points at me with her mug. "As your physical therapist, I'm living up to my promise to speak with your doctor about your remarkable progress."

The motion sensors at the front of the house indicate a car's coming up the drive. I let her precede me out the front door. I open the car door for her to get in then walk to the other side. The driver does a double take when he sees me.

God, I don't want to have to deal with my annoying fame again. Slipping into the vehicle, I reach across to the front. "Hi, I'm Bennett. Thanks so much for taking us to the helipad. Will you be picking us up as well?"

He smiles. "Yes. You were booked both ways."

"Great. How long does it take to get there from here?"

"It's fast. Only ten minutes once we get out of your development."

"Wonderful. Thanks for driving us." Niceties over, I turn to Jenna, who's busy watching the houses go by. I pick up her hand and kiss it. "Thank you."

Her lips purse. She either doesn't want me to touch her or—I'm hoping—doesn't appreciate PDA. Before her, I never did either.

When I buy Secluded Rest, I'll add a heliport on the side lawn. It'll make life so much easier.

When?

We arrive and are escorted into the waiting lounge. "I've never been on a helicopter before," she admits.

"It's fast. You get to see Manhattan from a bird's-eye view."

She sips her coffee, all the while throwing off standoffish vibes. The need to set things straight between us gnaws. "Last night was a clusterfuck."

Her eyebrow raises. "No arguments from me."

I pull her into a corner, keeping my back to any entering passengers. "I meant what I said. I haven't thought about Lissa in a decade. Not in that way. Whenever she did cross my mind, it was as a reminder not to get involved with anyone." I glance out the window as the helicopter lands. "Until you."

"Bennett, it's fine. I'm your physical therapist and you're leaving in a couple of days. I'll wish you well and return to my normal life, and you'll perform on stages across the world."

"You've changed me. The thought of returning to UC performances yawns with emptiness if you're not in my life." I suck in all the air. "I don't want to return to the *status quo*. I like who I am with you. Who you make me."

Lids close over her grey eyes in rapid succession. "Lissa's beautiful. She looks like the type of woman who belongs on your arm. Like the models usually there."

Two of my fingers tap on her chin, causing it to rise. "I have been with models, true. But you know who caught my eye ages ago, yet was unavailable to me? I won't lie and tell you I was jealous of Darren, but I did want what he had. I just didn't realize I wanted *exactly* who was on his arm. Now you're in my life, I can't forget you and walk away."

"Even if I were to agree, we lead very different lives."

I frown. My idea about meeting up during breaks and her flying to concerts isn't enough. "I'm not sure how, but I will do everything in my power to make things work between us." The same two fingers that tapped on her chin, now rub my own nose. "Do you want that?"

The million-dollar question hangs between us.

"The paparazzi will be ruthless."

"Tell me when they aren't," I counter. "Their job is to stir the pot. Mine is to not give a shit."

She steps back from me. Always stepping away. "I don't see how we could do this."

"Luke is going to meet us at the doctor's office. If you want to explore this with me, we should talk with him."

"I don't know what to think. You've pulled me off guard. Dragged me back into the pits of hell with all the media." She takes a breath.

"Then swept me off my feet like an avenging angel and made me forget all of these truths."

My knees bend so I can gaze directly into her eyes. "Sounds like you want to explore what's between us."

"I don't know." She shakes her head. "It's a lot. You're a lot."

"When I see something I want, I don't give up."

"I'm starting to see that."

The PA announces our flight to Manhattan is now boarding. Together, we take measured steps to the helicopter behind a few other passengers. Headsets on, we buckle up for the ride. Shortly afterward, we're carried away by the beauty that is New York City from above. Densely packed skyscrapers and pavement with bits of green space interspersed. The concrete jungle is an apt nickname, yet the life teeming below us is what sets this city apart.

"The City looks beautiful from up here," Jenna notes with a slice of wonder in her tone.

"So do you."

She turns her head toward me and rolls her eyes. Score! I have to be making progress with her since she didn't make any other comment.

Soon we land in Manhattan and are picked up by a black SUV, which takes us to the doctor's office. Luke stands as soon as we enter the waiting room.

"B!" He gives me a bro hug. "You're looking well. If I didn't know you'd pulled a muscle, I wouldn't think anything was amiss."

I wrap my arm around Jenna, who stiffens. "All thanks to this woman here."

Jenna disengages from my embrace and holds out her hand. "Luke."

Our manager glances between Jenna and me a few times before shaking her hand. "Happy to see our boy's been behaving."

She snorts, then covers up with a cough. "He is a handful, to be sure, but I've managed to keep him in line with PT. He's doing well."

"Good to hear." Luke turns appraising eyes on me. "I've already signed you in, so let's take a seat in the private waiting room. I'm sure we won't have to wait long."

Luke's prediction comes true as no sooner do we sit than I'm called in to get more tests. Soon, the three of us crowd the examining room where I sit on the table to give us some breathing room. Well, if Luke weren't here, I'd have a bunch of other ideas.

The doctor enters the room and the smirk falls off my face. This is the moment of truth. After introductions, he dives right in. "How's the groin pull, Mr. Hardy?"

"It's a lot better. Physical therapy is really helping me heal."

He nods his head. "Great. Miss Westfield, let's take a look at his progress."

Jenna moves around the room and stops next to me. "Sounds good, doctor."

The doctor makes me do several movements, feels my upper thigh—I *much* prefer it when Jenna does this—and asks a steady stream of questions. While my muscle twinges, it's not the searing pain from before, which has to be a good sign.

"Tomorrow night's the kickoff of your tour, right?"

Luke answers for me. "Yes. We haven't made a public announcement of his injury in the hope Bennett will be able to perform."

The doctor nods and makes notes. "I need to go and get your test results. Ms. Westfield, would you like to come with me so we can review them together?" She agrees and they leave the room.

As soon as the door closes, Luke dives in. "What the hell is going on? You *are* hooking up with Darren's ex."

"We're not hooking up."

Really.

Not much.

Yet.

Luke gives me the side-eye. "Right. And I haven't been UC's babysitter for nearly a decade."

I busy myself putting my sweats back on. I have more pressing matters to discuss with my manager. "Last night, my high school girlfriend appeared at the restaurant where Jenna and I were eating. She brought the paps with her."

"Ah, fuck. Seriously? You brought not one problem, but two?"

"First, Jenna is not a problem, full stop. Second, I need you to put the PR team on alert about Lissa Baker." I give him the rundown of what happened last night as well as our history. "She's nuts if she thinks I've been pining away for her."

"Crap. Please tell me you don't have any more skeletons in your closet. I've had to deal with this sort of shit from the rest of the guys, but you swore you were clean."

Images of my mother pop into my mind, but I shunt them away. She's remained under the radar this long; there's no need to think she'll be media fodder now. "No, that's it."

Luke taps on his phone, then focuses on me. "Tell me about you and Jenna. Don't try to say nothing's going on because I have eyes."

Luke is UC's manager. If I have my way and she joins us on tour, he needs to be armed with the facts. I sigh. "I think I'm falling in love with her."

His hand slaps his forehead. "Seriously, B? Even a grade three groin pull didn't make you keep it in your pants?"

I growl, "It's not like that, douche. She's . . . special."

"Didn't we already go through this with Darren?" At the firm set of my jaw, he continues, "Love? You don't do love."

"Maybe I was waiting to meet the right woman."

"How am I going to break the news to the guys? 007?"

"We can tell them the truth," I suggest. "They'll have to respect me."

"What about her? Does Jenna love you back?"

His question stops me short. I think so. At least, I hope she does. "I'm not sure."

"Great," he mutters under his breath but loud enough for me to hear. "What am I going to do with this?"

Our conversation is interrupted when the doctor and Jenna

return. The former looks satisfied while the latter wears a frown. What on earth did my tests show?

I don't have to wait long for my answer. The doctor speaks his medical jargon—I only pick up on the words "groin pull," "PT," and "grade three." Luke nods as if he's following while my attention remains on a disgruntled Jenna.

When the doctor stops talking, I ask the only thing that matters. "Am I cleared to go on tour, doc?"

A smile tugs at his lips. "Your PT has gone better than I even imagined. You've made remarkable progress, Mr. Hardy. So, yes, you can return to the stage for tomorrow's kickoff concert."

My fist pounds the air. Next to me, Luke's body sags.

"With one caveat."

I sit straighter. *This doesn't sound ominous or anything.*

The doctor continues, "You need to continue physical therapy while you're on the road." His prescription sinks into the room. "By this, I mean you must have a therapist with you on tour."

Now I understand Jenna's expression. However, instead of scowling, I'm wearing a huge smile. "I know exactly the therapist."

Luke and I turn toward Jenna, who raises her hands as if in surrender. Her words belie her actions. "I can't. I have a business to run, a new clinic to set up. Two, in fact."

The doctor checks his watch. "I'd like to see you back here in three months, to check on your recovery. Will you be in town then?"

Luke responds for the both of us. "We'll be on the other side of the country then, but I'll make sure Bennett catches a flight out here during one of our short breaks."

"Very good," the doctor replies. "I'll see you then. Keep up the great rehab." He looks at me. "Do you have any questions for me, Mr. Hardy?"

"As a matter of fact, I do. When can I resume normal sexual activities?"

Luke barks a chuckle, while Jenna gasps. Hey, I just want to hear it from the horse's mouth. So to speak. After all, he was the one who restricted me in the first place without so much as a peep.

The doctor doesn't appear flustered. "I'd say you need another fourteen days, minimum, assuming no setbacks."

I nod. Since setbacks are not in my vocabulary, I circle two weeks from today on my mental calendar. The day I can make Jenna mine.

Assuming she'll have me.

When no one else raises any other questions, the doctor walks out of the room, leaving me with Jenna and Luke. I don't waste any time. "Jenna, you have to keep up my therapy. You devised this strategy from the beginning. You don't want to turn your patient over to someone else at this stage." I bat my eyes.

"Oh brother," Luke says. "This is a decision to be made between the two of you. All I will say is you were able to keep up Darren's therapy by stopping in during the tour at various times. Maybe this could work now as well?"

"No, it can't." Jenna pulls her ponytail tighter to her head. "Bennett needs twice daily therapy, not bi-monthly like Darren did when he rejoined the tour."

"Which is why you have to do it," I argue. "Why should I work with someone else when I have the best?"

"Bennett, I can provide detailed instructions for whoever takes over your therapy. You won't even notice I'm gone."

I shove my body off the table. "You're the one who has overseen my rehab every step of the way. Remember when Austin had me do those skater steps? It was a complete disaster. I don't want anyone else but you helping me." Her chin wobbles. "I appreciate all you've done for me. Even the doctor complimented you on my progress. If you were to stay in Aroostook, all you'd be doing is working with contractors on your new clinic and scouting for your fourth location. King and Angie can help you with both things." They're real estate agents. Has to be in their job description.

"I do much more than that," she complains.

"I know you do a lot of oversight, which can be done online or through the phone, email, and texting. You told me yourself you don't see patients anymore, and how much you enjoyed working with me. Seems like you can do both things from the road." Unless she doesn't want to spend more time with a loser like me. *Please say that's not so.* Resisting the urge to get into her space, I lean back.

She glances around the sterile office. "I guess I could do a lot of my At Your Service PT work remotely."

Relief flows through me. Luke chooses this moment to insert himself. "Do you have a lot of employees?"

Her eyebrow quirks. "Enough."

"So you're familiar with the hiring process," Luke notes. "We're going to be interviewing a replacement for our guitar tech and could use your skills in deciding which candidate to hire."

I refrain from slapping him on the back. This is perfect—give her more things to do on the tour besides my PT.

"Oh, I don't know. I hate the interview process."

"You'll only have to sit in on one set of interviews. Because you know the rest of the band, your insight would be helpful." Luke offers an apologetic laugh. "Especially when they flake out on me."

"Hey," I interject. "I said I'd be there for the interviews."

"And I thank you for that, B. But another set of ears and eyes would be welcome."

"I don't know," she says. "You leave tomorrow and there's no way I could be ready so soon."

"Join us as soon as you can." I point to my thigh. "I can continue doing our exercises for a day or two. After that, I'd be lost."

Her hands go to her hips. "You need to keep up your PT. I expect you to be able to do skater leaps by next week."

My chest goes concave. Those things fucking hurt. "I won't promise anything."

Jenna looks between the two of us, and I read so many opposing emotions on her face—annoyance, excitement, fear—I honestly don't know which direction she's leaning. "Excuse me, I need to use the washroom." With that, she hustles away.

Luke and I walk out to the waiting room. "Don't take this the wrong way, B, but are you sure about this?"

"I definitely want Jenna with me. I know this will be a shock to the guys, especially 007, but she's a fantastic therapist." I duck my head. "Outside of PT, she's amazing too. I need to see where this goes."

Luke pauses for a moment. "Then we need to get her on the UC tour."

My head pops up and I meet his coffee-colored eyes. There's no guile in them. "You mean it?"

"Of course. If she's important to you, then she's important to me and UC. Give me tonight, though, to sort it out with the band."

"Thanks, man. We'll be joining up with you in the morning." I rub two fingers over my nose. "At least I will. I'm not sure where Jenna's head's at right now."

He puts his hand on the top of my shoulder. "She'll come around. I mean, what woman can resist *the* Bennett Hardy?"

I bark a laugh. "I'm positive she can."

"Then you better put your powers of persuasion into hyperdrive tonight."

The object of said powers reappears. "I haven't made up my mind," she cautions. "I need to talk with Court, my manager, to make sure this plan might work. I also have to discuss this with Ma. I honestly don't know what I'm going to do." She tucks her hands into her pockets.

I stand straighter. "I'll take indecision over a 'no' any day." My manager and I chuckle while Jenna shakes her head.

"Well, I'm heading back to the hotel," Luke announces. "Make sure you get plenty of sleep. The helicopter will be in the Hamptons tomorrow at noon." He slaps me on the back and surprises Jenna by giving her a hug. He whispers something in her ear, then walks out of the office.

After we collect my paperwork from the nurse, I ask what Luke whispered. She makes a zipping noise across her mouth. I'll get it out of her—or him—soon enough.

On the helicopter, Jenna twists toward my body. Into the headset, she says, "You're wrong, you know."

Okay. Many ideas flit through my mind but I simply don't know to which of the plethora she's referring. "Care to be a bit more specific?"

"Luke is your friend."

"No. We're acquaintances, nothing more."

Her lips purse. "You may think that, but I'm sure he doesn't. He gave you a hug and you reciprocated. That alone shows you're more than mere acquaintances."

"So? You hugged him too."

She continues as if I hadn't spoken. "He even has a nickname for you. 'B.' Again, friends."

"Nope. He doesn't know me beyond being the lead singer of UC. He knows what I tell him to handle media fallout. But not the real me." I point to my heart. "Not what's inside." Truth is, I've shared more with Jenna over less than two weeks than with Luke or all of UC in over a decade. I keep this factoid to myself as well.

"You have to let him in."

I shut her down, "No. I don't. The last time I did something as foolish as that was when I was back in high school and look how that turned out."

She swings her foot. "I'd like to be your friend."

She's said something like this to me before, and I distracted her. This time? I want her friendship more than a private jet taking us to UC concerts all over the world. I find my voice. "I'd like that."

We ride in silence until the helicopter lands. After unbuckling and depositing our headsets onto the seats, Jenna gets out. I take my time, holding onto the grab bars like an old guy, but without betraying my injury.

We walk through the waiting room and step out onto the sidewalk, looking for the car service to take us back to Secluded Rest. I have some decisions to make. So does Jenna.

A crowd rushes us, screaming unintelligible questions. I hear, "Are you getting back together with Lissa?" and "Have you been pining for her all this time?" and "Why are you with the Black Widow?"

It's the last one that draws my ire. I spin on my heel and would come crashing down on the pavement if not for Jenna's being at my side. She wraps her arm around my waist. "Ignore them. Let's get in the car."

Chapter Thirty-One

The ride back to the mansion is tense. My fucking leg throbs, but my heart hurts more. How *dare* they continue to call Jenna a "Black Widow"?

For her part, Jenna keeps her head down, deep in her own thoughts. Maybe she'd be better off without me. At least the paparazzi wouldn't follow her around like stink on trash. My heart twists at the possibility of her not being with me.

"Here you go. Safely back to your house," the driver announces.

"Thanks. Appreciate the ride." I pass him a hundred-dollar bill. "Have a good one." Don't want to give him any ammo to tell the circling vultures that I'm a cheap bastard.

Jenna's already inside the mansion by the time I get out of the car. I watch the car drive away, then limp up the stairs. Fuck, this hurts. How will I be able to perform on stage tomorrow night?

Going through the open door, I'm greeted by Jenna holding an ice pack.

Always an ice pack.

"Have a seat," she points to the chair in a nearby sitting room.

When I move in the direction, she says, "On second thought, take off your sweats."

Despite all the pain, despite all the crappy things reporters screamed at us, I smirk. "I didn't know you cared."

"Seriously? You reinjured yourself hours before you're set to take the stage." She pushes down on my shoulders. "Stop being a prima donna and sit."

The shock of her description, plus physically moving me, causes me to cave. My leg is put on a footstool and ice is on my thigh within seconds.

"What were you thinking back there? You've been making great progress."

"I was thinking the reporters were fucking out of line."

"You know they want to get a rise out of you. Why did you give them one?" Her fingers worm under the ice pack and massage my pulled muscle.

My head leans on the back of the tall chair. "God, that feels so damn good."

She huffs a laugh. "It's what you're paying me for."

I grab her wrist. "That's not true. You mean so much more to me than therapy." I stare into her eyes. "You have to believe me."

Her lips tighten. "I think the pull is relaxing. How's your pain level?"

I query my body. "About a six," I lie.

"Fine. Eight it is."

My gaze follows her movements as she sits across from me. "Jenna," I begin. "Lissa means nothing to me now. Back in high school, she was my world. Her and Curtiss. Until they put a wrecking ball to my life. I haven't thought of her in years, not in any romantic way. Perhaps they came through my mind as betrayal, but nothing more."

"I believe you."

Three simple words. Ones I've not heard from another person's mouth since Dad. He used to believe in me, but no one else has. Until Jenna.

I want to hug her until all the air between us evaporates. Bring her into my body and not let her disappear. This woman has the power to ruin me, and I'd gladly let her do it because I love her.

I can't contain my feelings any longer. With a clear conscience, I admit, "I love you."

Her hand flies in front of her face. "Bennett, no—"

I raise my palm toward her. "Shh. You don't have to say anything. I just wanted you to know."

She glances around the room, then focuses on the ice pack. Standing, she says, "I think you've had that on long enough." She removes the ice and takes it into the kitchen.

For once, I don't rip myself to shreds over my confession. The proverb "the truth will set you free" is one hundred percent correct. I can only hope she feels the same way. Someday.

Long minutes later, Jenna returns to the sitting room, pulling a different shirt over her scrubs. "Think you're ready for some PT?"

I'd do anything for her. With care, I get to my feet, relieved the pain from my groin pull has subsided. "Bring it on."

Two PT sessions and one delivery meal later, we find ourselves in the basement playing arcade games again. Due to her presence and the realization our time is drawing to a close, I can't concentrate. She has to join UC on tour. I won't accept any other answer.

I walk, without pain, to Donkey Kong. She's absorbed in the game so I take time to enjoy how she puts her entire body into it. Something goes wrong as she screams, "You suck!" and pounds the machine.

Chuckling, I ask, "Not the ending you wanted?"

"No." She pulls a disgusted face and I laugh. She may not have hair extensions, Botoxed lips, or surgically-enhanced boobs, but she's perfect. I love every single thing about her. She has to feel the same way about me.

She has to.

"Let's put on a movie." I walk over to an overstuffed sofa and a large screen TV by the jukebox. For once, I'm not in the mood to listen to music. I scroll through my Netflix account, stopping at *The Godfather*. I point to the screen. "Which one?"

She reaches behind her head only to realize she ditched her ponytail during dinner. Tucking some hair behind her ear, she replies, "It's your last night in Aroostook. You pick."

"Hmm. Hard decision." We settle in and Part II comes up on the screen. Her startled moan is my reward.

After a few minutes, she admits, "Luke told me not to break your heart." At my raised eyebrows, she adds, "When he whispered to me in the doctor's office."

My eyes close. Seems like Luke's watching out for me. "I promise never to hurt yours."

The movie rolls, but I can't concentrate on it. Nevada casinos and hotels provide the backdrop to my thoughts. I need her to agree to come with me on tour. During one of the shooting scenes—not the big one, of course—I play with her hair. "Say you'll join the tour."

"I have a lot of responsibilities here."

"Aren't I one of them?"

She sighs. "I know you still have a ways to go with your rehab."

I lean forward, placing my hands on her legs. "I need *you* to make that happen."

"What will the band say if they see me with you? I don't want to cause discord."

"Let Luke and me handle them. I'm sure they'd love to see you again." Darren's best friend 007 will be the hardest sell, but I'm sure we can get him to come around. Somehow.

Her head drops, studying my fingers making random musical notes on her legs. "I don't know if I want to open myself up to the media circus again. They were brutal the first time." She inhales. "This time hasn't been a walk in the park, either."

"I know. You'll have to ignore them, like I generally do." Except when they go after the woman I love.

"Doesn't seem like the restraining order did much good."

"If you agree, you'll be far away from here. UC's PR team will have tighter control." They better.

She worries her bottom lip and I have an unbearable desire to lick it.

"I'm not sure. I still need to talk with Court and Ma."

"Which you can do in the morning. Right now"—I lean in closer —"I need to soothe that lip of yours."

I don't wait for her response, simply mash our lips together. Like before, after a second, she opens up for me. My tongue sweeps through her mouth, tracing her bottom lip. Her little moan spurs me to envelop her in my arms and drag her to my body.

On screen, shots are fired but they don't come close to the fireworks raging through my body. When our tongues clash like an out-of-control inferno, I drag my fingers down her torso until I'm able to trace her boobs. Outline her bra. Go around her chest and work the hooks open even though she's still wearing her shirt.

Her hands skim down my torso and pull up my sweatshirt. I help her and soon we're both naked from the waist up. The way her boobs press against my chest is indescribable. More. I want more.

Grabbing her hips, I drag her across the sofa until she straddles me. My lips pay homage to her rosy nipples, biting and licking and sucking. Her lower half undulates over me and I clamp her down over my straining erection.

Pain shoots through my right leg and my eyes pop open. No. Fucking. Way. I ignore the unpleasant throbbing, focusing on how her nipples have pebbled for me. She shifts her weight over me and I let out a groan. Not of pleasure.

Above me, Jenna's eyelids reveal dazed grey irises. Which morph into an awareness. "Oh my God, Bennett. Are you all right?" She struggles to get off my lap and lands in a heap on my left side.

"I was better a second ago when you were on my lap." Even as I say these words, I know they're a lie. My hand massages my uncooperative groin.

"Let me get ice."

The thought of putting something so cold next to my rock-hard cock elicits an immediate response. "No way." I suck in air and pull her tight to my side. "Stay with me. You'll make it all better."

I can tell she wants to argue. Yet, the slumping of her body next to mine is all the response I need. A tentative palm lands on my chest. "I can feel your heart racing."

My cheeks inflate. "See what you do to me, Jenna? Stay."

I hold her for a long while, until her head lands on my upper pec and I kiss her forehead. "You mean so much to me," I whisper. When she doesn't reply, I check her gorgeous face and am rewarded with dark lashes covering the tops of her cheeks. She's asleep.

Damn.

I arrange her body, enjoying how her limbs fit into mine like they were made for each other. My muscle pull stops hurting after a while, and I reach for a throw blanket to cover us both. I've slept in much less comfortable places. With her at my side, there's nowhere else I'd rather be.

My alarm rings at seven in the morning, waking me. Jenna's head is still against my side and a longing to wake like this every day emerges. Well, perhaps not *exactly* like this considering we're still half-dressed on the sofa downstairs and not naked, in a proper bed. But I would wake like this for the rest of my life if I'm with her.

I kiss the top of her head. "Jenna," I whisper. "Time to get up."

I swear she kisses my upper pec. Her head flips to the opposite direction then she startles upright, the blanket falling to expose her beautiful boobs. "Oh no. Did we fall asleep down here?"

Eyes glued where my lips want to be, I reply, "Sure did."

She looks down, gasps, and pulls the blanket off my body to cover hers. "I can't imagine what you must think of me."

That you're not a groupie. Because if she were, we'd have done the nasty at least two or three times last night. We wouldn't be talking now either. I keep these thoughts to myself. "Your virtue's safe with me."

She pauses in the process of putting hair behind her ear. "How's your leg?"

"Doesn't hurt now."

"Good." She stares at my chest. "You UC boys sure are shredded."

While true, I don't like being lumped together with the band. "I'm sure my rehab is easier because of all the work I've put in at the gym."

"I agree." She scoots away, pulling the blanket totally off my body. I don't bother to hide my morning wood. After all, she's the cause.

"No pressure, but I need to get ready to head out. Will you be joining me?"

Her naked shoulders square. "What you said yesterday makes sense. Now is actually a good time for me to get away and work on your PT, since my two clinics basically run themselves and the third one is only in development. Angie and King can scope out a fourth location for me."

My heart races. "So you'll come?"

She holds up her hand. "Whoa. I'm not ready to commit, just pointing out the facts."

"All of which urge you to join me on tour."

"I still need to talk with my employees about it. Especially Court. Courtney. She might be willing to shoulder more duties if I'm away. Not to mention having a big discussion with Ma. Nothing's a done deal, but I'm more inclined than not to join you. Your doctor did prescribe PT while you're on tour."

"He did. He seemed impressed with you, by the way. He appreci-ated your initial diagnosis, which you did without any machines, might I note." I run a finger down her bare arm. "What did he say to you when he pulled you out of the office yesterday?"

She waves her opposite palm, not disturbing my fingers. "Nothing exciting. Mainly medical stuff, prognosis, exercises, that sort of thing. He seemed impressed you're not taking the meds." I shake my head, and she continues, "I get it. Thank you for your dedication to the exercises and for powering through them without artificial assistance."

I'm done talking about the doctor. Who said I can't have sex for another thirteen days. All I want is Jenna's agreement to be with me on tour. Well, and to sample more of her delicious wares.

"When will you have your final decision?" I leave in a few hours and want her at my side.

"Probably a couple of days."

Thud. "I'll be gone by then."

"There are such things as airplanes. I can meet up with UC wherever you are." She pauses. "Assuming that's my decision."

Days. I don't want to wait so long for her to be back in my arms. "What if I can't wait that long?"

"I'm sure you'll be fine." She taps my shoulder. "Promise me you'll keep up your exercises, no matter what."

"You know I will if you're riding my ass to get them done."

"Bennett."

I don't wait. I close the remaining distance between us and we kiss like never before. She hasn't agreed yet, but I know she's going to come with me. We'll tour the world together—I'll rock stadiums, and she'll rock my world. Once she fixes this muscle pull, which protests its awkward position. I separate from her and adjust my leg. Her eagle eyes land on me.

"Hurts?"

"Slightly." I wait a beat. "Maybe a three."

She stands, wrapping the blanket around her like a toga. "Let's do a set of exercises before you have to get on the helicopter, Rock Star. We'll take a shower after, and you'll be ready to leave."

I let her nickname for me pass. Rather, I zero in on the magic word. *"We'll* take a shower?"

"Separately."

"We'll see about that."

Together, we go into the gym and she oversees my PT regimen. Because I already was in my shorts and nothing else, I do the exercises half naked. Jenna, although again in her scrubs from last night, doesn't seem to mind.

I lie on the weight bench while she gets another ice pack. These exercises are challenging, but they're making things better. Can't wait until PT is over and I get to have Jenna all to myself for my own wicked reasons. Until then, I'll take her however I can get her.

She returns and the damn ice is put on my thigh. "While you let this sit, I'm going to take a shower."

As she's walking away, I grasp her fingertips and tug. She willingly returns to my side. "A kiss."

Without protest, she gives me a sweet kiss. I let her leave, savoring how her lips covered mine. This was the first time she initiated a lengthy kiss, even if I did demand it. Progress.

About five minutes later, my cell pings. I pick it up and wince. It's from 007:

> No fucking way. Luke just told us you're bringing Jenna on tour. I refuse to let that woman near me. What are you thinking?

I consider my response. While I want to tell him she's mine now, I'm sure his allegiance to Darren won't let him believe my truth. Instead, I type:

She's my physical therapist and I'm still not healed. I need her.

Find another therapist!

We've been working together for two weeks. She's really good. Remember how fast she got Darren back to touring?

And dead

I'm not taking any meds

Three dots bounce then stop. Twice. Finally, I get another text:

I don't want her on the tour

She's great at her job. Don't you want me to have the best possible care?

Dude

Sensing I'm getting through to him without explaining my feelings toward Jenna, I make my closing argument:

She's not how you remember her. She's quieter. I'm sure she'll keep to herself. Besides, she's not responsible for Darren's death. You know this.

. . .

Or I'll keep her locked with me. 007 doesn't need to know this until we're touring.

I still don't like it

I take this as a win and don't bother to respond. All I need now is to convince her that this tour is the best thing for her. And us.

Chapter Thirty-Two

I walk into the primary suite and it's quiet. If only she would've showered in here. I'd wash her back—and more.

Shucking my clothes, I open the bathroom door and stop short. Jenna, covered in bubbles, blinks. She leans forward, "I thought I'd be done before you got here. Your bathtub was so inviting and there's only a shower in my room."

If I didn't have any sexual restrictions, I would climb into the bathtub and make her scream my name in passion. Several times. I consider this option for a split second before shaking my head. No way am I healed enough to maneuver the high-lipped tub, let alone do anything more pleasurable.

Her eyes home in on my cock, which bounces in greeting. Her mouth drops open.

I strut to the tub. Dropping my voice to a low tenor, I rumble, "If my therapy was further along, I'd join you. You'd always remember my bathtub afterward."

Her cheeks flush.

I sit on the ledge. "Another reason you have to come with UC on tour. Who knows how many bathtubs we could christen." My hand plunges under the water to land on her leg. Her breathing hitches. "I could make you feel so good right now, though. Can I do that for you?" I trail my fingers toward her knee.

"You need to shower."

"Later. After I'm done with you, so long as you join me." I have no illusion this will happen, but—hey—nothing ventured, nothing gained, as they say.

Her legs swing shut, trapping my palm between them. She wails, "What are you doing to me?" Her head rests against the towel on the back of the tub.

I can take a hint. I reposition myself so I'm not in any danger of reinjuring myself. Using my free hand, I close the distance between our mouths in a kiss that's as wild as it is unrestrained. My other hand inches upward until my finger slips between her folds. Even though she's covered in bubbles, I'm sure she's wet because of me.

My fingers mimic how our tongues dance. I slide into her opening while my thumb circles her clit. Around her, the water moves as if it's a living thing, causing bubbles to flow into my chest and onto the marble floor. I don't care. The only thing that matters is making her feel good.

She moans.

Oh so good.

I pinch her nipple and her legs spread as wide as possible given the confines of the tub. Her breath comes in pants. My erection weeps in longing.

Our kisses deepen. My fingers rock in and out of her pussy. Water splashes overboard.

"Bennett!" Her body freezes, then she comes all over my hand. I prolong her bliss for as long as possible. When she slumps against the tub, I dry my fingers. In my mouth.

"I can't believe that happened."

Releasing my fingers, I stand, staring down into her languid grey eyes. "I can. It'll only get better, I promise."

I turn and walk into the shower positioned in front of the tub, my cock begging for relief. I turn on the spray, which fuels my need to get off right now. I stroke my erection and pretend it's her hand on me. My groan echoes through the bathroom.

Like I conjured her, the door to the shower opens and a blonde head appears before me. "Let me help you out." Her hand replaces mine on my shaft.

I know her professional ethics require we don't have a relationship. "I don't want you to compromise your principles."

Standing under the spray, she says, "I want to do this. For you. And me." Her mouth closes around my cock and all higher brain functioning ceases. She sucks and swallows and swirls her tongue around me. Her hand squeezes my shaft, then dips below to play with my balls.

I widen my stance, my thigh not issuing one complaint. My head almost explodes with the way her throat closes around me. In no time at all, I can't hold back any longer. "Jenna," I warn. "You need to step back."

Instead of doing what I told her, she hums around my cock. I can't stop what happens from here. Blindly, I reach out and cup the back of her head, guiding her to take all of me. With a final growl, I fly over the cliff.

When I return to my senses, I release her from my grip and my cock pops out of her mouth. She giggles.

The most beautiful sound I've ever heard.

"Come here, you." I pull her to my body. We kiss like I'm not leaving on tour in mere hours.

After we wash away our extracurricular activities, we wrap fluffy white towels around us and stand in front of the mirror. "You're amazing."

Pink slides up her neck. "You're not too shabby yourself."

Phones ringing pierce our happiness. Damn. Thought we'd have more time to do what we just did. Glancing at each other, we leave our steamy cocoon in search of our cells. I hear her say, "Hey Court, everything alright? I have something I want to discuss with you."

I answer my own phone, "Luke. This better be good."

Our manager replies, "B. PR is on it."

Nothing good comes after this statement. Ever. "What happened?"

Next to me, Jenna screams, "Oh my God!"

I turn to her as she clicks on a link Courtney obviously sent her. In my ear, Luke presses, "Seems it's been leaked Jenna's going to join UC on tour. Not the reason."

Jenna's eyes turn watery. "I can't believe this."

I demand, "What else?"

Luke pauses.

Jenna yells, "I have to leave!" She runs out of the room, her towel flapping behind her and jaw set at a hard angle.

Our manager says, "I can't believe they contacted Darren's family."

Darren?

Something is really, really wrong. "Send me the link," I snarl into the phone. The ping comes a second later.

Disconnecting the line, I read the story from *The Gossip*:

Black Widow Prepares to Strike Again

Rumor has it that Jenna Westfield, the former girlfriend of Darren Hilliard—original keyboardist in the hit band Untamed Coaster who overdosed nearly two years ago—will be going on the road again with the band. This time, she's set her sights on the lead singer, Bennett Hardy. Will he suffer the same fate?

Lately, Hardy has been seen in Aroostook, New York, home of reality TV stars King and Angie Hunte. It's also Westfield's home-town, where she owns a couple of physical therapy clinics called At Your Service PT.

According to Hardy's girlfriend, Lissa Baker, they were having dinner when Westfield appeared at their table. "I made it clear his songs are all about me," the buxom influencer states. Pushing her long, blonde hair behind her ear, she stares at this reporter with mesmerizing blue eyes. "Bennett has been in love with me since high school. We had a torrid love affair before UC started, which pulled him away. Since we've reconnected, no other woman will get between us."

Based on a tip Westfield is going to join the band on their first tour since Hilliard's death, we contacted the former keyboardist's mother for comment. We were not disappointed.

"That Westfield woman should be ashamed of herself," Ms. Hilliard responded. "She killed my poor son after getting him hooked on pain medicine. It was her failure to supervise him properly that led to his funeral. She shouldn't be allowed into a homeless shelter, let alone touring with the band she helped bring to its knees."

Her daughter, Hilliard's sister Marni Hilliard, agrees. "Westfield had Darren wrapped around her little finger." Her mother adds, "My poor son granted her every wish. I pray every night that Bennett is smart enough not to get caught in her web."

Only time will tell. We here at The Gossip will keep you posted —Stay tuned.

My head lands in my hands. Now what do I do?

Next up is the second book in the Passionate Beats trilogy, EXTENDED BRIDGE ~ *all from Jenna's point of view* ~ don't miss a beat, order it on Amazon today at https://geni.us/UntamedCoaster3!

Please stay up-to-date with me by joining my newsletter at https://geni.us/UCNewsletter!

A Note from Arell

Thank you so much for reading OPENING STRAINS, the first installment in the Passionate Beats trilogy, part of the Untamed Coaster series!

This story is told entirely from the point-of-view of the lead singer of Untamed Coaster, Bennett Hardy. He's super sexy. Incredibly talented. And so, so broken! Traumatized by his father's death, an awful mother, and high school girlfriend who abandoned him for his best friend, Bennett's traveling the world by himself. He doesn't consider his bandmates to be "family." Never has a girlfriend. Until Jenna Westfield turns him on his head!

Jenna was UC's keyboardist's girlfriend at the time of his overdose. They met when she was his physical therapist. Two major similarities with Bennett that they both struggle with. You have to keep reading the trilogy to get her her pov ~ book 2, EXTENDED BRIDGE, is up next!

As usual, some of my own life experiences appear in OPENING STRAINS ~

- I've visited the Hamptons a few times, and some of my travels have been incorporated into this story. Unfortunately, I've never taken a helicopter from NYC there, but Big Mike planned on proposing to me on one (the weather prevented it)!
- I've had the pleasure(?) of doing physical therapy a couple of times. Neither of my experiences were as nice as Bennett's, though!
- Guess who suffered a groin pull while working out? You got it! Unfortunately, I didn't get PT for it, and suffered for about a year. Happy that's over!

Please stay in touch! Subscribe to my newsletter at https://geni.us/UCNewsletter **or join Arell's Angels, my reader group on Facebook at** http://www.facebook.com/groups/arellsangels **~ or both!!**

If you have any questions, feel free to email me at http://Arell@ArellRivers.com. I love chatting with readers!

Thanks for devoting your precious time to OPENING STRAINS. I hope the beginning of Bennett and Jenna's story sucked you into the wild world of Untamed Coaster ... which is only getting started!

All my love,
Arell

Gratitude

Opening Strains couldn't have happened without so many awesome people!

First off, as usual, big thanks to my at-home support system ∽ my husband, Big Mike (plus our two cats Luna and Loki, with their unique brand of support!), and my Mom. They're small in number but off-the-charts in cheerleading abilities!

Opening Strains wouldn't be what it is without the fantastic group of editors I've assembled on my team. My plot coach, Theresa Leigh of The Fairy Plot Mother, developmental editor Trenda Lundin of It's Your Story Content Editing, editor Nancy Smay of Evident Ink, and proofreader Roxanne Blouin, all really made this story sing (haha see what I did there?) In addition, Dar Albert of Wicked Smart Designs sealed the deal with this truly delicious cover! Yum!!

I would like to give a shout out to Shauna and Becca of The Author Agency. They have provided so much guidance in how to best package this trilogy ∽ I couldn't have done this without them!

To my fantastic alpha readers Taylor Delong and Sandy Fear,

what can I say? Bennett and Jenna wouldn't be where they are without you!!

Big love to my ARC Team!! Each one of you warms my heart with how much enthusiasm you have for all of my projects, including this new band, Untamed Coaster. Thank you for taking the time to read, review, and share Opening Strains!!!

My Facebook reader's group, Arell's Angels, is my go-to place to hang out, check out hot photos, and simply just vent! Shout out to "Arell's Insiders" who post daily and keep the group rockin' with your wit and devotion. To all the Angels who participate in our Hotties of the Month, daily games, my crazy Facebook Lives, sneak peeks, collaborative stories, and author takeover Sundays ~ you make this journey so worthwhile! And there's always room for more angels!

I'm so lucky to have met, in person and virtually, so many wonderful authors who are so giving of their advice, support, and friendship. To my fellow Kissed by Romance Authors, Taylor Delong, Libby Waterford, Mary E. Montgomery, and Nicole Locke, you are the reason! ♥ Thanks, too, for all the support from Claire Marti, Darby Fox, Sophia Henry, Anne Lange, and Lilly Wilde!

To everyone who picks up this book, I hope you're "Strapped, locked, and loaded!" If you enjoyed Opening Strains, please share it with your friends and write a review on Amazon at https://geni.us/UntamedCoaster2 and/or GoodReads, https://geni.us/UC2GR. I can't wait for you to get Jenna's side in Extended Bridge!

Blessings,
Arell

About the Author

For as long as Arell Rivers can remember, she has been lost in a book. During her senior year in college, she picked up a romance novel … and instantly was hooked!

Arell started writing her first book because the characters were screaming at her to do so. The story came out in her dreams and attacked her in the shower, so she took to the computer to shut them up. But they kept talking.

Born and raised in New Jersey, Arell has what some may call a "checkered past." Prior to discovering her passion for writing romance, she practiced law, was a wedding and event planner and even dabbled in marketing. Arell lives with two adorable cats and a very supportive husband who doesn't care that the bed isn't made or dinner isn't on the table. When not in her writing cave, Arell is found cooking in the InstantPot, working out with Shaun T, or hitting the beach.

Want to keep up to date with Arell? Sign up for her newsletter at https://geni.us/SinsNewsletter. All new subscribers receive a special gift!

Also by Arell Rivers

Untamed Coaster

A found family/he falls first series following the rock band of the same name

SINFUL BEATS, http://geni.us/UntamedCoaster1 (Quinn and Callum)
(crossover from Sins of the Fathers)

Opening Strains, Passionate Beats trilogy (Bennett and Jenna, book 1)

Extended Bridge, http://geni.us/UntamedCoaster3 Passionate Beats trilogy
(Bennett and Jenna, book 2)

Mic Drop, http://geni.us/UntamedCoaster4 Passionate Beats trilogy
(Bennett and Jenna, book 3)

Animal Beats (Río and Hayden) - up next!

Sins of the Fathers

A billionaire series about the children of 3 notorious businessmen

VICE, http://geni.us/Sins1 (short story, originally published as "Tinsel
Bomb" in the 2021 anthology TINSEL AND TATAS)

ANGER, http://geni.us/Sins2 (Theo and Amelia)

PRIDE, http://geni.us/Sins3 (Xander and Madison)

IDLE, https://geni.us//Sins4 (Paige and Jesse)

The Hunte Family Series

*An enemies-to-lovers series about the dynasty created by rocker Braxon
Hunte*

Out of the Red, https://geni.us/OOTR (Brax and Sara, set in the mid 90s)

Out of the Shadow, https://geni.us/hunte2 (King and Angie)

Out of the Gold, https://geni.us/OOTR (Melody and Chase)

Out of the Blue, http://geni.us/Hunte4 (Trent and Cordelia)

Out of the Box, http://geni.us/OutoftheBox (box set of books 1-4 plus a bonus novella)

The Hold Series

A second chances series about rock star Cole Manchester, his publicist Rose Morgan, and their friends

Hold On, https://geni.us/HoldOn (prequel novella for Cole and Rose)

No One to Hold, https://geni.us/NOTH (Cole and Rose trilogy, book 1)

Hard to Hold, https://geni.us/HtoH (Cole and Rose trilogy, book 2)

To Have and to Hold, https://geni.us/THTH (Cole and Rose trilogy, book 3)

Take Hold of Me, https://geni.us/THOM (Wills and Emilie)

Hold Still, https://geni.us/GDwdlls (Ozzy and McKenna)

Hold Me, http://geni.us/HoldMeBoxSet (box set of books 1-3, 6, plus a bonus novella)

Kissed by Romance collections

Anthologies written by the Kissed by Romance authors: Taylor Delong, Nicole Locke, M.E. Montgomery, Libby Waterford ~ and me!

Steamy Shorts, https://books2read.com/SteamyShorts (4 quick reads guaranteed to bring the heat / my story is OUT OF THE SAND in the Hunte Family series world)

A Kiss at Midnight, https://books2read.com/AKAM (5 interconnected novellas about New Year's Eve at the Grandview Lodge / my story is OUT OF THE JADE in the Hunte Family series world)

Connect with Arell

- Subscribe to Arell's newsletter at https://geni.us/UCNewsletter
- Join Arell's Facebook Group, "Arell's Angels" at http://www.facebook.com/groups/ArellsAngels
- Like Arell's Facebook Page, http://www.Facebook.com/ArellRivers
- Follow Arell on Instagram, http://www.Instagram.com/AuthorArell
- Hang out with Arell on Amazon at https://geni.us/ArellRivers
- Check out Arell on Goodreads, https://geni.us/ARGoodReads
- Follow Arell on BookBub, https://geni.us/BookBubFollow
- Head over to Arell's website at http://www.ArellRivers.com
- Email Arell at http://Arell@ArellRivers.com

Out of the Shadow

Want to learn more about King and Angie Hunte, Bennett and Jenna's helpful real estate brokers in the Hamptons?

Read on to enjoy the first chapter of OUT OF THE SHADOW*, Book #2 in the Hunte Family series!*

All's fair in love, war...and reality TV

Nothing ever came easy to Angie Russo. Hard work, loyalty, and sheer grit made her the kick-ass realtor she is today. But when her best still isn't good enough, Angie decides to try something different. Maybe a stint on the new real estate reality show can give her the notoriety she needs to push her firm to #1. Her chances of winning the show's prize are high...until she meets the entitled, cavalier, and all-too-sexy jerk she's competing against.

Angie's big chance is King Hunte's rock bottom. He screwed up big, and he needs money fast. The silly real estate competition should be a breeze to win. Or, at least it would be, if not for the sassy, determined, and ridiculously desirable Angie. King's suddenly forced to work harder than he ever has, and he's shocked to find that he actually enjoys it...almost as much as he savors the combustible chemistry he shares with his prickly co-star.

Just as Angie discovers there's more to King than meets the eye, King realizes Angie could be the key to the life he's always secretly wanted. When a ghost from the past emerges to threaten their future together, Angie and King must overcome the obstacles the show—and life—throw at them, or see their shot at love end before the first commercial break.

Chapter 1 - King

I wake to my cell phone ringing in my ear. As I fumble with the device, a photo of Dad flashes in front of my face. Oh, fuck no. My brain, still pickled from my week-long jag in Mexico, isn't capable of talking with him. I decline the call and drop my hand on top of the plush Austin Horn silk bedding. *What a trip.*

My phone rings again. Really? What's his problem? I hit decline again. When he calls a third time, I relent. "Dad. What's up?"

"Did I wake you? It's fucking noon." His famous tenor voice is as irritating as an empty barbell hitting the floor.

I sit up in my bed, pillows scattering to the floor. "Got in late last night. Or, rather, early this morning." Why do I have to justify my actions to this man? It's not like he's been around for his firstborn since...ever.

"From Mexico, I see."

My eyebrows pull together. "Yes, I was on Max's yacht off Puerto Vallarta with a bunch of friends." I pause, searching my barely-functioning brain for something redeeming to say about my hedonistic trip. "Trevor was there."

A snort soars through the phone. "Yeah, I see that loser right there with you."

I run my hand through my hair. A kneejerk defense of Trevor is on the tip of my tongue—at least he's been there for me well, usually —but something snags my attention. It sounds like Dad's looking at a picture. "Where are you seeing all these things?"

"The internet has some amazing sites, King."

I review the events of the past week, but can't think of anything that would've made him this mad. Better bite the bullet. "Like I said, what's up?"

"What's up, *son*, is there's a photo of you and your good friend Trevor on *The Gossip*."

I shrug. "That's nothing new. The papps love to follow us around and put us on their site. Harmless."

"Oh, really? The photo I'm looking at is not harmless. At all."

An unusual twang in his voice makes me nervous. My father has been pissed at quite a few of my many antics, but this tone—resignation?—is one I've never heard in all my thirty-three years. What the hell did the papps catch this time? I shake my head and put the phone on speaker so I can load *The Gossip*.

Crap. It better not be...

The site loads. In huge letters, the headline screams—"SNOW IN MEXICO!" Below the damming photo, the caption reads, "Socialite King Hunte and Los Angeles real estate agent Trevor Stern snapped doing lines of cocaine on the beaches of Puerto Vallarta with heiress twins Lacey and London Toalle." The photo is too crystal-clear for me to attempt denying it.

"Fuck."

"You can say that again." Heavy breathing comes through my phone. I picture my father's hands, calloused from decades of playing guitar, turning white as he grips the arm of his favorite chair. "King, you know my stance on drugs."

I can't deny it. Hunte—my father's uber-successful band—famously lost their first drummer to an overdose when I was an infant. No one in the band touched drugs again. Dad wasn't around much when I was growing up, but he instilled that lesson in me many, many, *many* times.

"Dad, it's not what it looks like." Embarrassingly, my voice cracks.

"Oh, really? From where I'm sitting, it looks like you and Trevor were snorting cocaine with two barely-dressed women. They didn't need to bother with the caption. The photo shows it all."

"Listen, I can explain—"

"I don't want to hear your excuses any more. You're a fucking adult. I've let this go on for far too long."

What is he talking about? Let what go on? This is the first time I've been caught doing drugs, and it's not like it happens often. I only partake occasionally, always with Trevor. Maybe once every few months. Or so.

"Dad. I don't make a habit of doing drugs. I don't—"

"King. I love you. But Sara has told me for years—"

At the mention of my stepmother, my stomach tightens and I cut him off. "What does *she* have to do with anything?" She's such a ball-buster. How she ever ensnared my father, I'll never understand. Well, he did knock her up, but it's not like having me was motivation enough for him to stay married to my mother. Not that the first Mrs. Hunte's a prize, either. However, I've been waiting for him to see the light for twenty-five years now, and it's pretty obvious he's never going to dump wife number two.

My father ignores me and plows ahead. "You dropped out of college. Fine. I understand schooling isn't for everyone. But what, exactly, have you done with your life except live off your trust fund and party all over the world?" He pauses. "Nothing. That's what you've done."

"That's a lie and you know it," I say on reflex. "I've done a lot of positive things."

"Really? Name one."

I search my memory and don't have to go far. "Diego. I've been a Big Brother to that kid for ten years, helping him through some difficult shit."

"I'm glad he got his act together. But that's on him, not on you. You, personally, haven't done squat with all the gifts you've been given. And now you're taking drugs? This is the final straw. I've tried hard to give you the benefit of the doubt, but I've been enabling you. My own father was a fuck up, and you're headed down the same path. I'm done, King. Done. I've already called and cut off your trust fund. I'm not giving you any more handouts. I love you. I do. But you need to get your shit together. Get a job." He disconnects the call.

I stare at my phone in disbelief. What the fuck just happened? No way in hell did he really cut off my allowance. Heart racing, I call my trust fund's administrator. "This is King Hunte. I'm calling because I received an unusual phone call and I need to check that everything is still in order with my trust fund?"

The woman on the other end of the line clears her throat. "Mr. Hunte, I have been advised by Mr. Braxton Hunte himself that you are no longer to receive your monthly payments. I'm sorry."

I don't say another word, just kill the call. He did it. He really did it. All because of his bitch of a wife. The saintly Sara.

And Trevor. Like a douche, I asked him to join me in Mexico because we hadn't hung out in a while. The very first night, he offered me the coke—which I did, thinking it was a one-time thing to kick off our vacation. Unlike me, he kept partying the whole trip, so much the others noticed his drugged-out rude behavior. I practically begged him to stop and go to rehab because, after all, it was my "loan" he was snorting. His response? "Fuck you, I'll party if I want to!" Look where that's landed me now.

Blinded by rage, I call my errant "friend," but it goes straight to voicemail. "You asshole. You had to get snow in Mexico. Have you seen what *The Gossip* posted? Now I have to deal with a pissed-off Braxton Hunte." I hit the red button and fling my phone across the bed.

Ice runs through my veins. Where am I with money? The condo is paid off, so no worries there. Same for my car, although I was thinking of getting a new one since the Lamborghini is already over two years old.

Retrieving my phone, I go on my bank app and pull up my balance. I have five grand. And that's it. No more allowance coming at the end of the month.

At least I still have my social media sponsorships.

The sound of a text arriving draws my attention back down to my cell, and it's from one of my sponsors. I open it and find out they're canceling my contract under the "moral turpitude" clause due to that damn photo. A second sponsor texts, but I don't have to read it to know they're following the same path.

Now what the fuck am I supposed to do for money?

Dad's parting words about getting a job ring in my ears.

What can I do? I guess I could be a personal trainer, but how much does a job like that pay? And don't they have to be at their jobs at least five days a week? I hold back a gag and collapse back onto the feather-light bed.

My phone rings again. It better be Trevor so I can give him a real big piece of my mind. I roll over on my bed and check the screen. Despite the shitshow of a morning I've had, I can't help but smile at the sight of Diego's face. Forcing an upbeat tone, I answer, "Hey, Diego. How's it hanging?"

"Good. I mean *real* good."

I've known Diego since he was eight and a bunch of my buddies decided to join Big Brothers. While the rest of my friends dropped out, I made a real connection with the kid. Maybe because he was being raised by a single mother, although his mom did take an interest in him. Perhaps it was his dad, who only showed up for birthdays and Christmases but didn't care to know the super kid he had spawned. Diego's situation hit home.

Sitting up, I rest my head against the grey upholstered headboard. "What's up?"

"I got in."

I suck in my breath. "I knew NYU wouldn't turn down such an accomplished scholar."

He chuckles. "I know that's what you said and all, but until I received their letter, I couldn't even let myself hope. I followed your advice, and it worked." His beaming smile reaches me all the way across the country. "Want to know the best part?"

"I can't imagine what could top you getting into the college of your dreams, but hit me."

"One word. Scholarship." At his words, a tiny piece of my heart expands.

Not able to remain in bed any longer, I throw the covers off my naked body and pace around my bedroom. "Way to go. That's super, Diego. I'm so proud of you."

"Thank you. I mean that. If it weren't for you, I don't know what I'd be doing right now."

I scoff at his praise. "Really, you did everything. I only gave you a couple of nudges in the right direction." Slipping commando into a pair of workout shorts, I ask, "What did your mother say when you showed her the letter?"

"After she finished crying, she hugged the shit out of me. I'll be the first in my family to go to college."

"I know. The world's going to be your oyster, man." Diego has always been interested in filmmaking—I've been able to hook him up with some of my friends in Hollywood, who gave him practical experience. Now, he'll be able to hone his skills and make the necessary connections to become a great director someday. I feel like calling Dad back to tell him. I *have* done something good.

"I can't thank you enough for offering to cover the cost of my room and board and books. The scholarship only covers tuition."

I still at his words. How am I going to help him now, without my trust fund? I flex my biceps. "Well—"

"When can we get together to celebrate?"

Still reeling about this new development, I toss out, "How about

Thursday? I don't have anything on my schedule since I just got back from Mexico."

He laughs. "Nice life, King. Weren't you in Hawaii a few weeks ago?"

"I was." A fantastic trip with a new set of friends. My mind goes back to the villa we all stayed at, owned by the family of a guy I met in Cannes two months ago. Sun, exercise, and lots of drinks and sex. What could be better? "But that was so last month, you know?"

I won't be going anywhere next month, a thought so depressing I flop onto an overstuffed chair to wallow.

"Well, Thursday works for me. I want to take you to someplace special, not our regular spot. I'll arrange everything and text you, okay?"

"Sounds like a plan." We usually hit up SmashBurger, so I can't wait to see his "special" choice. I normally pay for our meals, but maybe this once I can let him? *Crap.* I hate this. "I look forward to it. I can't wait to share everything I know about New York City with you. And, hey, you're going to own that school."

I disconnect the line and text Trevor—again—telling him that I want the last loan I gave him repaid pronto. Heading into my kitchen, I make a protein shake and head down to the beach for my morning exercise, despite the fact that it's after noon. I need to get out and clear my head.

After my workout, I run back to the condo, sweaty from pushing my body hard, and take a long shower. I spend a few minutes shaving my stubble to get the perfect three-day look, then work some product into my hair and examine my nails. It's been five days—time for a manicure. How much does that cost? Well, maybe it can wait a couple of days...

I toss on a pair of Prada grey sweats and, sans shirt, head to my kitchen. Since my fridge contains beer and ketchup, I have no choice but to order lunch like usual. When the delivery guys shows up half an hour later, I go to pull a twenty out to give him as a tip, but—

feeling like an ass—give him a five-dollar bill instead. Desperate times and all that.

As I eat my chicken, I review my options, none of which are appealing. How am I going to survive without my trust fund and sponsorships? My PR needs to change, like yesterday. This sucks in a real bad way. And it's all because of some blow.

My mind bounces from coke pusher Trevor to Blaine, our other childhood buddy. Who's producing a new TV show about real estate and asked both of us to screen test. At the time, I scoffed at the idea, but hell. Maybe I should?

After all, I've gained the reputation of being a "house match-maker" over the years. Whenever someone I know is looking to sell or move, they always whisper in my ear to see if I know of anyone who might be a good match. I've enjoyed hooking people up.

Blaine's TV gig has to be better than getting a "real" job.

Putting my dishes into the sink, I pull up Blaine's number and make idle chitchat about his wife, Jewel—also a childhood friend—and their kids. When we finish shooting the shit, I get around to the point of my call. "So, have you made any final decisions about your new show? The one about real estate?"

"Not yet. Trevor was in here today. He looked good."

At Trevor's name, my resolve strengthens. No way am I going to let him get this gig. "I was wondering—" I let my last statement hang out there, waiting for him to take the bait. Which he does.

"Wondering what?"

I scrunch up my face, knowing he can't see me. "I was thinking I might be interested in trying out for your show after all. Since you're still looking, after all."

"Buddy, that would be great," he says, and I can tell he means it. "I'd love to have you come in for a screen test, but it has to be tomor-row. We're about to make our decision as to who goes on to the next round."

"Perfect." My nails catch my eye, and I decide to make an

appointment with my manicurist today after all. "What time should I be there?"

"Come by around ten. And King, I think you're perfect for this role. We'll be filming out in the Hamptons. I'll tell you all about it tomorrow."

We hang up and I collapse back onto the couch. I can do the Hamptons. Been there, done many of the ladies. I smirk. If I have to get a job, this sounds like it'll be right up my alley. Not to mention I can pull the rug out from under Trevor, the asshole who ripped away my trust fund.

―――――

Read the rest of King and Angie's story on Amazon! https://geni.us/hunte2